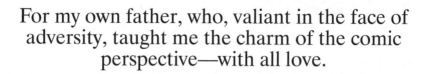
For my own father, who, valiant in the face of adversity, taught me the charm of the comic perspective—with all love.

MR GOLIGHTLY'S HOLIDAY

Salley Vickers

CHIVERS PRESS
BATH

First published 2003
by
Fourth Estate
This Large Print edition published 2003
by
BBC Audiobooks Ltd
by arrangement with
Fourth Estate
a division of HarperCollins *Publishers*

ISBN 0 7540 9353 0

British Library Cataloguing in Publication Data available

Printed and bound in Great Britain by
Antony Rowe Ltd., Chippenham, Wiltshire

Take hold lightly, let go lightly; this is
one of the great secrets of felicity in love . . .
                    ROBERT ORAGE

MARCH

CHAPTER ONE

One afternoon in mid March, when the green-white snowdrops had blown ragged under the tangled hawthorn hedges, the pale constellations of primroses had ceased to be a novelty, and the more robust, sun-reflecting daffodils were in their heyday, an old half-timbered Traveller van drove into the village of Great Calne. There was, in fact, no other Calne, great or small, in the county of Devon; or if there ever had been, it had long since vanished into the indifferent encroachments of the moor. Great Calne stands at the edge of Dartmoor, one of the ancient tracts of land which still, in the twenty-first century, lends out its grazing free to the common people of England—though it must be said that the 'common people' are something of a scarcity these days.

Sam Noble, out walking his bitch, Daphne, named for his mother's still-born twin sister, and having nothing better to do, watched with naked curiosity as the driver of the car negotiated the corner by the Stag and Badger—where, thanks to the pub's garden wall, the passage was tight and drivers often came a cropper. He was mildly disappointed when nothing untoward occurred. Sam's was not an especially malicious nature, but Great Calne did not provide the thrills he had once been used to. Before his retirement, Sam had been a film director, and had had hopes of winning the Palme d'Or at Cannes with a film about women jockeys which had subsequently made waves. However, for the past five years he had lived in

Great Calne, where the principal excitement was provided by Morning Claxon's plans to transform the tearooms into an alternative health centre.

There was another witness to the arrival of the car, a less obvious one. Johnny Spence had, as usual, skipped school and it wasn't safe for him to show his face till after four o'clock. During the stranger's arrival, Johnny was hiding, as was his habit, in the upper branches of a yew tree which spread its antique shade over the churchyard wall and on to the garden of the Reverend Meredith Fisher, the latest occupant of the rectory. Johnny, whose researches were thorough, knew that the lady vicar was off doing her counselling training down in Plymouth, and would not be back before six. So he was free to watch the old Morris—which from his calculations must be worth a bit—being brought skilfully round the corner and into the front garden of Spring Cottage, which since the death of Emily Pope had been let out by her daughter, Nicky, to holidaymakers.

Emily Pope had been dead long enough for Nicky to discover that Spring Cottage did not let easily. So far, it had been rented by a couple of families who complained about the out-of-date facilities, and the damp. One woman, from Clapham, claimed to have found toadstools. It had been something of a relief to receive a request via Nicky's new website—www.moorvacs.co.uk—from the gentleman who had described himself as 'a writer in need of a peaceful situation within easy walking distance of shops and pub'. Spring Cottage filled the bill nicely. Writers were notoriously careless people—very likely this one would smoke in the bedroom, but then again he was a man, and

4

mightn't notice that the back plates on the kitchen hob were dodgy, or that the avocado suite in the bathroom (once the pride of Emily Pope) was now badly out of fashion. Nicky, in the first flush of holiday letting, had splashed out on a Norwegian wood-burning stove, sold to her by a travelling salesman who had hinted at further attractions. These had never materialised, and the stove, prominent in the website details, filled the downstairs rooms with smoke when the wind was in the wrong direction. The Clapham woman had complained about this too; but Nadia Fawns, who ran an antiques store over in Backen, had sold Nicky a couple of convector heaters which she hoped would put paid to the heating problems.

Sam Noble, with several backward glances, had made his way with Daphne through the main street of Great Calne and up towards the moor by the time the driver came to unload the Traveller van. Only Johnny Spence was there to observe him more closely. Johnny's powers of reconnaissance were keen; had he been asked he would have described the stranger as 'a fattish old guy who looked as if he hadn't had a proper shave'. But Johnny's position on the yew bough would not have afforded a view of the newcomer's most striking feature—a pair of eyes whose true colour was hard to discern, since they had a quality of shifting from the brooding shades of a storm-crushed sea to the limpid freshness of a dawn sky.

It appeared that the visitor was at any rate physically strong since he emptied the Traveller in double-quick time. The contents were comparatively few: a knocked-about suitcase, a baggy holdall, a laptop computer, a rather loud-looking portable stereo and some cardboard boxes, one of which bore the name of a well-known wine store. A drinking man, at least, Colin Drover, who managed the local inn, might have remarked. The visitor had brought his own alcohol—which might have been a disappointment to a publican. But with drink, as with so much else, inclination in one quarter usually leads to exploration of others.

And the publican's optimism would have been confirmed. When the stranger had unpacked the van, and distributed some of his belongings in the cramped interior of Spring Cottage, he strolled up the main street to the inn, paused a moment to inspect the menu displayed outside, which promised *Tasty Snacks & Bar Lunches*, and then pushed open the solid double doors to enter the fire-lit warmth within.

CHAPTER TWO

The name of Great Calne's inn was the Stag and Badger—known to locals as the Stag and Badge—and its manager, Colin Drover, was out the back hurrying up Paula over the prawns when Mr Golightly made his way to the bar. Customers liked their prawns better 'shell-off' but it was God's own task to get Paula in the kitchen to shell them. There was always some excuse—if not her periods it was her boyfriend's back, though what the devil that had to do with anything Colin Drover couldn't imagine, as if 'boy' was what you could call Jackson anyway! Jackson had been at school with Colin Drover and both had seen the best side of fifty. As usual with any encounter with Paula, her employer had got the worst of it and this made him of a mind to try that bit harder with the person he now saw seated at one of the bars.

'Good evening, what can I get you?' The publican infused his greeting with a special concern, unconsciously hoping that this might act as antidote to any inhospitable shelliness in the Stag and Badger's prawns.

The new customer smiled back. He had an agreeable expression and, thickset and sensibly dressed in an old tweed jacket and woollen shirt, had the appearance of a country person himself. But when he spoke Colin couldn't place the accent. Welsh, maybe, he thought, or a trace of Derbyshire? Colin had family, on his mother's side, in the Peak District.

'Thank you. A pint of your special bitter, if you'd be so kind.'

Colin Drover had never lost his pleasure in drawing a pint of really good ale. He was proud of his beer, which he still reckoned king among the alcoholic beverages. People nowadays went overboard for wine, but in Colin Drover's view you couldn't beat a decent pint of real ale. A solid no-nonsense beer drinker was always welcome in the Stag and Badger.

He drew the beer to a foaming head and set it down delicately on the bar where the foam rocked and then slopped gently over the glass's side. The man on the other side of the bar treated the drink with equal care, lifting the glass to his lips to sip the dark gold liquor beneath the creamy rim and Colin Drover watched, anxious to see how his beer went down.

The stranger sipped and sighed, and the landlord of the Stag and Badger sighed too with vicarious enjoyment. 'Nothing like a good pint, I always say,' he remarked with the subdued enjoyment that a satisfactory sale always brought.

'Nothing like it, except perhaps another one!' the stranger promisingly agreed. He seemed a self-sufficient sort, not chatty, but not one of your gloomy types either. He sat quietly absorbing the atmosphere, his eyes half lidded over as if to keep a veil over his thoughts. Not the kind to give much away but could make a valuable customer, was Colin Drover's conclusion as he forced himself back to the kitchen to take up the cudgels again with Paula.

The newcomer looked about him, apparently taking in his surroundings. The inn was prosperous-looking: mahogany fittings, brass lights, and wallpaper with a leafy National Trust motif in the restaurant area, where tables were set out for dinner guests. It was in this part of the pub, where the stranger was sitting, that a few stools were available for the more elevated drinkers. But it seemed that the stranger did not include himself in this category for after another sip of beer he slid down and made his way round to the public bar, just as a thin young man with an earring and a close-fitting woolly cap came through the door.

The young man took up a place as if this was a regular perch. Luke Weatherall was a poet, who comforted or rewarded himself, depending on the day's output, most evenings about this time. This particular evening was one for comfort—his long, narrative poem, based on a Creation myth of the North American Indians, had stuck fast. Luke had pinned the sheet of paper he had covered in useless stanzas to the stud wall of his room—in Lavinia Galsworthy's barn conversion just outside the village, where Luke rented a studio flat—and thrown darts at it before making his way down the hill to the Stag and Badger. It was at times like this that Luke wondered if he mightn't have done better to choose the other Indians for his poem— the Eastern ones—about whom there was more known and less room for artistic confusion.

'Evening, there,' he said to the man who now came and sat beside him. Luke had a friendly nature, but he also hoped to have his mind taken off the worries of creation.

The other man acknowledged the greeting with a slight nod of his head and for half a second there flashed across Luke's mind an image of a mountain lake in which there was perfectly reflected a pellucid gentian sky. Perhaps the stanzas hadn't been so bad, after all.

'Golightly's the name. What can I get you?'

'Hey, thanks, man. A bitter'd be great.'

The stranger waved a hand at the barmaid, a slight girl with long red hair demurely caught back in a velvet band.

Mr Golightly, who liked all prettiness, gave an affable glance in her direction and ordered. 'How's the weather been round here?' he enquired, showing he was a thoroughbred Englishman and knew what bar talk entailed.

The girl set down the glasses so that not a drop slopped over the rim on to the polished surface of the bar.

'Middling only, there's been terrible rain but there's been some God days, too.'

9

'She means the odd sunny one,' explained Luke, alive to the dangers of social exclusion.

But his concern for his new acquaintance was unnecessary, as once again Mr Golightly gave his accommodating smile. 'Ah, yes,' he agreed, 'I know those!'

He seemed disinclined to chat further, so Luke turned to the back of the newspaper, which was kept for the customers, and started in on the crossword. The North American myth of Creation had cruelly reduced his circumstances; the only chance of a paper was when he walked down in the evening to the Stag.

The door opened again, letting in the cleansing draught of a March wind and an apricot spaniel dog who trotted ahead of her owner. Sam Noble, the former film-maker, was also a regular at the pub. There was no need for him to speak his order and a gin and tonic was wordlessly laid before him by the red-headed barmaid.

Sam hesitated a moment as if unsure whether in betraying curiosity he mightn't betray rather more, and then ostentatiously sat himself on the other side of Mr Golightly. 'Evening,' he said. 'Visiting these parts?'

The question was unnecessary since he had witnessed Mr Golightly's arrival at Spring Cottage earlier that afternoon. Perhaps Mr Golightly guessed this. In any case, he merely agreed that he was staying in the area.

'In the village, is it?' Sam asked. It was part of his social ritual to pretend to know at once more and less than he really did about his neighbours. 'Holiday?' he asked again.

But Sam's project of enquiry was doomed, as all

the other did was renew his opaque smile. He appeared more taken by the spaniel, who had sidled up and was rubbing her parts seductively against his boot.

'Nice dog you've got there. Bitch, is she?'

'Daphne, yes,' agreed Sam, slightly affronted that his pet was making more impact than himself. But then the newcomer didn't know about the Palme d'Or. Time enough to bring that up later. 'Named for my aunt,' he added. 'My mother was a twin and lost her sister when she was born. Nowadays it would count as trauma.' He was quietly proud of the tragedy which hung over the family psyche.

But even the account of this disaster did not disturb the newcomer's humour. 'Ah,' he agreed, 'it would, I suppose.' He spoke as if he might have added that in his day they saw such matters differently—life and death, his demeanour seemed to suggest, were not so important that they should interrupt a quiet pint.

Sam Noble, sensing that conversation was drained dry, turned to the man who had approached the bar to ask for 'twenty Lambert and Butlers'.

Jackson, the so-called 'boyfriend' of Paula out-the-back, was Great Calne's handyman, though 'handy' was hardly the word to describe his skills. Residents of the village would frequently ask, on the matter of Jackson, why on earth they bothered—something of an existential question, as Jackson, like most who work in the building trade, dealt in promises of doubtful validity. No one in their right mind seriously believes a builder when he tells you he will be with you next Wednesday;

certainly not when accompanied by the rider, 'on the dot of nine'. As all the world knows, to a builder 'next Wednesday' means in a couple of months if you're lucky, and no man or woman born and bred in Britain would seriously count on it being otherwise.

Jackson, however, took this licence to extremes, interpreting 'next Wednesday' to mean as much as a couple of years off. Nor, when he finally arrived to do a job, could the results be said to be satisfactory. He had set up old Emily Pope's electric shower, down in Spring Cottage—in the days before it was let to holidaymakers—so that the first time she used it a jolt of electric current went through her naked body which people said had very likely contributed to her being carried off altogether the following year.

Jackson's chief interest in life was baiting badgers, and girls. In the latter case, if not one of nature's gentlemen he was at least one of her democrats. He had no fine feelings about what a girl looked like provided she was willing to drop her knickers with no fuss. Of course, it was a bonus if they were lookers too, but not essential to his general aim.

What happened to a girl once she had come across was another story. Paula had made history by keeping Jackson's attention long after she had become unpredictable in the knickers department. Jackson himself did not wholly understand the reasons for his unusual constancy. Like many apparently aggressive men, he was frightened of violence and wasn't at all sure what a dumped Paula mightn't do. More than once, she had darkly referred to the collection of kitchen knives which

12

were kept at the Stag and Badger for slicing cold meats. Jackson had an uneasy feeling that Paula's mind, if sufficiently stirred, might turn to ideas of slicing other kinds of flesh. It was well to keep in with her; the badgers were a different matter.

In the days before Paula, Jackson had a vague scheme to get his leg over Mary Simms, the red-headed barmaid. But Mary herself had higher ideals. She had recently enrolled in an Open University course on Romantic poetry and had no plans to waste her time with a layabout like Jackson. 'How are you getting on?' she asked Luke who was frowning at the crossword. Luke was a poet and the course on Romantic poetry was not entirely coincidental.

' "This Old Testament prophet gets cut off short in drought"—five letters?' he queried aloud, oblivious to who was speaking. He was on unfamiliar territory with the Bible—American Indians were his thing.

Sam Noble decided to have a go at Jackson. 'Any chance of you getting round to fixing the pond?' he asked. This was a routine question; the pond had been waiting to be 'fixed' since the day Sam had moved into the village, leaving behind his showbiz career.

Jackson, who reserved a special contempt for townies, contracted his little red eyes as if in fierce thought. 'Be with you Thursday—' he announced oracularly—'Friday latest. Right?'

'Very good,' said Sam primly. 'I shall expect you not later than Friday noon.' After five years he was still prone to the error of imagining that his former position and class made any headway with Jackson.

A family party, parents and two small children,

13

now arrived and flustered Colin Drover by ordering the prawns 'shell-off'. The publican made a sortie out the back—to Paula's domain—and returned red-faced to suggest that 'shell-on' could be had for a 'pound off'. 'Mu-um,' the small boy whined, catching on that here was a chance for a scene, 'I don't like them with shells.'

'Of course not, darling,' said his mother. 'I'm sure the nice man will get us some without.'

'Nonsense,' said his father. 'Shells are fun! Daisy thinks they're fun, don't you, Daisy?' He beamed at his daughter, calculating that if they all had the prawns with shells on the meal would be four quid less. He wanted to get back home for the match on TV; the evening out had not been his idea.

'Don't like shells,' his son stubbornly maintained. Daisy was only four—what did she know? She didn't eat grown-up food anyway.

Mr Golightly, who had been looking at nothing in particular, now turned his glance in the direction of the restaurant, and the boy piped down and shuffled his shoes against the table leg. They were new shoes, bought during the half-term which was almost over. He didn't want to go back to school where he was bullied in the playground and had had his head pushed down one of the girls' toilets.

'Shells are fun!' his father repeated. Like most repetition this was not convincing. But at that minute a grinning Colin Drover emerged from out the back with four plates of naked, steaming, rosy prawns. Inexplicably, Paula had buckled to and shelled them.

'There now,' the father spoke with wooden cheer, the promise of four quid saved disappearing with the arrival of the prawns. But by Monday the kids would be back at school and the half-term horror would be over. 'Wasn't that kind of the man, Daisy?' he prompted, more enthusiastically.

Mr Golightly had turned his eyes from the table but the boy continued to watch him. He looked a bit like that picture of the man feeding birds, in olden times, his teacher had up in the classroom.

Mr Golightly finished his pint, lowered himself from the tall stool and stood looking round as if to take his leave of the company at the Stag and Badger.

'Old Testament prophet six down,' he said, passing behind Luke Weatherall to the door. 'Hosea. Not a bad sort,' he added.

CHAPTER THREE

Spring Cottage was named for the natural water supply which seeped up through the Devon soil and occasionally made its way through the porous walls of the old dwelling. The cottage stood in a run-to-seed garden, which looked across to hills and ran towards fields which sloped down to the River Dart. This, thanks to recent rains, was roaring like a hungry lion when Mr Golightly stepped outside his back door the following morning.

It was early, not yet six; the stars had yet to disappear and the near-full moon hung still, like a yellow paper lantern, in the west. Over the hills, black clouds made portentous shapes suggesting Eastern tales: dragons, strange-beaked birds, perilous cliffs. Behind the clouds, a veined-marble sky was streaked dim green and pearl. An

15

experienced watcher of weather could have predicted that the day would be a bright one, for beyond, in the east, a thin patina of gold hinted at imminent light.

Mr Golightly snuffed the air like a hunter. It smelled to him of animal life and sappy growth, of burgeoning country things which gave a lift to his heart. All hearts need a lift from time to time and Mr Golightly's was no exception. He had come to Great Calne to take a holiday. It had been many years since his duties had allowed such an indulgence, but for some time he had been thinking that a project he had started long ago was due for reappraisal. Quite why Great Calne had been chosen as the place to set about this project was a question that Mr Golightly himself may not have been able to answer. But he understood, perhaps better than most, that all important questions are unanswerable.

The intricacies of the World Wide Web were still a mystery to Mr Golightly who, despite his business experience, with many other pressures and concerns to attend to, was not yet practised at using it. One of his valuable aides had entered his requirements—'Holiday let in peaceful rural setting'—into the search engine, Alphaomega, coming up with Spring Cottage via Nicky Pope's website.

So far the result appeared satisfactory. In any event, Mr Golightly did not give the impression of being a choosy sort. On the contrary, he emanated some sense that all places were alike to him. He gave every sign of being content with the simple accommodation—a bedroom (referred to in the website details as the master), which was almost filled by the iron, black-painted double bedstead, a boxroom (bedroom two) stuffed with old curtains, magazines, rugs, a fender, an exercise bike and supermarket bags full of the late Emily Pope's correspondence with the taxman, which Nicky Pope, who as a single mother had her hands full already, meant to get around to when she could only find a moment.

Downstairs, there was a parlour (lounge-diner) which boasted an oak gateleg table, a couple of floral-covered comfy chairs, a spine-challenging orange sofa bed, bought by Emily Pope during a short mid-life crisis in the sixties, a black-and-white TV, and the state-of-the-art wood-burning stove from Norway; also a narrow scullery (fitted kitchen with mod cons) which housed a microwave oven, an erratic hob, some Formica cupboards containing a medley of crockery, and a whining fridge which, as Nicky Pope had had to run off before she had quite seen that all was in order, still contained a tub of low-cost margarine, a dried-up half of a lemon and five of a 'six-pack' of Cokes, a legacy of the Clapham woman's stay.

In the days before planning permission, the scullery had been tacked rakishly on to the side of the cottage and roofed, in a slapdash manner, with corrugated asbestos, which nowadays would have drawn down imprecations from a dutiful Health and Safety inspector. Lucky, then, for Nicky Pope, that Mr Golightly had none of the Clapham woman's self-preserving assertiveness; or it may have been that health and safety were not issues for him.

When the rain fell it made a timpani of the scullery roof, a sound which Mr Golightly had yet

17

to discover whether he found enchanting or distracting. A rickety fence, with a wicket gate let into it, which led through to the garden, ran beside the scullery. But this morning Mr Golightly was troubled by none of those things: he stood listening to the sound of the rushing brook, which ran through the lower meadows, and noting how the hills formed a gentle cleavage through which the River Dart found its way to the sea.

Grazing in the field, to which the untidy garden sloped, was a stocky brown horse with a white flash down its nose. Beyond, bounded by a beech hedge, where the leaves independently maintained their autumnal rust, lay further fields, where young spring wheat was forming a green glaze over the soil.

A batch of rooks was already out scouring the earth for food, while a band of their less diligent kin sat in the bare-fanned branches of an ash tree, making clean silhouettes against the gathering light. As Mr Golightly watched, a pair of magpies swooped gleaming down, balancing with their long tails and settling among the rooks to add a touch of Old Master cachet to the scene.

'One for sorrow, two for joy.'

Mr Golightly spoke the words aloud. It was an ancient saying, old as any of the works of man, and he could not now recall when he had first heard it. But, like many country-bred people, he did not let reason oust superstition: the sight of the swaggering piebald birds gave an added fillip to his spirits.

And now, as if to add fuel to this fire, a sliver of sun appeared above one of the breast-like hills, a mere slice of orange which rapidly grew to an incandescent globe. Rifts of glowing red infiltrated the green-grey sky which began to take on further intimations of light.

'Be praised!' said Mr Golightly.

He did not speak aloud, but as if to a beloved intimate whose understanding had no need of outward hearing.

Samson, the horse, perhaps catching the drift of the unspoken words, made its way up to the wire which formed a boundary to Spring Cottage's garden. 'Hello, old boy.' Mr Golightly ran a finger down the long plush nose and wished he had thought to bring sugar lumps. The cardboard box he had brought was packed with some of the items he might have difficulty finding in the average English village shop: tins of anchovies, jars of pickled walnuts, Marmite, a pot of moist Stilton, chillies, pine kernels, a French sausage, Frank Cooper's Oxford marmalade, sugared almonds— but despite these latter items Mr Golightly did not, in general, have a sweet tooth. He had not been raised on sugar and consequently it did not form part of his regular diet.

'Sorry, old chap.' He spoke regretfully: he liked to indulge animals who rarely bore resentment if one failed to do as they wished.

As if in response to his apology, a ribald cackling made itself heard and Mr Golightly turned away from Samson and towards the direction of the noise. The next-door garden was fenced by heavy barbed wire. Through the wire Mr Golightly could see a female figure among white geese with glistening orange bills and some farmyard ducks.

Mr Golightly was naturally courteous; but he was concerned, too, to establish peace with his

19

neighbours so that there should be no threat to his tranquillity. His work had too often been a battle; he had no wish for his holiday to be marred by warfare. War between neighbours, he knew from long experience, is often of the most disruptive kind.

'Hello,' he said, and offered his hand across the barbed-wire fence.

The other said nothing but only stared. It was the kind of stare which might have perturbed anyone with an uneasy conscience; but if Mr Golightly's conscience was uneasy he didn't betray the fact. He held the gaze steadily till the woman relaxed and held out a hand.

'Watch the spikes on the fence.'

'Good fences make good neighbours.'

Mr Golightly could not have explained why he had made this remark. He was not in the modern habit of constantly enquiring into the workings of his own mind but tended to say whatever came into his head.

'Ellen Thomas,' said his neighbour, apparently ignoring his comment, and turned away.

'Golightly,' said Mr Golightly, looking after her; the grey eyes of Ellen Thomas were those of a creature in pain.

Back in the cottage, he unpacked the box of provisions and arranged these tidily in the Formica cupboards. He looked about for a kettle which he eventually found in the cupboard under the sink. No plug. Better make a shopping list, he decided.

Up in the bedroom he completed his unpacking. His possessions were simple: a couple of nightshirts, a pair of slippers, some woollies, a number of warm shirts, wool socks, underwear. His zip-up sponge bag, rather the worse for wear, was already in the avocado bathroom. No tie—this was a holiday. Among the other items there was a small travelling photograph holder which framed the picture of a young man with a piteous face.

Mr Golightly looked at the face as he placed the picture beside the bed. Love is the price of love, he thought, as, observing the warning on a note tacked up by Nicky Pope, he minded his head down the steep stairs to the parlour where he prepared to do combat with a book of instructions lying beside the Norwegian woodstove.

Books of instructions were things with which Mr Golightly had little patience. He opened the booklet entitled 'Norpine Stoves: the extra modern way to be old-fashioned' and read: *The flue towards the left-handed side of the upper orifice is to be unclosed while the material fires is being laid down.*

What the hell did all that mean?

CHAPTER FOUR

Ellen Thomas lay on her sofa looking across to where the sheep stood making enigmatic runes on the hillside. She was reflecting that if she could read these runes she might become wise.

No living soul knew this but, shortly after her husband, Robert, died, Ellen had had a strange encounter with a gorse bush. She had been walking her dog, Wilfred, across the moor and, as usual when she walked in the days after Robert's death, she had been crying. Although she had no inhibition about crying over Robert, the tears only

21

seemed to come when she was mobile. While she was stationary they stayed dammed up inside her, causing unbearable pressure around the heart.

There was something about striding across the tough moorland grasses, through the plashy bogs and past the pale lichen-coated brakes of thorn, which made a breach in her constraining inner structures; so that when she had climbed to the stony outcrop of the tor she was able to stand against the wind on the spine of the skyline and howl like a banshee.

She was returning from just such a venting early one afternoon, a time when most people were eating lunch, when Wilfred began to sniff and whine round a patch of gorse. Supposing voles or rabbits, Ellen had put Wilfred on his lead and tried to drag the dog past the bush. But he pulled so hard the lead slipped from her grasp, and Wilfred, barking frantically, bolted for home.

Ellen, about to hurry after him, was arrested by a strong sense that the gorse concealed more than a vole or a rabbit. A violent burning sensation leapt like a ravaging tiger at her heart and a voice, sweet and terrible, spoke from the golden bush.

'I am love,' it said.

Ellen was not of a religious disposition. If asked, she would have said she was an atheist, an agnostic at best, so these words startled her and at first she believed there must have been some mistake.

'I am Ellen Thomas,' she had offered, diffidently, in return, and waited, expecting to be dismissed. But the dismissal came in the form of a further surprise.

'Tell them.'

'What?' Ellen asked.

22

'Tell them!' said the voice again in its tender, commanding tone.

Ellen waited for more but no further utterances issued from the gorse. She walked home, dry-eyed, after Wilfred.

Ellen had no idea how to obey the injunction she had been given. She had no clue as to what the cryptic words might mean. Whatever they meant it was not—she was sure of this—that she should go about preaching to people. No being, not even one whose essence was love, would suborn her, Ellen Thomas, as a preacher in its cause. She wondered if what she was being asked was to write about the experience, but that seemed hardly more likely. Robert had been a journalist and had occasionally run stuff past her for comments; but aside from that, and the jottings she sometimes wrote in her grandmother's recipe book, since school, where she had not excelled, she had had no practice in writing.

To be asked to tell of love is a tall enough order; to be asked such a thing when one has not even the habit of belief is awful. The magnitude and impossibility of the task she had been assigned felled Ellen.

The loss of Robert had awoken her to the innate treachery of all certainties. Her husband's enduring sympathy had made life seem unchangeable. With Robert gone this illusion, along with all human ties, vanished too. Yet even in his absence, the knowledge of Robert's steady love had conferred upon her a sense of life's consistency. But the enigmatic order from the gorse bush robbed Ellen of her old self and the sureties that had survived Robert's death. She took to walking, day and night, seeking not so much a solution to the problem she had been unwillingly set as escape.

The walks left her overwhelmingly fatigued. The friendly countryside she had once enjoyed took on a menacing aspect. The foliage in the trees became baleful, dropping leaves and icy water on her as she passed. The hedges murmured threateningly in the wind, which rushed at her, haranguing her like some invisible prosecutor. Metal gates clanged horribly, bruising the calves of her legs, or making violent grating noises, shocking to her ears. The sun, red and glowering, plunged down the sky in pursuit of her. Outside or in she felt alarmingly afraid.

Gradually, as rats are said to leave a sinking ship, her everyday capacities had begun to slink away, leaving her a remnant, a hapless passenger on the derelict wreck of her old personality, which now appeared to float on perilous and alien waters. She seemed to feel her feet sliding under her, sensed the deck shudder and tip her dangerously off balance, downwards to an icy darkness, where lurked shapeless, unformed things, and where death looked a blessed relief and disintegration easier than resistance.

With the last dregs of her failing resources, she dragged herself to sell Brook Farm, the farmhouse she had lived in with Robert for over twenty years, and move to the small, plain, characterless bungalow where obscurely she felt she might be safe. And here—after the anguish of disposing of the furniture over which she and Robert had laughed, planned, bickered, made love and acted all the multifacets of a long marriage, for there was no way the accumulation of a shared life would fit

24

into her new home—she had hidden herself away, for what she found she chiefly could not bear was other people's company.

From the long sofa, which, scraping the bottom of the barrel of her energy, she had made the object of a last-ditch shopping effort, she lay, unrecognisable to herself, gazing out in those moments of passionless lucidity which afflict the mortally wounded. It seemed to her, at such moments, that she might never rise again, but would simply freeze there upon her long perch, like some stray migrant bird forced to winter over in a cold and alien land.

One morning, while she was engaged in looking out—if 'engaged' could be the right word for something which so much resembled the loosening of all former ties—she became aware that the nature of what she saw had undergone some alchemical change.

Ellen had been a watercolour artist, and made a successful living selling her paintings at local craft shops. She had an accurate eye and a patient hand, and the world, as she was used to seeing it, had beauty and charm. But now everything she had once seen as colourful, lyrical, dramatic, even, was subsumed into a vast, unquenchable litany of light.

The months that she had by now spent lying on the sofa had brought Ellen no further towards solving the problem she had been set by the presence in the gorse bush. But the vision of the changed world, rather than diminishing her sense of inadequacy, became a reproach. She looked outside to where the trees and hills and sheep apparently continued their former existence, but in the infinitude of space around and between them,

25

she now knew there lay the inscrutable and uncompromising powers of love and mercy, and she, Ellen Thomas, had been enjoined to make them known.

The intense and brilliant light Ellen had seen at the centre of all things probed her being like a surgeon's knife. There seemed no safety outside herself and no refuge within. She could tell no one what had occurred—lest she be taken for a lunatic. She feared to show herself to anyone for she felt there must be a savour of madness about her.

During the day, apart from the sparest of attentions to economic necessities, she gazed out of the window, a shadow between two worlds, surveying the landscape, waiting for the awful injunction to return, for she knew that having been a prey to truth it would never leave her, but would make itself felt at any cost. At night she lay in a kind of dead-and-alive doze, apprehensive that the voice might call on her again.

The assault of love upon Ellen Thomas had been savage rather than sweet, and, like many caught in its toils, she longed to have been spared the experience.

CHAPTER FIVE

After forty-five minutes of fruitless struggle Mr Golightly had reached the view that the instructions for the up-to-the-minute stove had probably been produced and marketed by his business rival. He had not admitted this to anyone at the office, but he had been troubled, lately, by recent signs that his rival's business was beginning to supersede his own. It was a business formed upon the back of his own global enterprise, and this made its proliferation especially galling. To distract his mind from this unwelcome line of thought, he began to check out the rest of Spring Cottage's equipment.

He found the two convector heaters, slightly chipped and rusting, in the cupboard under the stairs. Well, that was a blessing, anyway. He could afford to take a more cavalier position with the stove. In one of the Formica cupboards there was a toaster, thank goodness with a plug attached; a broken machine, apparently designed for grinding; in the cupboard beneath the stairs an iron which had seen better days, and an impossible ironing board. There had been times when he might have gone in for grinding, but not on his holiday. Nor, since his secretary was not there to pass comment, was there any call to iron. Toast, now, was a different kettle of fish: toast fingers, with a boiled egg, was something which Mr Golightly was partial to . . .

It was nearly nine and a walk to the shop would give the opportunity to assess what provisions were available in Great Calne. He hoped not to have to drive too far afield. The Traveller could play up and he didn't want the bother of having to find a mechanic who could fix it. Of course, he could always send for someone to come down from the office, but it was to get away from all of that that he had come away for his holiday.

Putting on a green parka, Mr Golightly walked up the hill towards the Post Office Stores where a young man with a straggly beard was stacking

27

oranges in the window.

'Good morning,' said Mr Golightly. And he spoke truly for the fully risen sun was unreservedly lighting the village of Great Calne.

'Depends who you are,' rejoined the beard, stepping back from the window. 'Shit!' as the oranges rebelled and rolled down and all over the floor.

Oh dear. Mr Golightly spoke only to himself. He had selected milk, fresh and 'untreated'—he didn't hold with 'dead' milk in cartons—half a dozen eggs, some local cheese, tomatoes and a couple of brown rolls.

'You staying at Spring Cott?' asked the young man, cramming too many tomatoes into a tiny paper bag.

'Yes, indeed. A pretty location.'

'All right for toads! Damp as hell. Wouldn't catch me there, that's for sure.'

Why this is hell, nor am I out of it . . .

As Mr Golightly walked back down the hill, some words, which had always struck him as particularly grim, rang in his mind. But better not to meet trouble halfway—there were boiled eggs and toast to look forward to, he was on holiday and here to revise his great work.

Many years earlier Mr Golightly had written a work of dramatic fiction which, after slow initial sales, had gradually grown to become a best-seller. In time, the by-products of this enterprise had expanded to form the basis of a worldwide business. The work had been based on his observations of human life—its loves, hopes, fears, lusts, idiocies, anxieties, false securities, vanities, dishonesties, fantasies, cruelties and general

28

tendency to inveterate folly. Mr Golightly, in his droll way, liked to describe his work as a 'comedy'; but in this, he had discovered, he resembled the playwright Chekhov.

Chekhov, attending the dress rehearsal of one his plays, was surprised to find that the director, none other than the great Russian Stanislavsky, was playing it as a tragedy. There were no laughs, Chekhov was tickled to find, except those provided by the single audience of the humorous playwright himself.

Mr Golightly's magnum opus had something of *The Cherry Orchard*'s ambiguity. Perhaps it was this, or perhaps it was the gradually reducing sales—though to be sure it had had a good enough run: for years it had been an international sensation—which had determined him to rewrite the work. The idea had come to him when, one evening, he had turned on the TV and had become engrossed in one of the many soap operas which run there.

Mr Golightly's business was so time-consuming that often he remained ignorant of the rapid developments of modern culture. His philosophy was that if a thing was going to catch on it would, in the fullness of time, catch up with him. That millions of people organised their lives so as not to miss their personal 'soap' was news to Mr Golightly.

But herein lay one of the gifts which made him unique in his sphere. Far from being shocked, or taking an 'it wasn't like that in my day' attitude (a common trap among the older generation), he saw at once the advantages. His own work, he felt, after sampling the current TV output, had many of the

29

features of a modern soap—it was merely the idiom and the episodes which needed bringing up to date. The characters in his original drama were only apparently unlike those of the present day. Human nature hadn't changed, of course, but custom had, and the times.

And then there was that delightful notion of a holiday . . .

Mr Golightly had been taken by an item concerning 'stress in the office' which had followed *Neighbours*, the soap his secretary watched and for which he had found he himself developing a liking. Stress, it seemed, was a recently discovered malady and one, Mr Golightly couldn't help feeling, that he could be a candidate for. It seemed there were all kind of palliatives available to combat it—t'ai chi, reiki, Pilates, yoga, reflexology, hypnosis, homeopathy, psychotherapy, acupuncture, massage— but something in Mr Golightly baulked at these remedies which, so far as he was able to grasp them, struck him as somewhat invasive.

But a 'holiday' was a different story: that harked back to a former era—a time when he had been able to rest on his laurels and had taken delight in all he had achieved. And what better plan than to combine a long overdue rest with a reworking of his great enterprise?

No one but an artist knows the peculiar delight of being summoned by a work which, as yet unborn, lies, with all its potential undisclosed, within the dormant darkness of the creating heart. Mr Golightly's tread had a secret bounce as he made his way down the hill and towards his awaiting soap opera. He would boil the eggs, pour a mug of coffee, with the unpasteurised milk he had bought at the miserable young man's stores, and set up the laptop, the use of which Mike had instructed him in before his departure.

Mike, it was agreed by all at the office, was a perfect angel. His patience was a byword and he had promised, if necessary, to come down to Great Calne himself should Mr Golightly encounter any technical problem with the newly installed e-mail system.

Mr Golightly had drunk his coffee from the Spiderman mug he had found among the medley of crockery, before he opened up his laptop to check his e-mails. Mike had explained that the system called for an e-mail address and something called a 'server'. He had set up golightly@golightly.com which allowed, he suggested, for expansion into a website. For some time Mike had been of the view that a website would make a valuable innovation for the Golightly Enterprises and was hoping to take advantage of this holiday to persuade the boss of its commercial advantages.

Connecting the laptop to the phone involved some fiddling about with the leads which Mike had had the foresight to include, so that by the time Mr Golightly was ready to dial up it was past ten o'clock. Plenty of time, though, to start work—the day was still young.

Several e-mails, accompanied by a sound effect, appeared on the screen. The first was a message from the server, cosmos.com, and offered Mr Golightly the benefit of bargain travel services, including a cheap offer to go diving in the Red Sea.

In his younger, more forceful days Mr Golightly had often visited that part of the world. But the greener, less turbulent pastures of England, were,

31

he felt, a more soothing environment for his recreational plans. The Red Sea would take him too far down memory lane, a route to be avoided when one was set upon change.

The second message was from Bill, his handsome PA, and concerned some charity, to do with Third World aid, to which Mr Golightly had agreed to lend the firm's name.

The third was from no recognisable name or address.

by what way is the light parted?

was the disconcerting message.

Scientific questions had not troubled Mr Golightly greatly over the years. In the past, when questions had been asked at all, it was he who had tended to do the asking. His secretary, Martha, the one who had put him on to *Neighbours*, would probably say that this was 'very like a man'. Comments along these lines from Martha had been more forthcoming lately. She had worked faithfully for the Golightly firm for many years but latterly she seemed to have picked up the modern woman's tendency—an unfortunate one, Mr Golightly couldn't help sometimes feeling—to criticise the male; or perhaps criticise him openly was more accurate, since Mr Golightly was too shrewd a judge of human nature to suppose that men had ever, in women's private thoughts, got off scot-free.

What would Martha make of the enigmatic question which now confronted him? It seemed to contain a sly play on his name. And who on earth could have sent it? His usual movements, for the purpose of the smooth running of the firm, were shrouded in a certain mystery; he was unused to being confronted with barefaced questions, especially ones which touched obliquely on his own person.

Mr Golightly had set up his computer on the gateleg table with a view on to the garden and down to the field below. Looking out, he saw the horse standing in the sun, taking the benefit of its warmth on his chestnut coat. There was something reassuring about the horse's stance. Not quite meaning to, Mr Golightly got up from the table and wandered outside.

Samson, observing activity, walked over to investigate. Mr Golightly felt regretful again over the sugar lumps. But no doubt the horse's owner would anyway disapprove. It was discouraging how few of the world's prodigal comforts were nowadays available for enjoyment. Mr Golightly had been cautioned by Martha against exceeding the recommended number of 'units' of alcohol he drank in a week. There had been times when her boss had supped of the vine in a manner which would throw a modern health practitioner into a frenzy, and yet, Mr Golightly couldn't help feeling, he was not obviously any the worse for his past excesses.

*   *   *

Next door, Ellen Thomas was lying on her sofa. She looked out to where the rooks were dredging the fields clean of the new-sown wheat. A saying of her late husband's drifted into her mind. 'Forbear not sowing because of the birds,' he had used to say, when counselling against needless caution. Her new neighbour, with his big head, reminded her a little of Robert. She might give him some of the duck eggs, azure, like the sky's watery reflection in the puddle which had collected on the upturned barrel she had put outside for some purpose she couldn't now remember.

What did 'remember' mean? Robert had told her this once, too. Wasn't it putting back together the body's members which had been torn asunder . . . ?

CHAPTER SIX

It was Thursday, and consequently the yew tree was not a safe hiding place for Johnny Spence. The Reverend Meredith Fisher was at home and would be back and forth, sticking her nose into other people's business or attending to her parish duties, depending on your point of view. Johnny's attitude was laissez-faire: he didn't mind what the lady vicar did so long as she didn't interfere with his use of the churchyard.

The concept of sanctuary is an old one and in using the environs of the Lord for this purpose Johnny followed a long and venerable tradition. But he was not the first to be ousted from safe-hiding by one of the Lord's appointed. Who can say how far the Lord Himself, were He to be consulted, would sanction the attitudes of those who undertake to speak on His behalf? As it was, Johnny had to look for an alternative place of concealment.

Great Calne's church, with its square Norman tower, stood flanked on one side by the rectory and

34

on the other by the Post Office Stores. A little way down the hill, on the opposite side of the road, lay Spring Cottage where only the previous day Johnny had watched the arrival of Mr Golightly.

Johnny had practised being invisible since his mum took up with his stepdad. Like all early training, this stood him in sound stead. At school his absences were so regular as to be generally overlooked and often his name was omitted entirely from any official register. A conviction that one is nothing acts as a powerful charm against being perceived, but Johnny was experienced enough in the ways of the world to know that you mustn't take anything for granted. Despite the fact that, to the authorities, he didn't exist, that didn't mean he should be careless. Like a young tomcat, he whipped down the street and inside the gateway of Spring Cottage. He felt cautiously well disposed towards the bloke he had spied on and he wanted, anyway, to get a closer look at the Traveller.

The sky had turned indigo and the sun set up at once a contesting sheet of light. A cloud of rooks, with the mysterious concordance of flocking birds, rose, hovered in the petrol-coloured sky, gathered together again, then, as suddenly, parted into factions to flutter like confetti from some Satanic wedding on to the fields, or settle in the stands of reddening beech. Splashes of sunlight on the birds' plumage made fitful, darting gleams. And now the sky, as if surrendering to an eloquent seducer, cleared rapidly again, stretches of blue wash appeared and scraps of cloud, as picturesquely puffed as any on a painted Italian ceiling, began to scud wantonly across the renewing sky.

Mr Golightly, sitting before his laptop, watched

this drama. It was amazing what could be accomplished if you simply left a system to run itself. This was the policy he tried to operate in his business. In the early days, he had held the reins more tightly, managing everything more or less single-handed. But that was before the catastrophe which had changed everything. These days, as the office knew, delegation was his watchword. And it was precisely this which made it possible for him to take this holiday and rewrite his great work into the soap opera, which he had decided to call—he was a little proud of the title—*That's How Life Is*.

But, how, in God's name, to begin?

For a start he needed the cast of characters. Until recently, he would have written these down in a small, leather-bound notebook, which he still carried about with him in case he should wish to jot down a passing thought or useful saying. But now that he had the services of a computer he supposed he'd best adopt new practices . . .

He opened a file, as Mike had shown him, and 'saved' it as 'THLI'. Then, typing slowly, he spelled out 'Cast of Characters' and paused, debating whether that didn't belong better in a file marked 'Prelims'—a piece of technical advice about organising his material which he had picked up at the office, from Muriel in Accounts.

Muriel was less in the forefront of office affairs than Mike, or Bill. She was a retiring soul, who kept herself to herself, but she'd been part of the firm since its inception. Muriel had a capacious memory. If Mr Golightly wasn't one hundred per cent sure how a word was spelled, he would check with Muriel. Thinking of her, he remembered he must rescue his *Oxford English Dictionary*, which he

36

had jammed under the passenger seat of the Traveller. Bill had suggested that Mike could load on to the laptop a CD-ROM of the *OED*, which would apparently furnish every word in the English language anyone could wish to check. But in Mr Golightly's view, a computer screen was no substitute for a solid book you could get your hands around. It was his habit to read the dictionary in bed, an activity which he suspected neither Mike nor Bill would fully understand. Slightly evasively— he didn't like to have to defend his preferences— he had stuffed the two volumes of the *Shorter OED* into the Traveller at the last moment of departure.

The office could tell you that when the boss got his dander up he could spit fire and hailstones, but these days, for the most part, Mr Golightly was a pacific sort and his inner state was reflected in his physical movements. Johnny Spence, who from years of cohabiting with his stepdad could detect a human tread quicker than any cat, only saw Mr Golightly as he came round the side of the cottage. Johnny shot under the Traveller and lay pulling the hood of his baggy top well over his face.

Mr Golightly stood for some minutes by the open car door, straightening out a dog-ear from a page of Vol. II Marl–Z. As he did so he whistled. He was senior enough to have tuned in regularly to a radio programme, *Whistle While You Work*, on the old BBC Light, and the injunction had infiltrated his habits.

Johnny Spence, crammed under the van, heard the bars from *Fidelio* and was strangely reassured. He was not familiar with Beethoven's single opera, but those who fight for freedom are joined by more than temporal bonds and Johnny perhaps

37

recognised, in the long-departed composer's music, a theme in tune with his own revolutionary aims.

Mr Golightly had finished smoothing out the crumpled page and, still whistling, paused a while longer to read the definition of a word he had forgotten. His memory, once capacious, had been playing up lately. He had disguised this from the office, but there were times when he found himself suffering worrying blanks and lapses when he couldn't find a familiar word or place a name. But, he comforted himself, even the most efficient memory cannot retain everything and a less than perfect memory had benefits. It lessened the likelihood of grudge bearing. A tendency to bear grudges was a habit which, when he encountered it, embarrassed Mr Golightly; it reminded him too much of former times.

Johnny Spence lay dead still under the van. The old bloke hadn't moved off—from where he was lying he could see his shoes, the kind with little holes in the toes, scuffed but posh leather. He needed a pee—what the fuck was the old bastard doing just standing there?

Mr Golightly's attention had been caught by a word on the crumpled page of the dictionary: 'uberty', pronounced, as he now read, like 'puberty', it meant full of bounteous kindness, a state which he was disposed to approve of. Here was another forgotten joy of authorship: the chance to stow away a likely-looking word and make occasion to use it. A pity that the word was too obscure for his soap opera. Bill and Mike were too respectful to let it slip, but he had picked up from Martha, whose pronouncements tended less towards 'uberty', that the language of his original work was considered antiquated and abstruse.

For all the forgetfulness, Mr Golightly's mind still ran easily on parallel lines, and as he mused on the perils of authorship he wondered what to do about the young boy in the hooded garment hidden under the Traveller.

His first instinct on seeing Johnny duck under the van's carriage had been to ignore him. Latterly, live and let live was one of his mottoes, and if the boy wanted to make the Morris a hiding place it was nothing to him. But a flashing impression of the face, as it dived beneath the van, had affected him. It brought to mind another boy child, so grippingly that he couldn't tear himself away to return to the laptop.

Although he liked to think of himself as essentially creative, it was in fact many years since Mr Golightly had tried to put his ideas into effect. Perhaps he felt a certain forbidding fear at re-embarking on this insecure enterprise. Or perhaps it was the memory evoked by Johnny Spence which made him say, 'I wonder whether you'd care for some refreshment?'

Johnny Spence did not at first take these words as meant for him. Without an introduction, Mr Golightly had adopted an over-formal mode of address. Hearing himself, he adjusted his style.

'Hey, you, boy under the car, fancy a Coke?'

This was spoken in a tone which made Johnny shoot out from under the Traveller before he was aware of what he was doing. He lay on the ground, half on his side, squinnying up at Mr Golightly. Sure as fuck the old guy would hand him over to his stepdad, or the social services.

The sun which had gone behind a cloud

39

reappeared at this moment and casually dropped a ray upon the little earth, transfiguring the upturned face of young Johnny Spence. Mr Golightly swallowed hard and held out a hand.

'There's Coke in the fridge. If you want biscuits one of us'll have to go up to the shop.'

'Not me,' said Johnny Spence. Ignoring the hand he got to his feet. Whatever was going on he wasn't going to show himself out of school time to that Steve Meadows at the post office, thank you very much!

'Well, if you can manage without . . .' It had been Mr Golightly's theory that the modern child only ate biscuits; but there was bread and Marmite and the Frank Cooper's marmalade if the boy was hungry. With his still outstretched hand, he touched the boy lightly on his shoulder. 'Come along inside, why don't you?' he suggested.

CHAPTER SEVEN

On the opposite side of the street to Spring Cottage, set back from the road and fronted by an ugly, untended garden, was a long low building which bore a painted sun-peeled sign, NUTKIN'S TEAROOMS. This, despite a further legend which promised 'Full Devon Cream Teas', was well on the way to becoming derelict. In fact, the only takers for teas now, cream or any kind, were the brown rats whose scampering depredations had so scared Paula's mum that she had had to give up her little cleaning job, while those who owned it made up their minds what they were going to do with the blamed place!

In the past, the tearooms had provided a useful, if limited, source of income for those residents of Great Calne who were neither retired nor living on social security and consequently barred from able-bodied work. During the holiday season, coachloads of tourists had visited regularly and the people of Great Calne had themselves liked to take an occasional light snack there when the services offered extended to a soup and salad luncheon with choice of white or brown 'fresh-baked' bread rolls (delivered twice weekly from Bunn's Bakery, in nearby Oakburton).

In those days the tearooms had been run by Patsy and Joanne, a lesbian couple of the old school. They had left Great Calne after there had been talk that Patsy had made a pass at Nicky Pope's daughter Tessa. Tessa was known to be fanciful, and feeling among the village—after the departure of the two women, who in their quiet way were popular—ran high. It was felt by some that justice would have been better served if Tessa Pope, rather than being offered counselling by the lady vicar, had been smacked hard for her lying ways.

The tearooms were bought by a retired couple from London, Hugh and Heather Wright, who also took over the name of 'Nutkins' for their house at the top of the village. But after Heather ran off with a lecturer in medieval social history—he had come to do research on vanished villages of Dartmoor and vanished instead with Mrs 'Nutkin'—Hugh had found consolation with Morning Claxon, a practitioner in crystal healing. A committed campaigner for health foods, she had turned Hugh against cream—indeed against cholesterol of any kind.

Among the residents of Great Calne, 'Morning' was not a name which inspired confidence. The example of Patsy and Joanne had induced tolerance of homosexuality—indeed, sexual proclivities of most varieties were generally accepted—but the village was inclined to be mistrustful of anything 'hippie'. A name like 'Morning' didn't command sympathy. It had been the devil of a job to get those long-haired squatters out of the rectory, when it was empty all that time after Rector Malcolm died of Parkinson's. The lager cans and quantities of roll-up butts had become local legend. Morning's plans to turn the tearooms into an alternative health clinic had attracted suspicion rather than support. And there was the question of the car park, which butted on to Sam Noble's garden.

The tearooms' car park was placed, somewhat anomalously, up the hill and across the road from the tearooms. It stood behind the village hall bearing a sign TEAROOMS PARKING ONLY and was mostly used by the children of Great Calne when learning to ride their bikes. Sam, a man who read both the *Guardian* and the *Daily Telegraph* and was well versed in his rights, was adamant that an alternative health centre would bring unacceptable noise levels to the proximity of his bedroom.

A meeting of the parish council had been called at which Morning had spoken, passionately, of the benefits of Indian head massage. Not properly a resident—she only came down for weekends, when she had Hugh Wright out in the garden all day, getting a dig, people said, at the old wife by having him unearth all the shrubs she had planted—her right to speak was questioned and her words did not carry weight.

The car park was, in fact, a prime building site. It was Sam's nightmare that a speculator would buy it and try to engineer a profitable development. While planning permission in the area was granted rarely, there was nothing, Sam knew, that money couldn't buy. That Indian massage woman was flaky. Even if she had no plans for developing the car park herself, a speculator could easily get hold of her, cross a few palms with silver and then where would their peace and quiet be? No, by far the best plan would be for the village collectively to buy back the tearooms from Hugh Wright; then Sam could oversee the car park.

To this end, Sam had run a cost-benefit analysis which he had printed out on his computer. He proposed to call on all the village personally and drum up support.

The Morris Traveller was parked in the front when Sam called on Spring Cottage and banged on the door with the flat of his hand. There was no bell or knocker; when Emily Pope had lived there folk always went round the back; but the new tenant had not been installed long enough for proprieties to be dispensed with.

Johnny Spence was on his second can of Coke when Sam knocked and Johnny's reaction was to look for a place to hide. There was a cupboard under the stairs but his eye had hardly found it before Mr Golightly laid a hand again on his shoulder. Placing a finger to his lips, he mouthed conspiratorially, 'Wait there!'

Johnny found himself obeying his host who

43

walked with his peculiar silent tread to the hallway.

Opening the front door took a bit of shoving: the door was used infrequently, and the wood had swollen in the winter damp so that in opening it Mr Golightly almost staggered into the man standing outside.

'Morning there. Sam Noble—we met the other evening up at the Stag.'

A hand was being proffered, but Mr Golightly was annoyed at having his conversation with Johnny interrupted and his response was lukewarm.

'Yes?'

He hoped this visit would not form a precedent. He must be careful not to convey an impression that Spring Cottage was a home for social chit-chat.

'Pleased to meet you again. I'm calling about the tearooms.'

'The tearooms?' Mr Golightly's face was a disobliging blank. Tea gave him a headache—he rarely touched the stuff.

'All here,' said Sam, 'cost-benefit analysis.' He slapped a furled bundle of papers on the palm of his hand. 'Scheme for the village. I'd be glad of your views.'

'Ah, yes,' said Mr Golightly, ambiguously. It was to escape the affairs of the world that he had come to Great Calne. The last thing he wanted was to be involved in local politics—indeed, politics of any kind.

Johnny Spence, after an initial obedience to Mr Golightly's directive, had nipped up to the bedroom to check it out. The room didn't look like a perve's. Not that Johnny specially cared. That jerk who slept in the caravan all last summer, up in

44

the parking place on the edge of the moor by old Lavinia Galsworthy's house where you weren't supposed to park, had tried something on him and Johnny had kneed him in the balls. If this bloke had any ideas Johnny was prepared. But somehow he didn't give off that kind of feeling.

Mr Golightly's employees could have told Johnny that to pry undiscovered was a lost cause. The boss had supersubtle powers of observation. It was said that their business rival had once, long ago, worked for him and got himself sacked that way; on the other hand, there were rumours they had fallen out over some woman. Those who knew the boss felt that this last was unlikely—certainly the idea of some inexcusable interference fitted the picture better. When Martha had once, quite innocently, moved some of his archaeological specimens to give them a thorough clean, she had received a dressing down which had led to bad feeling for several weeks. Since then, the boss had tidied his own desk, which, as Martha said, behind his back, meant those nasty old stones, dating back from God knew when, merely gathered more and more dust, which was murder for her asthma.

Mr Golightly, having seen Sam off, looked in the direction of the stairs. If he sensed Johnny's investigations—and it would be hard to see how he could—he must have decided not to mention it since he merely said, 'Is there anything I can do for you, before you go?'

The idea of leaving made Johnny's stomach lurch, like when his mum had gone in for her operation and he'd had to sleep on the sofa over at his Auntie Jean's. Not that Jean was really his 'auntie': she was his mum's friend from when he was a kid and he and his mum and Auntie Jean lived together over Plymouth way. That time, when his mum was in the hospital, Uncle Glenn, his Auntie Jean's live-in boyfriend, had driven Johnny in his convertible to see her.

'Can I have a go in your car?'

Mr Golightly inwardly sighed. What about his writing schedule? But the boy's hazel eyes looked at him with frank beseechment.

A dart of pain touched Mr Golightly in the upper quarter of his left ribcage. Subduing irritation, he said, 'Well, we can't go far but . . . maybe you could direct me to the nearest place for decent shopping?'

That was easy. Oakburton was three miles down the road and full of all the supermarkets and wine stores anyone could desire. Under Johnny's guidance, they reached Oakburton in remarkable time, given the age of the Traveller, and soon Johnny was guiding his new acquaintance round Somerfield.

Not that any of the foodstuffs seemed to have had much to do with fields, or with summer, Mr Golightly observed to himself. He bought a plastic bag of seedy-looking potatoes, some tins of tomatoes on special offer (four for the price of three), lavatory paper, kitchen roll, and a kitchen cleanser called Mr Muscle, a name which took his fancy. When they got to the till Johnny, who had been dragging round behind, surprised him.

'Seven pound ninety-four.'

'Seven ninety-four,' the cashier, with bored inattention, repeated a second later.

Mr Golightly forked out a ten-pound note and they went next door to the Oak Deli. Johnny wandered off, leaving Mr Golightly to buy a brie, some slices of garlic sausage, olive oil, wine vinegar and some stuffed olives. These delicacies in hand, he looked for the small hardware store which, painted in a green gloss, had caught his eye as they drove into the town.

'Paint', 'Timber', Glass', 'Keys' promised one window, while its twin announced, 'Gas', 'Houseware', 'Plumbing', 'Fancies'.

Mr Golightly was taken by the idea of 'Fancies'. He liked the look of this shop and entering felt at once at home among the curious collection of bric-a-brac. Here were dyes, bath plugs, colanders, tea cosies, flour sieves, screws and hooks and brass bolts of all sizes, slug pellets, hot-water bottles, jam covers, lemon squeezers, thermos flasks and hurricane lanterns. In particular there was a milk jug in the likeness of a cow. Mr Golightly lingered a little over the cow but in the end he bought a hot-water bottle with a knitted cover, some clothes pegs, shaped like little wooden people with stiff legs, some electric plugs and a packet of firelighters.

The door of the shop was fitted with an old-fashioned bell which raucously announced the arrival of Johnny. Mr Golightly pointed out the cow. 'Me mum would like that,' Johnny observed. 'Eight pound forty-nine,' he said, before the elderly man at the till had had time to ring up the items.

'How did you work that out?' Mr Golightly asked.

'Did it in me head.'

'Did you now,' said Mr Golightly. He had heard about savage child geniuses and hoped to goodness he hadn't got one on his hands.

47

CHAPTER EIGHT

Sam Noble had been disappointed that his brief conversation with the tenant at Spring Cottage had offered no purchase for the story of the Palme d'Or. The residents of Great Calne had all heard about it—many several times.

The opportunities to repeat the account of his brush with success had diminished over the five years since Sam had moved from London to the village after his divorce from Irene. Sam sometimes regretted parting from Irene. At the time the world had presented itself as his oyster. The separation had occurred after the near miss at Cannes and had been speeded on its way by a temporary association with an air hostess from Malta. But the oyster seemed to have clammed up since, and such pearls as may have been lying in wait remained ungarnered.

It was true that Irene had not been inspiring: she had wittered on, and long before the intervention of the air hostess Sam had ceased to pay her attention. But nowadays he sometimes missed her chattiness, her observations about the garden and whether they should use chemical pesticides on the patio moss, or go for something organic. There were times when he even missed her warm, comfortably ageing body in the bed beside him.

Sleeping alone in the double bed—which, since it had become available for legitimate double occupancy, had remained depressingly single—had eroded Sam's confidence. He dreamed fitfully about naked women jockeys and woke in the mornings too early. Dr Rhys at the Oakburton surgery had even discussed Prozac with him but, in the end, Sam decided he preferred to go it alone without anything chemical. After all, he still had a brain—or liked to think he did!

Dr Rhys was young and handsome and believed in the Hippocratic oath. That, and his sympathetic manner, meant he got lumbered with all the psychological stuff. He had suggested that maybe Sam might like to 'talk' to somebody. But Sam feared the 'somebody' might mean the lady vicar, who was training as a counsellor. Everyone knew she had a bee in her bonnet about male sexual performance. She had alarmed George, who dug the graves and helped out down at Folly Farm with the lambing, during bereavement counselling by asking questions which were hardly decent when you thought that his wife of fifty years was barely cold in her grave. And the grave dug lovingly by her grieving husband's own two hands too! But these days it was all live-in sex and what the lady vicar worryingly referred to as 'seeing to yourself', with precious little about the rites of holy matrimony.

Sam had no particular concerns about the Church of England's attitude to sexual habits, or to anything else for that matter. He had lived most of his working life in Hampstead and was a confirmed social atheist. But he didn't care to be asked about his morning erections, particularly not by a lady vicar. George, it was rumoured, had been encouraged to plot a graph.

In any case, it was not attentions of that kind he necessarily craved; it was intellectual stimulus. The empty early mornings had produced a new idea for a creative project—a film about sheep dog trials.

49

According to Nicky Pope, this chap who'd moved into Spring Cottage was a writer. He would probably welcome a chance to hear about Sam's contacts in the film trade.

*   *   *

Mr Golightly's first day of writing had been a washout. The shopping excursion with Johnny had protracted into lunch. The cottage had been chilly on their return, and the boy, off his own bat, had read, and apparently comprehended, the instruction book for the wood-burning stove. A miracle, Mr Golightly couldn't help thinking, and far more useful than some he had known. The impossible-looking diagrams had seemingly been clear as daylight to Johnny, who had flicked, switched and adjusted knobs and had even managed to open the firelighters, which were packed so impenetrably that they defeated Mr Golightly. After that it would have been churlish not to offer to share his modest lunch, though, from the way Johnny had wolfed down the rolls, they could have done with the species of miracle which multiplies.

Johnny had left just after four and by the time Mr Golightly had washed up and checked his e-mails again, dealt with a question from Muriel—it was shocking what the government took you for VAT these days—it was far too late to begin a day's work. Instead, he strolled up to the Stag and Badger, where he adroitly avoided conversation with Sam Noble by helping out the young poet in the woolly hat again with his crossword.

Mr Golightly was a crossword addict, a passion

he shared with Muriel at the office and over the years he had fallen into the habit of doing *The Times* crossword with her. One reason for reading the dictionary was to pick up unusual vocabulary which might crop up, since it is well known that crossword setters are of the tribe of fiends. It had once been put to him that in the beginning was the word, and although in his own view things were both simpler and more complicated than that, it was a theory he had sympathy for.

Long ago Mr Golightly had discovered the principle of synchronicity, the law of meaningful coincidence, and it was following its signs in his business practices which was perhaps responsible for their general success. So he was not too surprised when four down in *The Times* read, 'a deprived adolescence provides succour (6)'.

'Uberty!' said Mr Golightly, blatantly disregarding Luke's chance to have a shot at the clue.

Luckily, Luke was not competitive. 'What's that? Never heard of it.'

But at that moment a thickset young man with a loud jacket, exuding a smell of aftershave, equally loud, made his way towards the bar.

'Evening. Wolford, Brian Wolford.' The man held out a well-cushioned hand. Perhaps it was the overpowering smell of the aftershave but Mr Golightly withheld his own. Rather deliberately he picked up his pint mug.

'Golightly,' he said. 'You know Mr Weatherall?'

'You're the writer chappie,' said Wolford, ignoring Luke. He made it sound like an accusation.

'My friend is a writer too,' said Mr Golightly,

distinctly.

But Luke was more interested in the crossword clue. 'So what's it mean, then?'

'Funny thing', said Wolford, 'I work up at the prison yonder. You come across some pretty weird stuff there. I've often thought of writing a book about it. Might drop round your place and have a natter. We've all got a novel in us, right?'

'Uberty?' Mr Golightly said, pointedly addressing only Luke. 'It's the milk of human kindness,' he explained, a trifle vaingloriously.

*　　　*　　　*

The next morning saw Mr Golightly more than ever determined to get the soap opera under way. Staring out of the window for inspiration he saw the horse, Samson, standing four-square in the greensward. Columns of fine rain were blowing in misty battalions across the fields. A kestrel, resting magisterially on pillows of air, circled above the low-falling rain. Kingdom of daylight's dapple-drawn dawn falcon . . . Mr Golightly found he was suddenly overcome by a need for coffee.

But, maddeningly, he had forgotten that the boy had finished off all the milk yesterday.

Up at the shop the bearded Steve said, with evident satisfaction, 'Out of milk, I'm afraid, even the long-life. Got soya, though, that do you? Weather's all right for those as has webbed feet.'

Mr Golightly did not care for soya in his coffee. He bought a small tin of evaporated milk and returned glumly down the hill. Yesterday's buoyancy had deserted him. The unwritten soap opera had become an unresponsive lover, one who

52

resists the most ardent attentions.

Coffee with evaporated milk did not improve his mood but, nevertheless, by 10 a.m. Mr Golightly was once again seated at the gateleg table. Better check the e-mails in case there was something at the office . . .

Three messages, heralded by their zippy musical accompaniment, materialised in the 'Inbox'. One from Muriel, to do with one of the many unpaid accounts they were increasingly having to hassle for, one from a firm selling timeshares in Spain— Mr Golightly paused to wonder how 'time', which was indivisible, could conceivably be 'shared'—and one from yesterday's anonymous correspondent:

hath the rain a father?

it asked.

Mr Golightly did not know what to think. He was too unpractised in the art of e-mail to be able to decipher any clue to the questioner's identity, and while he didn't want to reveal that he was the victim of an anonymous correspondent perhaps an e-mail to Mike was called for.

He thought a moment then tapped out:

'Dear Mike,
If someone e-mails me how do I know who they are? And how do I reply to them?'

He pondered a moment more and then concluded:

'Yours ever, Golightly'.

Mr Golightly had never had occasion to write to

Mike before, or any of the office staff. It made him realise how little he really knew about ordinary channels of communication. Alone in Spring Cottage, with no one by to protect or defend him, he experienced an unfamiliar sense of vulnerability. The marching columns of rain had dissolved into a uniform drizzle and Mr Golightly thought he might stretch his legs before starting work. The River Dart was flowing into hills covered today by a modest décolleté of mist and seagulls had winged their way inland suggesting rough weather out at sea. The air was laden with moisture, but Mr Golightly had spent much of his existence under sun-parched skies and the cool wash of English country air was a welcome balm.

He stood with the mild wetness anointing his face. He had to admit it, he was rattled: not merely by the fact of the phantom e-mailer but by the nature of the message. The references to fatherhood and the coincidence of the rain gave the impression that his unknown correspondent was peering at him knowingly—a feeling that challenged his usual security.

Back inside, the 'Inbox' announced that he had received another e-mail. Opening it, he read:

> boss,
> scroll down and you'll see name of sender and address—bring cursor to 'reply' box, click and space for message will appear— compose message then click on 'send'— simple!
> cheers, mox

There was something unsettling in this

communication too. Mike seemed to have dispensed with the normal rudiments of style, with capital letters for example. And then the tone, while not actually disrespectful, was uncharacteristically familiar—that circle and cross by the signature, presumably betokening kisses and so forth. Presumably such endearments were part of e-mail etiquette. In which case, was he expected to do likewise?

Following Mike's instructions he scrolled down the anonymous message to find nemo@nemo.com. Whoever the someone was, they had an ancient language in common. Nemo; evidently, the someone who was 'no one' didn't wish to be known.

Slightly trepidatious, Mr Golightly clicked on the 'Reply' box and at once a space appeared ready to record his answer. But what in the name of heaven to say to an anonymous correspondent? Mike had mentioned, in passing, the propensity of e-mailers sometimes to get into over-intimate communications. Mr Golightly had given this information short shrift—it was hardly the kind of mess he had foreseen himself getting into. But might he not be about to fall into just such a trap?

And yet he had to admit he was curious about the anonymous mailer.

He sat motionless for a minute and then found he had typed:

who is this that darkeneth counsel?

Mr Golightly was not quite sure himself where these words had come from. But then many things which emanated from him emerged without consideration. 'Consider'—now there was a word the phantom e-mailer might also understand . . . *con sidere*—with the stars. Was that how the e-mails travelled, through the upper reaches of the ether? He pictured himself, wearing a pair of silver shoes, strolling soundlessly through the quiet chilly regions of the far-flung universes . . .

At this moment a loud banging at the back door and a raised voice penetrated his musing.

'Hell-oah! Anybody at home?'

*   *   *

'Someone, I know, who's in the know, said there was some kind of handkerchief-pankerchief with the judges.'

Sam Noble had been at Spring Cottage for nearly an hour. Mr Golightly had, slightly maliciously, directed his visitor to the orange sofa, but a challenge to the spine is no deterrent to the determinedly garrulous. Sam had accepted, and drunk, two coffees from the Spiderman mug, and was well launched into the history of *What's a Nice Girl?*, his film about female jockeys.

'Everyone said it was in the bag.' A piece of luck for this Golightly chap, Sam thought, that he was able to put him in the frame about the movie business.

Mr Golightly, who, by and large, believed in the virtues of politeness, was suffering in silence. Protected as he had been by his faithful staff, he was rarely exposed to unwanted company and lacked the social know-how to rid himself of an unwelcome guest.

'Of course, it was a set-up,' Sam reaffirmed. 'Everyone knew the Palme should have gone to

56

Nice Girl.'

'Yes?' asked Mr Golightly.

'No question.'

There was a pause during which Mr Golightly said nothing. He had had no idea how mind-numbing self-absorption could be.

'So, what are you up to then?' asked Sam, mustering some faint recollection that social engagement was supposed to entail dialogue.

'Up to?' The question had an intrusive flavour; it reminded Mr Golightly of the anonymous e-mailer's challenges.

'Yes, what are you writing, then? Novel, is it?' Sam gambled. It was usually a novel that chaps like this were engaged in when they came to out-of-the-way parts like Great Calne. They all thought they'd got one in them!

'Not exactly,' said Mr Golightly, stiffly.

'If it was a script, then if there was any way I could—'

'Not a script,' said Mr Golightly. 'Thank you,' he added. He did not cross his fingers behind his back because he regarded such superstitions as childish. But he felt indignant that he had been driven to fib.

'—because if it was a script then I'm your man.'

Mr Golightly had observed over the years that there are occasions when a truth cannot be told. On the whole, his policy had been tell the truth and shame the Devil, but there were also occasions when a truth can act as a lie.

'It's a dramatic epic,' he averred, 'which seeks to unfold the moral and spiritual history of human civilisation.' That should do the trick. No one in their right mind could share an interest in such an undertaking.

'Really?' said Sam Noble. 'The young chap up at Lavinia's barn is writing a narrative poem. Tell you what, we should form a writers' group. Read each other's work, swap ideas. What d'you say?'

*   *   *

There were no e-mails waiting for him when Mr Golightly was released by his visitor's departure back to the laptop. Since Sam Noble had drained the tin of evaporated milk dry, if there was to be coffee, it meant another trip to the shop.

Immanuel Kant, Mr Golightly had heard, formed such a dependency upon coffee that, on an occasion when it was slow to arrive, he was heard to mutter, 'Well, we can die after all; it is but dying, and in the next world, thank God, there is no coffee and consequently no waiting for it.' Mr Golightly had begun to experience a fellow feeling with the querulous philosopher. It seemed impossible that he should embark on the revision of the work he had ironically represented to Sam Noble without the stimulus of caffeine. But after his caller he really couldn't stomach another encounter with the bearded one up at the Post Office Stores. Maybe he would drive into Oakburton, fill the Traveller with petrol and get in some more supplies before getting down to work?

Being Friday, it was the Reverend Meredith Fisher's day for Plymouth and Johnny Spence was lodged again in the yew tree. Its foliage was thick, little of the drizzling rain penetrated to the tree's occupant, who lay in the fork of the trunk looking down like a watchful jaguar.

The jaguar gaze registered Mr Golightly

manoeuvring the Traveller into the street. It crossed Johnny's mind to ask for another lift; but, like any other wild animal, the coil of Johnny's instinct was caution. His encounter with Spring Cottage's occupant had turned out surprisingly well. But Johnny's life to date had shown that if you trusted anyone on this earth you needed your head examined.

In any case, with the old bloke out of the way, he could get inside the house and have another snoop round.

Johnny slithered down the yew tree and nipped warily across the road and round the back of Spring Cottage, where he had noted from his first visit that the window was left unfastened. No probs—he could get in easy.

Samson sauntered over to the wire fence and stood watching as the boy creature swung his leg up and on to the sill, reached an arm inside an open window and disappeared inside.

On the other side of the window Johnny found the laptop on the gateleg table. It took five minutes to work out the means to find the password. Rapidly, he scanned the contents. Nothing interesting. No porn. A few e-mails, no sex or love stuff. There was someone called herself Muriel but she didn't seem to amount to much.

Upstairs offered no new discoveries either. A book by the bed; *Jeeves in the Offing*. Nothing else different.

Downstairs there was a box of stuff. More books: *Ethics* by Spinoza, *The Sermons of John Donne*, *The Odyssey*, Shakespeare, Jane Austen, George Eliot, Damon Runyon, Raymond Chandler, Philip Pullman, a load of poetry books, *The Wind in the*

Willows—which was a kids' book—and another book for kids Johnny's mum had given him when he was seven, *Alice*. Maybe the old guy was a perve after all?

Johnny cast around looking for another unexplored quarter to assuage his curiosity. Next to the music centre there was a box of tapes and CDs—classical stuff and some rock—Ella Fitzgerald, Peggy Lee, Elvis, David Bowie, the kind of stuff old ravers went for—no rap or thrash, not that you'd expect that.

Mr Golightly had driven out of the village before he remembered his credit card. As a rule, he carried no cash or card as his staff attended to all money matters for him. But part of the point of the holiday was supposed to be an opportunity to sample the pleasures of self-sufficiency. Bill, his PA, had organised a special 'Gold' card. There had been talk of 'Platinum' but Mr Golightly had rejected this—platinum, with no poetic tradition behind it, he regarded as inferior to the nobler virtues of gold. However, in assembling the usual furniture of the inner pocket of his jacket—notebook, fountain pen, propelling pencil—he had forgotten to include the neat case in which, expensively sheathed, the card had arrived from the credit-card agency. As Martha would say, he would forget his own name next!

Johnny had memories of Elvis because before his mum met his stepdad she had used to dance to a tape, *Elvis: the Greatest Hits*, with Johnny in her arms. Mr Golightly, returning to retrieve the card, was greeted by a familiar bass-baritone declaiming that you could do anything you chose except step on his blue suede shoes. 'Ah,' he said, entering the parlour where he was met by a terrified young face, 'a fellow fan . . . !'

There were some Cokes still left over from the six-pack in the fridge. Johnny drank one of these while Mr Golightly made himself a cup of black coffee and they both listened to the King. However, when it came to one track, Mr Golightly made a pretext to leave the room.

The lyrics never failed to remind him of someone who was always on his mind.

CHAPTER NINE

Mr Golightly's CD session with Johnny had concluded, to Johnny's surprise, with no questions asked about his presence in Spring Cottage. It was as if his weird host believed the purpose of the call was to establish a musical bond. He had played Johnny some other CDs which, once Johnny had got over the shock of being offered a Coke, rather than a smack round the head, he found quite entertaining. Mr Golightly sounded pleased when his guest asked the name of one of the pieces.

'Steve Reich's "Music for 18 Musicians"—an innovative work. Who is your own favourite?'

Johnny said he liked Badly Drawn Boy.

'Any special number I should look out for?' enquired Mr Golightly.

Johnny suggested his latest album, *Have You Fed The Fish?*, was cool.

'I'll make a note of it. Next time you visit I must play you some Schubert songs, the *Winterreise* are particularly fine. But now I have things pressing and no doubt you have your own engagements to attend to . . . ?'

It was nearly lunchtime and Johnny resumed his jaguar position in the yew tree while his host returned to the gateleg table prepared to start afresh. Coffee first. But hell and damnation, he still had no milk!

Mr Golightly consulted his watch. There was no help for it, a trip up to the shop and the aggressive young man with the beard. But a notice in green biro, also somewhat aggressive, met him, stating baldly that the shop was closed between the hours of one and two. To go in to Oakburton now would take up yet more of a day in which he had promised himself faithfully he would commence work. But to work without coffee . . . more and more Mr Golightly found himself in sympathy with the cantankerous philosopher.

Ellen Thomas lying on her sofa heard the wind chimes in the pear tree. A man was standing outside the glass door which made a fragile barrier between her and the terrible incandescence beyond. With the sun behind his head making a bright coronet, she thought at first he was the Angel of Death come to grant her release. Then she saw it was just her new neighbour with the funny name.

Ellen tried to throw off the overwhelming sense of listlessness which, like a heavy rug, covered every bit of her. She raised her body carefully from the sofa. Everything she did now she did slowly because she knew if she moved too fast she would shatter into a million fragments.

'I've disturbed you,' said Mr Golightly. He rocked slightly on the balls of his feet in embarrassment. 'I'm sorry.' He held in his hand a small pale pink jug, slightly cracked about the lip.

'No,' said Ellen truthfully. Nothing could disturb her more than she had already been disturbed.

'Only,' said her neighbour, 'I have stupidly run out of milk.'

'Oh, milk . . .' said Ellen Thomas. She made it sound as if it was a concept foreign to her.

'It sounds daft,' Mr Golightly went on, 'but I find I can't get down to work without coffee. And the shop is closed for lunch so I just wondered . . .' He held out the jug awkwardly, like a small boy making a peace-offering.

'I can give you a cup of coffee, if that's what you want.' Whatever possessed her to say that?

Mr Golightly paused. It was not what he wanted. What he wanted more than anything was to get started on his project. But Ellen Thomas was being neighbourly—it seemed churlish to refuse. 'Thank you,' he said, politely.

He stepped past his hostess through the door into a room which put him in mind of a ship's cabin: clean and orderly, with little furniture other than two sofas arranged at right angles. There were no pictures on the walls, other than one he recognised of some crows flying through a field of violent yellow corn. The woman herself seemed out of place.

'Till last year I lived in a much grander house.' She was the sort who read your thoughts, then.

'I was grand once,' said Mr Golightly, a touch regretfully.

'You know,' said Ellen, her mind flickering vaguely to the fridge—was there any milk in it? She hadn't the least idea—'I've heard it said that as we

63

get older we should guard against a sense of lowered consequence, but I find I prefer obscurity.'

'Where is the dancing and the noise of dancers' feet, the banquets and the festivals?' asked Mr Golightly. The question was purely rhetorical: it was reassuring to find his neighbour so sanguine about her altered circumstances.

Ellen Thomas opened her mouth and was startled to find further unsolicited words issuing from it. 'You can stay for lunch, if there's any food.' And, more from the nervous rush that the speech produced than any wish to charm, she smiled.

Ellen Thomas had never been a beautiful woman; if her appearance was commented on at all she was described as 'pleasant-looking'. But when she smiled her face was transformed in a way which her husband had found irresistible. Mr Golightly, who had determined to resist anything which would detain him further, also found himself unequal to the smile.

And I would have had to eat lunch anyway, he excused himself, stepping back over the wire to Spring Cottage for a bottle of light Moselle from the wine carton.

Ellen rediscovered table mats and linen napkins in the drawer of the oak sideboard, a legacy of Robert's godmother, and, under his hostess's instructions, Mr Golightly laid the table. He found there was something soothing about obeying orders.

In the kitchen, Ellen cracked duck eggs. I have been an emptied-out eggshell, she thought. She chopped sorrel, gathered from the garden, and beat the eggs to a froth in a white bowl. Yellow and white, the colours of the narcissi she had planted beneath the pear tree.

'Are you sitting up?' she called through to the other room, where her guest was seated, a linen napkin tucked into the top of his shirt. 'You have to eat an omelette like lightning or it ruins . . .'

Conversation over lunch was cordial but formal. Mr Golightly was greatly relieved to find his neighbour seemed not to want his help over any writing project or to press him into action over some scheme for Great Calne's improvement. Instead, she described the local features: the stream, which ran through the meadow beneath them, for instance, called Holy Brook because once a hermit had preached there to a congregation of otters.

Mr Golightly was impressed. Otters, he said, were famously unbiddable—the hermit must have been a man of rare influence or had an uncommon way with words.

They moved on to the unpredictable spring weather, the asinine EEC regulations threatening a local variety of apple and the current world crisis, although Mr Golightly apologised for not wishing to pursue this topic.

Ellen was pleased at an opportunity to exercise forbearance. There was enough she preferred not to be exposed to herself. Deftly, she turned the conversation. She explained that she had been an artist, making a living from painting local landscapes, but gave her guest to understand that, as with much else, she had abandoned this activity after her husband's death.

'I am sorry,' Mr Golightly said sincerely. He was familiar with the sapping effects of grief.

By the end of lunch he felt unusually sleepy.

Between them he and his hostess had polished off the bottle of Moselle. He dallied a little over coffee, then made his regrets and under Samson's unblinking gaze stepped cautiously over the barbed wire and back into the garden of Spring Cottage.

Returning to his seat at the gateleg table he found he had some problem with the focus of his eyes. A short lie-down would do no harm—it would refresh him, pep him up for starting work on the soap opera.

Next door, Ellen Thomas washed up the glasses, the cutlery and crockery. She laid away the table mats and linen napkins carefully in the sideboard drawer. What a mercy at the last minute she had kept it back from the furniture sale. Lunch had been more than she had been used to eating—and she supposed it must be the wine which had gone to her head.

All at once, she wanted nothing more than to be outside. For too long she had managed no more than to creep out, with Wilfred, at dusk, like a felon on the run—it had hardly deserved the name of a 'walk'. Now she felt a brisk stroll was just what she needed.

Summoning the black Labrador, they went out together and up the lane which rose towards the moor. As she watched the dog sniff along the hedgerow, her trained eye spotted tiny flowers like snowflakes, and she crouched to put her nose to their sequestered sweetness. There are few blessings, thought Ellen Thomas—her head a little dizzy from the wine and from bending—as welcome as white violets.

CHAPTER TEN

The Reverend Meredith Fisher never economised with her conscience. She nursed it as a proud mother nurses a precocious child. And, like many such mothers, she was not parsimonious with the cherished one's talents.

No event in Great Calne passed unnoted by its vigilant parish priest and so significant a matter as the arrival of a new tenant at Spring Cottage could hardly have been overlooked. If she had not yet made a welcoming visit this was not because she was idle.

Meredith Fisher took her pastoral work strenuously. On Wednesdays and Fridays, she attended the South Devon counselling training at Plymouth College, which had the virtue that it freed the yew tree by the rectory wall to harbour Johnny Spence.

It might be hoped that the vicar's training provided other benefits too. But it is a sad fact that a zest for human psychology is not always shared by the objects of its concern. Meredith Fisher's attempts to counsel the parish of Great Calne had fallen on stony ground. Statistics indicated that it was improbable that Great Calne had escaped its share of sexual abuse—but if so, its victims and perpetrators were joined in some unholy pact to keep quiet about it. And adultery, though certainly rife, was, if not actually applauded, apparently tolerated. It appeared there was no Christian means of helping the afflicted.

The arrival, therefore, of a brand new

opportunity to adjust a psyche to normality (it was well known that writers were neurotic and this one was single, which, in a man, generally meant some kind of sexual dysfunction) was a bonus for the vicar. Hers was essentially a doctrine of light; there was no darkly noisome corner of the human psyche the Reverend Meredith Fisher felt unequal to illuminating.

The chance to cast light upon her neighbour's darker corners presented itself on Saturday over her breakfast of Weetabix, toast and jam.

'Been to see the writer chap over the road?' her husband, Keith, asked casually behind the *Express*. He was keen to run down to Newton Abbot and lay a bet on 'Banoffee Pie' which was running seven to one in the 2.15. To accomplish this successfully his wife's attention had to be diverted. There had been a worrying trend recently to make Saturday the day they 'did things together' which Keith was hoping to nip in the bud.

The common weal, and other large causes, can generally be relied on to outweigh lesser domestic concerns and Keith was relieved to see his wife already at the door of Spring Cottage as he reversed the Renault down and out of the front drive. He could wing it into Newton Abbot, place the bet on Banoffee Pie and then pick up some brownie points with She-Who-Must-Be-Obeyed by hopping down to Tesco's to do the weekend shop.

Mr Golightly had already switched on the kettle for a second cup of coffee and was about to put on Clifford Curzon playing the Schubert impromptus when there was a rap at the door. The lunch with Ellen Thomas had been nourishing, and entertaining, but it had not forwarded his writing plan. He had shut his eyes for a mere five minutes and already it was evening . . . But sufficient unto the day is the evil thereof was his motto and that morning he had woken bright and early and ready to work.

The effort at opening the front door to Sam Noble had eased the tendency to stick; a fact which Mr Golightly regretted when he saw he had yet another visitor, one who was engaged, it appeared, in robbing the garden of its crop of harmless wildflowers. Unless it was the gardener Nicky Pope had warned him to expect.

The Reverend Fisher held out a frankly earthy hand—in the other she held a bunch of wilting dandelions.

'Hi there. Meredith Fisher.'

'Golightly,' said Mr Golightly, somewhat emphasising the syllables of his name.

'I'm the rector—don't fall down dead with shock!'

'No,' said Mr Golightly. If anyone was about to fall down dead it certainly wouldn't be he.

'I'll leave the weeds here, shall I?' asked Meredith, rubbing earth enthusiastically into the other hand. 'Better late than never! I've come to welcome you to the parish of Great Calne.'

*   *   *

'What I like to stress to my clients,' the Reverend Meredith was saying, 'is that love is a *verb*.'

'Ah,' said Mr Golightly, trying his best not to show his attention was drifting.

Once he, too, had believed that he knew much about love. That a woman with a dog collar

69

(though this morning the Reverend Fisher wore only a roll-neck sweater to indicate her calling) should beard him on the subject struck him as faintly absurd.

'You see, it's the active ingredient which counts.'

Mr Golightly had thought much about love's multiple complexities. Like the vicar, there was a time when he had been strenuous in his loving. For years he had given his support to people in return for their absolute loyalty—but when, as was inevitable, given the instability of all things, this loyalty had flagged or wavered, he had reacted with a vehemence he now deplored.

'Is it?' he heard himself say. A mistake. He knew enough about human nature to be sure that he had let himself in for an argument.

'Oh, I think so,' said the Reverend Meredith, and her eyes gleamed with what Mr Golightly recognised, with an inward shudder, as zeal. Zeal, like vehemence, was nowadays a condition he fought shy of. 'You see . . .'

Years ago, when Mr Golightly had gone about more in the world, he had encountered people like the Reverend Fisher. It seemed to him they spelled trouble. They had to put their fingers in every pie and could not leave well alone.

In the past, it had been his habit to try to steer such people into situations where their conviction had fuller scope. Some, he was sorry to say it now, he had employed to promote his business. But since the catastrophe he had become mistrustful of all endeavour which tried to improve the human lot. The world was no longer a theatre for his grand gestures. That idea now seemed unspeakably grandiose . . .

The worst thing about such people was that it was the Devil's own job to escape the running fire of their counsels. The Reverend Fisher drew breath only on sufferance. She was delivering an enthusiastic account of the 'meaning of the Gospels', which, Mr Golightly dazedly gathered, were packed with emotional prophylactics and helpful panaceas, until the sound of a car outside distracted her. That, she explained, must be her husband, Keith, back from the shops.

Mr Golightly felt towards Keith something of the gratitude of a dog who sees a stranger about to remove a troublesome thorn from its paw. He conducted the vicar to the door, but she hung on still, promising a future visit accompanied by contemporary feminist exegeses of the parables. 'I'll get Keith to pop across and help you with all of this,' she declared finally, gesturing at the crop of harmless dandelions.

'No,' said Mr Golightly firmly. 'Golden lads and girls . . .' He was fond of these reminders that all humanity must come at last to dust.

'Sorry?'

'Dandelions. When the blooms go they become like chimney sweepers' brushes,' he added, confusingly.

'It will be good for Keith—for his health,' said the Reverend Meredith, ignoring this incomprehensible irrelevance.

'But not for mine.'

'Well, if you're sure . . .?' asked his neighbour, fired up by the sense she had a fight on her hands.

'Sure as eggs!' said Mr Golightly and pulled the door to smartly.

It was a while since he had checked his e-mails.

He had been about to when that pesky woman had called. He dialled up and waited for the sound as the messages arrived. But instead of a now familiar 'plop' an ugly noise heralded an announcement that the 'domain' wasn't answering.

Mr Golightly experienced a bewildering sense of impotence. He was unused to being denied information. Information about any corner of his global enterprise, relayed by his band of assiduous aides, had been to hand whenever he required it. At a loss, he went to the telephone to ring the office. But hell and damnation, he had forgotten it was Saturday—the day the staff by long tradition took off! He left a curt request for someone to ring him back and dialled up again. This time the ugly noise prefaced an announcement that the 'server' did not 'recognise his name'.

Mr Golightly was the first to acknowledge that all wayward things are best met with patience. Yet had the Reverend Fisher been present, and reminded her neighbour of the gospel saying 'In your patience possess ye your souls', she might have got a dusty response. If you are in the way of presiding over a large empire, or even a small one, it is disturbing to find an area where your influence is nothing. Mr Golightly was unused to such discouragements and the effect was to make him suddenly famished.

The visit from Reverend Fisher had taken up the best part of the morning and it was close to lunchtime; he decided to kill two birds and walk up to the Stag and Badger for a pint and a cold sausage, to stay his hunger and work off his wrath.

Luke Weatherall had also suffered creative frustration that morning. His poem had not

72

advanced; or rather it had advanced by three stanzas but these on rereading had been too patently influenced by the rhythms of *Hiawatha*. Luke had read Longfellow's *Hiawatha* while researching his own narrative poem and had found his head taken over by its insistent rhythms. A trip to the Stag and Badge offered an antidote.

Mr Golightly and Luke met as they approached the inn; one thing led to another and the older man offered to buy the younger a drink. Luke had provided his first social exchange in Great Calne. Mr Golightly might not have fully recognised the sentiment but what he was feeling was that at a time of insecurity here was a friend.

Mary Simms remarked, when she popped out the back to have a peek at her hair and touch up her lipstick, that the writer from Spring Cottage was in. She made no mention of Luke; she had plans for him, and no woman worth her salt lets slip her plans about anyone of the opposite sex. But Paula's negative intuition was fine-tuned.

'That Luke Weatherall in, is he?'

Paula had her own reasons for asking this. If she could get someone to rent her room she could leave home and move in with Jackson. Looking around, she had lighted upon Luke as the best bet. After all, he would be nearer the village, and the Stag and Badge, and that Lavinia Galsworthy was a fussy cow. Luke ought to be glad to leave her poxy ways and her crappy studio flat!

Paula's plan to move in with Jackson was born of determination rather than any warmer emotion. She didn't like Jackson; rather the reverse. But she had detected Jackson's desire to be rid of her, and also his fear of her, and the combination made a

73

powerful draw. Years ago, her dad had left her mum, leaving her mum to lean on her. If Paula moved in with Jackson she could get her own back on the lot of them.

Mary flushed. 'I didn't notice.'

'Like fuck, you didn't!' said Paula, expertly banging down a sharp steel knife on a cherry tomato. 'Anyone with half a mind can see you can't wait to have him up you!' Mary Simms got on her nerves.

Luke Weatherall found the tenant of Spring Cottage sympathetic when Luke confided, over a pint of Brewer's Best, the problem he was having over *Hiawatha*. Mr Golightly had been growing aware himself of the potential inhibiting influence of another work of art. Was he not finding just such a handicap himself? His dramatic epic, which had made such an impact, acted now as a dismaying block to his new idea which, he had begun to worry, might never match the success of the original.

Luke finished his pint and asked if he could return the compliment. It seemed impolite to refuse. The conversation had brought up thoughts in Mr Golightly of whether he mightn't have bitten off more than he could chew. There was comfort in comradeship, the young man's company was agreeable and another pint would hardly detain him for long.

Mary Simms said, 'It's the mire I'd be worried about if I were him, poor soul.'

There had been an escape reported from Dartmoor prison and Sam Noble and Barty Clarke were discussing the news with whoever wanted to join in.

'What's he in for, then?' This was Paula's mum

74

who had popped in for a word with Paula and was taking the weight off her feet with a half of sweet cider and some cheese-and-onion crisps.

'Child molester,' said Barty Clarke.

Barty, a tall man with a yellow-white moustache and mild blue eyes, was the local auctioneer, who also published his own newspaper. Called the *Backenbridge Review*, and known locally as the *Backbiter*, its chief purpose was the vicious promulgation of local gossip.

'No, it was rape, my Brian told me.' This was Cherie Wolford, the prison officer's mother, who lived next to Paula and her mum in Rabbit Row. Although Wolford had his own house over at Princetown, near the prison, he was a frequent visitor to Calne, where his mother still kept his old room for whenever he chose to stay. Brian, as Cherie was fond of telling everyone, had been to university, where he had been popular at student parties with his disc jockey skills. He had even toyed with becoming a disc jockey full-time, his mother said, but in the end the prison service offered a pension and more stability. Great Calne—Cherie Wolford anyway—was proud of his achievements

'Same difference,' insisted Barty, piqued that his role as the fount of bad news was being usurped.

Mary Simms tried to draw Luke into the conversation. 'Listen to them,' she said, putting her copper-coloured head on one side. A boy she'd been out with once had said she looked winning when she did that. 'You'd think they'd never been in trouble theirselves . . .' Mary's was a soft heart. She didn't like to think of those men all shut away in that nasty cold prison with no one to give them a cuddle.

But Luke was too preoccupied with the problems of art to care about a real-life drama. 'The way I see it,' he was saying, 'is that once you get the plot blocked in you free yourself up for the dialogue, right?'

Mr Golightly had no notion of whether this was right or wrong. The truth was he felt a little out of his depth. The young man seemed full of enthusiasm but also full of unfamiliar terminology. And around him the conversation plucked worrying chords.

They were all chatting, eagerly now, about the escaped prisoner. Colin Drover remarked that in his view it all came about through lack of corporal punishment for the young; Paula's mum said it was a shame you had to discipline children but look what happened when you didn't; Cherie Wolford said in her son Brian's view all rapists should be castrated; and Paula, who had popped out for a word with her mum, said there would be no need for that if he came anywhere near her!

Only Mary Simms, who had said, to no one in particular, that she didn't like to think of anyone coming to harm, listened when Mr Golightly remarked, 'Hatred is like alcohol or cigarettes. We don't know how dependent we are on it till we try to give it up.'

'Oh, yes,' she said eagerly, leaning across the bar. 'It's true. But, please, why is that?'

Mr Golightly turned to look at the barmaid. Mary Simms had green eyes, and the midday sun, which was storming the window panes she had polished that morning, made bold bright gleams on her copper hair. Look on this, it said, and rejoice!

76

'Perhaps we underestimate the powers that can destroy us,' he suggested.

One sad thought generally leads to another. Mr Golightly's mind, dwelling on the human taste for disaster, had also brought up the image, never far beneath its surface, of his own boy who, like the pretty barmaid, had also been such a one for saying 'Yes'. That had been half the trouble, the boy's disregarding unequivocal affirmation, which had led to the catastrophe.

It was three o'clock when Luke and Mr Golightly finally left the Stag and Badger. He had lingered beyond the time he had allowed for his lunch break; but the exchange with Mary Simms, and the lurking thoughts following in its wake, made the prospect of a return to solitude a bleak one.

'Coffee?' he suggested.

Luke was on for a cup. He had a few more ideas about the Myth of Creation to run past his new friend.

Together they walked down the hill towards Spring Cottage. Clouds, passing over the face of the sun, raced long combs of rippling shadow over the green fields. Mr Golightly, observing nature's gentle chiaroscuro, felt the beginnings of a restoration of the peace which the conversation in the pub had disturbed. The natural play of light and shade over the landscape was restful after the brooding thoughts.

Though they weren't unwelcome; they were as welcome as the rainbow, for was not any memory of his son the purest sunlight and water?

CHAPTER ELEVEN

The brake of thorn bushes gave no substantial cover but it provided a screen of shadow along which the man ran. As he ran he bent low, in a kind of creeping lope, more like a driven creature—a beaten dog, a mangy tiger escaped from a rackety travelling circus, or a wolf from a down-at-heel zoo—than a human being. The light was still low and the mist made weird shapes in the depressions and hollows of the moorland terrain.

The man was making for the beacon which had begun as a dark speck in the misty distance and now looked to be just a short run ahead. Yet each short darting burst he made seemed to bring him no nearer to reaching it. His breath scraped in his throat, like gravel in danger of being sucked too deeply into his struggling lungs.

At the far edge of the long thorn brake he stopped and cramped down his big body into the smallest bundle he could make of it. His ears, like those of any hunted beast, were super-alert, and he had caught, more a feeling than a sound, the faintest tremble of movement on the air.

As he crouched, his ears pinned, his heart contracted to a painful pulse, he felt, as he had felt before, the desire to walk out of the cover and give himself up to whoever or whatever was approaching his hiding place. But he did not surrender to the impulse. He had lived night and day with the serpent voice which offered him the solace of betrayal.

Sunday was a day when Mr Golightly, from long habit, was used to taking a break from administering his business. Though when he woke on this particular Sunday morning, in the small cold bedroom of his holiday home, he hardly felt that a rest was what he deserved.

Another twenty-four hours seemed to have slipped by without him writing a word. He had enjoyed doing what Luke referred to as 'chewing the fat' yesterday afternoon, over several cups of coffee and, on Luke's part, most of a packet of Silk Cut, till it had seemed the most natural thing in the world to stroll back with the young man up to the Stag and Badger for an early evening pint which had somehow extended to another one.

Looking out of the window at the back, he saw Samson dancing around an audience of rooks. Luke had referred to a gym down at Newton Abbot. He could do with a spot of exercise himself.

It was chilly outside. The houses of Great Calne lay comfortably asleep beneath a soft blanket of white mist. All the residents appeared to be abed too except for Ellen Thomas's dog, Wilfred, who was already out patrolling the hedgerow for voles but eagerly abandoned this activity with the offer of better adventures.

Along the lane, Wilfred continued to make bounding sorties after scuttling shapes of fur and bone. Beside the cattle grid, which marked the boundary to the moor, stood Lavinia Galsworthy's house where Luke Weatherall rented his studio flat, but Mr Golightly did not consider calling in. It was too early for a social call and for the time being he'd had enough of human nature.

Wilfred, devout in his discipleship of tooth-and-claw, raced ahead in the hope of rabbits. Mr Golightly walked sedately, following the muddy track between the gorse bushes. He observed, in passing, the line of ghostly lichen-plated thorn trees, bent, like a unanimous jury, in the direction of the prevailing wind.

The man, sweating in the cold morning air, stayed hunkered down as the dog lumbered lightly forwards; a black dog, like the one his aunt had said she could see on his shoulder when he was a boy. Gingerly, he put out his hand and the dog came towards it and stood, his pink tongue lolling across the cruel teeth, staring with brown, unworldly eyes. The crouching man and the Labrador dog faced each other. Then the dog, making some oracular choice, licked the man's hand and moved away from the thorn.

'Good dog,' Mr Golightly said absently as Wilfred bounded back. If answers to unanswerable questions were to be found they might be found on the moor, where nature worked away without need of human encouragements.

And as if to demonstrate this inhuman industry, suddenly, from nowhere, the sun appeared and, borrowing from the swept sky, dashed down into a puddle a reckless sheet of sheer blue; a peacock butterfly, confused in its dates, fluttered crazily past, its brilliant raggedy reflection erratically flickering in the mirror of the peaty water; and somewhere a yellowhammer offered a future mate 'a little bit of bread and no cheese'.

The other birds, scornful of the yellowhammer's humble courtship offering, began to sound their own invitations to prospective partners, setting up a tuneful chain of eager pre-nuptial clamour.

The man behind the thorns heard the birds' song and paused, allowing himself a fractional remission from the consuming fear. The birds themselves, afire with the ruthless drive of procreation, forced this respite on him, their thin, sweet voices pinking at his ear, drilling holes which let in, momentarily, the vast invisible space which encompasses the limits of this world and where music is forever playing.

Mr Golightly heard the same music and paused on the boggy track. People sometimes asked what the point of a thing was—for him it was the very pointlessness of the birds which filled him with satisfaction. Wilfred had come to a halt beside him, the gleaming rabbit pellets on the track suggesting that the objects of his own worship would not be far away. The dog waited patiently, recognising that here was another creature caught for a moment in its peculiar form of praise.

*   *   *

The Reverend Meredith Fisher had finished her sermon and the congregation had given voice, somewhat thinly, to the final hymn: 'We plough the fields and scatter / The good seed on the land . . .' She had taken the prospect of the hymn as an opportunity to speak in her sermon about the dangers of unprotected sex. For a while now she had been waging a campaign to have a vending machine selling condoms installed in the Stag and Badger, but Colin Drover's wife, Kath, had been brought up Roman Catholic. She was lapsed

81

herself but it had given her principles.

The Reverend Fisher—also from principle—was averse to all aversion, especially of a sexual kind. Her programme of enlightenment discouraged the notion that any physical act between consenting adults could be distasteful. However, there were realities to consider—Aids and venereal diseases were contingencies no modern Christian could afford to overlook.

She had put this thought to the drowsing congregation which this morning had consisted of Paula's mum and her Auntie Edna, who'd come for a weekend's country air to get over the death of Uncle Ron, a couple of the old bell-ringers, who turned up because Rector Malcolm had told them, before he became incoherent, they were to 'mind' the new incumbent and they owed him that at least, and Tessa, Nicky Pope's daughter. Tessa was going through a religious phase and had had a vision of the Virgin during a lesson on Bosnia and, as a consequence, had been sent to the sick room to lie down.

And there was also Barty Clarke, the auctioneer and editor of the *Backenbridge Review*.

It was as well, the Reverend Fisher thought, that Mr Clarke was there. His distinguished form stood upright among the more recumbent members of the congregation. He ploughed the fields and scattered in a vigorous bass, and he paid flattering attention to the sermon, apparently taking notes.

In following her vocation, Meredith Fisher had bravely set her face against disheartenment. The path of a modern Christian, particularly a female one, was bound to be uphill. Had our Lord been a woman Himself He could scarcely have been set a

82

more challenging one to tread. Nevertheless, it made a welcome change to have a member of the congregation take such an interest as Mr Clarke.

Barty took the vicar aside at the end of the service after she had shaken hands with all her parishioners—which to one of a less optimistic turn of mind than hers might have seemed to take dispiritingly little time—and questioned her about her pronouncements on gay sex. He seemed impressed when she explained how they were all born of her own experience. It was encouraging to the vicar to encounter a fellow pilgrim—a man as well—on the hard road to enlightenment.

*   *   *

Up on the moor, Mr Golightly was sitting on the high granite bench of the tor, with Wilfred beside him. The moss made plump emerald pillows on the rocky outcrop, and the delicate leaves and petals of the saxifrages formed fine-cut cameos at his feet. Mr Golightly smelled the moist earth and let the clean light bathe his eyes. He surveyed the scene before him: the green and brown and gold chequered moorland floor, the reservoir ahead, where light shone like polished silver on the water, the steep fall below, where humps of trees and glowing brambles tumbled to extinguish themselves in the rampaging River Dart.

All this, he observed, was good. So what was wrong? Why were nature's creations so gracious and vital compared to humankind? Humankind was part of nature too. But unlike the rest of nature it seemed so prone to litter the world with error and blunder, with noxious insinuations and

83

captious demands which could never—surely reason would say so?—be fulfilled. Reason was supposed to be the prerogative of human beings but, of course, all really important things had little to do with reason.

He returned to Spring Cottage in low spirits to find a call registering on the answerphone.

'Hi there, Boss! Got your call, I'll give you a bell later. Cheers!'

Drat! He had forgotten all about the wretched e-mail. He wondered whether he could be bothered with it. These modern systems of communication seemed to be two-edged swords—they were tiresome to administer and exposed you to unwarranted intrusion. He went over to the gateleg table and opened the laptop. This time the e-mail started up with no trouble and within seconds the 'Inbox' displayed the news that there were three messages waiting.

The first was from Mike.

> boss—keep trying with the server—it goes AWOL from time to time but don't you fret—I'll give you a buzz—mox

Yes, well, more of the same. Nevertheless, Mike was right, the wayward server had righted itself.

The next message was from Martha who said she wanted to 'do diaries' over some future engagements.

The third said:

> as for darkness, where is the place thereof?

CHAPTER TWELVE

Morning Claxon, over to spend the weekend with Hugh up at 'Nutkins', was out, that Sunday, for her morning run. Like Mr Golightly, she did not attend the service at the village church. Morning was a pagan and it was rumoured that she had danced naked, to see the sun up, on Widecombe Moor last midsummer. Gossip also claimed that the stone circle where she danced was the one put up by Jackson, when the people from Channel Four wanted a location for a film about Satanic rites.

Morning was broad-minded and sympathetic towards the Christian faith. It was her belief that Jesus was really a pagan, and she had been thrilled to hear in a lecture, given at Totnes, that one of the Gnostic sects—which it was widely believed, in Totnes, that Jesus belonged to—had been in the way of consuming a sacred drink, made up of menstrual blood and semen. Known to be a favourite among pagans, menstrual blood and semen had not yet hit the taste of Great Calne where communicants still favoured the more familiar wine and wafer; though, even for these, takers were somewhat slender, as the Sunday's congregation showed.

Morning paced herself going down the hill where you could turn an ankle. Passing the church she was in time to see the Reverend Meredith talking to Barty Clarke. A pity when women didn't keep up appearances, Morning ruminated, raising her pace as she came down on to the flat. The vicar would look so much better with more fashionable glasses and eye make-up.

A barking Labrador bounded towards her.

'Wilfred!' reprimanded Ellen Thomas, who had come out into the street to look for her dog.

The black Labrador had made his way under the barbed-wire fence into the garden of Spring Cottage. Mr Golightly, finding the dog there after their walk on the moor, was returning him for a second time.

Morning pulled in her stomach muscles and lengthened her spine, conscious that good posture shows a woman's breasts to advantage. A man of late middle age, altogether unremarkable in appearance, was not the stuff to bring out any special response in her. Still, a man was a man, and no opportunity to further her plans should be wasted. She had not given up the fight to transform the tearooms to an alternative health centre and was hopeful of instituting a Pilates class.

Mr Golightly's was a nature adapted to finding pleasure wherever pleasure was honestly to be found. He enjoyed the sight of a shapely bosom and his eyes now rested on Morning Claxon's, much as, a little earlier, he had paused to admire a crop of shining yellow celandines. 'Good morning,' he said. Had he had a hat he might have raised it, so statuesque was the young woman who stood before him.

Morning Claxon smiled on her elderly admirer. 'My friends will tell you otherwise but if you can't be good be careful, I always say!'

Mr Golightly looked politely puzzled.

'My name's Morning,' explained his new acquaintance. This was not strictly the case: her given forename was Maureen but this had not translated well to the alternative culture of the South-West.

'Ah,' said Mr Golightly.

Ellen Thomas turned to go inside.

'Oh, Mrs Thomas,' Morning said, remembering why she had made Ellen's the final point of her run.

Morning had overheard Nicky Pope, up at the Post Office Stores, mention that Ellen Thomas was 'poorly'. From the sight of her it looked as if the woman might have ME, some sort of food intolerances certainly. Taking in the name of the house they stood outside—'Foxgloves'—Morning remembered she had been meaning to have a word with the post office about getting the name of Hugh's house, 'Nutkins', changed to 'Morning Glory'.

'Might I just pop in for a mo?' she asked, unleashing her most empathic smile.

Mr Golightly discerned a look of panic in Ellen Thomas's eyes. He had returned from his outing in a mood to roll up his sleeves and start in at once on his soap opera. But Ellen Thomas had been neighbourly and a woman in distress spoke to his sense of protectiveness.

'Ah, I was wondering if I, too, might have a word . . .?'

'Of course . . .' There was relief in Ellen Thomas's glance at Mr Golightly as she vaguely gestured both guests inside.

*   *   *

'And then,' Morning Claxon's voice had something of the swimming-bath attendant about it, 'there's

87

colonic irrigation . . .'

Mr Golightly, whose bowels needed no regulating, looked across at Ellen Thomas who was staring blankly out of the window.

'I'm so sorry to interrupt,' he said to Morning, 'but I need a word with Mrs Thomas, ah, about the matter we talked of last time I was here . . .'

'What matter?' asked Ellen Thomas, almost rudely. Morning's animated smiles had brought on fantasies of self-mutilation.

'The, ah . . .' he shot a look in the direction of the intruder. 'I'm afraid it is private,' he said, feebly.

'Oh, please,' said Morning, 'don't you two mind me. I must be off or Hughie will be frantic. He gets in a state when he doesn't know where I've got to.' With her back held in the correct postural alignment she rose from the sofa. 'No, don't get up—I can see my own way out.' Obviously, there was a *tendresse* between the dear old pair—she was the last person to get in the way of Cupid's work!

When the front door had been heard to close Ellen Thomas put her hands over her face.

Mr Golightly sat saying nothing, looking first at the picture of the crows flying over the cornfield and then across at the sheep, on the unpainted hills, which looked no more real than the painting of the landscape—like toy creatures set out on a child's play farm.

After a while Ellen said, 'You see, since my husband died . . .' and gave up. It wasn't really Robert. For some reason, to Mr Golightly, even by omission, she didn't want to lie.

'You see,' she said, again, 'I have been asked, told . . .' How could she explain . . .? And yet, somehow she wanted to explain to him. 'I have been told to tell people . . . about love,' she concluded, lamely.

Mr Golightly, who knew minutely the truth and terror of this emotion, and its capacity to inspire and to ruin, looked at her but still said nothing.

'I don't know how to do it,' said Ellen Thomas. She felt suddenly savage, thinking of the impossible task she had had forced upon her.

'Yes,' said Mr Golightly, 'without great wisdom and strength humankind should pray to be spared the experience of love.' And he sighed, feeling he was in a unique position to know how impenetrable that condition is, perhaps most of all to those whom it masters.

'I mean,' said Ellen Thomas, taking courage from her fiat of anger, 'why me? What, for God's sake, do I know?'

'Well,' said Mr Golightly, 'since you ask,' and his gaze, with its peculiar shifting quality, which had bent on her with unusual directness, now settled again in the direction of the dark crows, 'I would say that perhaps what you know—it is a hard thing to explain—is that love is larger than life.'

*   *   *

The drawn bow of the moon had soared austerely into the sky by the time the man left the beacon. He had accomplished what he had come for and now he must find food—his belly was clanking like an iron-clappered bell. The day and night spent in flight had raided his strength which the years of captivity had depleted. His limbs trembled with hunger and exhaustion as he made his way down the valley's steep side, catching his ankle in the arm of a twisted bramble which ripped at his skin.

The lights in Ellen Thomas's sitting room were out because she had not troubled to put them on in the first place. After her neighbour left she had remained lying on the sofa. He had protected her, shown her solicitude and, now he was gone, she missed him. Tears slid down her face as she stared into the colourless dark.

'Die? Die?' suggested the young moon enticingly.

Samson was safely stabled, but the ghost horse, who knew no stables, was making shadowy ellipses. It was some weeks since, towards evening, she had begun to see him cantering occasionally beside Samson—a white horse, the colour of old ivory.

The audience of one became two as the man walked quietly towards the French windows and felt the back of his neck prick. As he turned to witness the circles made by the shaggy hooves and flowing mane, the slight movement caught Ellen Thomas's eye.

The man approached the windows and felt with his hand to see if he could ease them open. They slid smoothly and he stepped inside.

Ellen Thomas shifted her limbs fractionally to be more comfortable for death. Well, it had come at last. She waited for the touch, sudden and appalling, praying that Robert might be on hand to see her safely through.

The man, not seeing the still figure on the sofa, stole towards the farther door revealed in the cool moonshine. Feeling along the wall, he found his way to the kitchen. Nothing much in the fridge but a starving man is not fussy. He pushed aside a cut-glass bowl with three tinned prunes in it and plucked out a couple of hard-boiled eggs.

He had crushed the shells of the eggs between his palms when a light was turned on and he was clean caught in the sudden illumination.

APRIL

CHAPTER ONE

Mr Golightly had made little progress with his soap opera. In the early evening, he turned on the black-and-white TV set, for which he had to adjust the aerial many times, and watched *Neighbours*, hoping to pick up tips. There was no doubt about it, the writers of the series had a knack he lacked. When, after a simple supper, he took his regular evening stroll up to the Stag and Badger, to do the crossword with Luke and compare notes (somewhat pessimistic ones) about the day's output, he heard all round him, in the talk of the people of Great Calne, just the kind of everyday dramas that he was vainly trying to work into his script.

This raised a question in his mind. Did the characters on television talk the way they did because that was how people naturally thought and talked? Or was it, he wondered, the other way round? Did flesh-and-blood people come to resemble fictional characters, imitating what they heard on the TV or cinema screen or read in fiction? In which case, how you wrote and what you wrote about was God's own responsibility.

Perhaps it was the weight of this burden which held up Mr Golightly's project. He woke each morning with firm intentions. After a walk round the garden, during which he would inspect the sky for signs of the coming weather (he had little faith in forecasters), he would chat to Samson before returning inside where he put on music. (He had become keen on some of the minor Italians and was currently on Corelli which, rather enterprisingly, he couldn't help feeling, he had ordered from Amazon.) Then he washed and shaved and made a cup of coffee and, very often, another. After all this, he was ready to sit at the gateleg table.

But try as he might, as the days passed, he could not get beyond the re-creation—or regeneration rather—of the original cast of characters. These he could see clearly in his mind's eye.

The eye of Mr Golightly's mind was no near-sighted one and it was easy enough to bring before it the familiar forms and faces of the characters he had created all that time ago. The action, after all, was, as Luke would say, already 'blocked in' from the original work. Put like that, the task he had set himself should be child's play. But where to find a child? he ruefully asked himself one morning.

His own son, now . . . he had retained the childlike mentality he was after, had kept, to an extraordinary degree, that uncompromising quality which was so often a thorn in the parental side. Children, in fact, were very like characters in fiction: you couldn't legislate for, never mind predict, how they might turn out. Once you'd created them they took on an independent, and often defiant, turn of life.

The drama he had written all that time ago, for example. How far had he been responsible for all the upsets and disasters? Could it have turned out differently? And the love story—which he had hoped might redeem the tragic elements in the plot and had ended so ambiguously—was that all down to him? The tale, and the participants, had gathered its own momentum, which had moved under laws he had certainly created but seemed to have passed beyond his control.

He sighed and pressed the start on the CD player. 'Well, if your baby leaves you,/And you've gotta tale to tell—'

Here, now, was another thing. The pain which seemed such an inevitable accompaniment of all relationships. Mr Golightly's foot swung to the beat of the music which obscured the sound of a rap at the door. The rapping was repeated more insistently.

'Hell!' exclaimed Mr Golightly, not altogether sincerely, for he had come to a point in his procrastinations where interruptions were something of a mercy.

When he had finally kicked open the front door, which had swollen again in the April rains, Mr Golightly saw before him a figure he vaguely recognised: an athletic-looking, ginger-haired young man wearing a large-checked sports jacket.

'Brian Wolford. We met up at the Stag.'

The prison officer from Princetown, recalled Mr Golightly, wondering what he wanted.

Whatever it was, Brian Wolford didn't wait to be invited but walked straight on in. Mr Golightly put 'Heartbreak Hotel' on 'Pause' and offered coffee.

'Thank you, sir, never touch it.'

'Coke?' There was a can left over from the six-pack.

'Not offering me a line, are you, sir? 'Scuse my little joke. No, I don't touch sugar or artificial sweeteners either.' Wolford revealed perfect teeth.

Mr Golightly's teeth were almost antique, and he rarely showed them, but his grin now had the look of an aged dog trying to outwit an annoying master.

'Milk?'

'Fat-free diet, I'm afraid!' Wolford, whose manner did not suggest fear, massaged his chest. The gesture gave an impression that what lay beneath the shirt was as indisputably hairy as the hand.

'Water?'

'I won't if it hasn't been filtered, sir, begging your pardon.'

'Not at all,' said Mr Golightly. He was intrigued to note how the refusal of hospitality was creating more attention than a demand for it.

'Mind if I take a pew?'

'I'm so sorry . . .' His social skills had run their course but the man's over-sureness invited rudeness.

'Sorry to trouble you, sir, it's this character we've got who's done a runner,' said Wolford, confidentially. As he spoke his tongue flicked lightly between his teeth.

There was no one about to hear them in the dust-dancing sunlit parlour but a tone of confidentiality, Mr Golightly observed to himself, has more to do with the speaker's sense of self-importance than a wish for privacy. 'Yes?'

'Thing is, up there we don't see how he could've got away from the area. We got a cordon round the moor quick as scratch your bum—' Mr Golightly shifted his buttocks uncomfortably—'so we're asking around again, getting folk to search their memories, know what I mean?'

Earlier in his existence, as Mr Golightly was the first to acknowledge, his character had included a punitive streak, but time had softened his responses and nowadays he tried to let tenderness rule. His son had had a liking for miscreants and malefactors—had even sought out their company in preference to the well-to-do intelligentsia where he could easily have held his own among the best of them. The image of the escaped prisoner, hunted like a beast by men like Wolford, brought in its wake painful memories of other persecutions.

Perhaps detecting some unspoken dissent, the prison officer assumed a more official manner.

'Just thought I'd call by, ask you to keep a look out. You're new to the area. Familiarity breeds contempt.' Wolford showed more of the superior teeth. 'You might notice something which folk round here wouldn't.'

'When are we speaking of?' enquired Mr Golightly. His memory may have been failing him lately but he recalled the date of the escape perfectly: it was the day at the Stag and Badger when the sun had glinted on Mary Simms's hair. A prison officer would have no official role in the search. The visit, Mr Golightly guessed, had more to do with nosy curiosity, or, heaven help him, with yet another request to assist with some wretched form of creative writing.

'Now I've got you in my clutches, if you'll pardon the liberty, sir, there's this idea I had for a book. Stop me if you've heard it,' requested Wolford, sitting back confidently in the easy chair.

*   *   *

From his post in the yew tree, Johnny Spence had been spying on the various comings and goings of Great Calne. It was the Easter holidays, so for the time being he had no obvious need of concealment. But his stepdad was off work, and his mum had gone somewhere, so there was no safety at home. And Johnny hadn't many friends—none now he'd knocked Dave Sparrow's teeth down his head for him for saying he was queer. Partly out of boredom, and unwilling to waste an opportunity, Johnny elected to see if there was anything worth nicking from the church.

As Johnny slid jaguar-style from the tree, Brian Wolford was leaving Spring Cottage. The idea for the novel, about a sex offender doing life, had yielded no response from Golightly. He had made it pretty plain that he wasn't much interested. Probably jealousy. Those writer johnnies were touchy as hell about their status.

Wolford's own temper was uncertain; as a child he had knowingly starved his pet rabbits and his mother's cat knew to keep out of his way when he was in a bad mood. Spotting Johnny Spence, Wolford quickened his stride and was in time to grab hold of the boy at the church door.

'Whatcha do that for?' Johnny asked, balefully rubbing his arm. Wolford's grip was strong enough to have bruised the flesh. Up at the prison, it was common knowledge that it was wise to stay on the right side of Wolford.

'What you up to going into the church, then?'

'Just going in there, aren't I?' Johnny knew what Wolford did. His stepdad was fond of telling him how he'd land inside himself one day.

'Oh, a churchgoer, are we?'

'Said I'd go there for the chappie yonder?' said Johnny quickly, nodding his head towards Spring Cottage.

'Oh yes,' said Wolford. 'What does Mr Golightly want you to do that for, then?'

Inspiration is democratic—it abandons great artists without a backward glance and alights on the shoulders of ragamuffins. 'Wanted me to get him a hymn book, didn't he?' Elvis had been religious.

'Oh, really?' Wolford's eyebrows signalled pleasure at this patent fiction. 'Hymn books, is it? We'll see what Mr Golightly says when I ask him, won't we?'

'Yeah,' said Johnny, uneasily.

Wolford looked at his victim's face more closely. 'You live up Storey Lane, don't you? Your dad know what you're doing?' He knew Phil Spence by reputation—a drunk and a layabout, probably a 'domestic violent' too.

'Yeah,' said Johnny, too quickly this time.

'Well, now, you get back to your hymn books then, Mister Spence, and maybe I'll pay your dad a visit. I'll be asking questions about you, don't you worry.'

Johnny's sense of danger was acute: he knew that it wasn't safe to tangle with a sadist. As he and the screw were speaking, he'd seen, in his peripheral vision, the tenant of Spring Cottage go out of the house and off up the street. Mr Golightly had been OK. Maybe his best bet was to go after him and explain. If Wolford spoke to his stepdad he'd be for it—and so would his mum.

*   *   *

The prison officer's visit had left Mr Golightly feeling the need for a change of air. He had not cared for Wolford, nor his fiction proposal, which struck Mr Golightly as based on something unsavoury into which he did not wish to delve. And the mention of the escaped prisoner had touched off those insidious feelings which so haunted and perplexed him.

The fact was that Mr Golightly had a secret—or rather, not a secret exactly, because it was not that he was hiding it from anyone—certainly not himself, which is often the way with a secret. But there was no one he could tell, or talk over with, the matter which was always on his mind.

The idea which he could not shake off was that he had in some way been responsible for the catastrophe which had deprived him of his beloved son and had had such widespread consequences. Not for one second, since he had watched his boy die, had he been free from the carking sense that he had been crucial in that unbearable end. Not that the appalling affair had been—could ever have been—his plan for his boy; but the lad had somehow got it into his head that to embark on the course he had taken was what his father expected of him . . .

There had been complicating factors: Mr Golightly had been about other business at the time; regrettably, he had trusted to others to see that the boy—who, from the first, had shown a reckless disregard for consequences—came to no harm. The boy's mother, for instance. Somehow he had supposed that a woman's sense would have . . . but what was the use in going down that regretful road? His mother had been devastated too; as had all the women the boy had collected around him. There was no doubt the lad had been attractive to women, as any man who is careless of his own

102

safety will be. And of course, whenever he opened his mouth he attracted not just women—but people of all kinds. He had a way that drew every type to him, far more effectively than his father had managed. Indeed, Mr Golightly mused, it was his own foolish imperviousness to human psychology which in part caused the trouble in the first place . . .

He dug out his walking shoes and went out into the lane where Wilfred bounded to meet him as if he were an old friend. It was a while since they had walked up to the moor together, and he had returned to rescue the dog's owner from the woman with the impressive bosom who had shown such concern for his bowels.

Wilfred had taken an animal's unilateral decision and run on ahead. The banks the dog was exploring had thickened with foliage since Mr Golightly had last walked there. Nettles were unfurling tender green leaves. Dock and sorrel were shooting up. Tiny violets, purple, mauve and white, grew scattered among the green growth, like wanton gems dropped by some ebullient and careless woman. Azure-headed chaffinches with apricot breasts pinked ecstatically along the dark, white-blossomed branches of blackthorn and flew ahead in dipping waves as he followed the Labrador up the lane. The April air was gentle and seductive. Nothing is so beautiful as spring, Mr Golightly said to himself.

It was vexing, therefore, to meet Sam Noble at the cattle grid.

Sam Noble had not forgotten his suggestion to Mr Golightly that the cultural arm of Great Calne would be strengthened by the formation of a writers' group. Nor had he forgotten that it was he

103

who had undertaken to get it going. What luck he had all that experience with the Mummers in Kensal Rise! He greeted Mr Golightly with enthusiasm, explaining that he had dropped by to canvass Luke—not about the car park, he wouldn't want Golightly to think that his mind was not sometimes on 'higher things'!—but about his idea for a writers' group. 'You're the busy fellow—any day'll suit us,' Sam declared.

'Ah,' said Mr Golightly, who was unfamiliar with the unsolicited largesse which corrals. He wondered if he could refer to a business appointment in town; but with the date of the proposed meeting in his own control how could he arrange for it also to take place in his absence? This was just the kind of nuisance his staff had dealt with. For a second his mind turned regretfully to Martha: despite her temperamental behaviour, she would have come up with some saving strategy.

'Luke's keen,' Sam announced.

This was not quite true. Luke had been woken after a disturbed night, passed under the influence of *Hiawatha*'s insistent rhythms, by a phone call from Mary Simms, who wondered if he could possibly give her a hand with her Open University assignment. Aside from Longfellow, Luke knew very little about poetry. From being wakened suddenly, he had answered Mary awkwardly, Mary had rung off discouraged, and both parties had been left with the depressing sense of inadequacy brought on by a failed communication.

The arrival of Sam Noble was at least a distraction and Luke was mildly flattered to be asked to join a writers' group; but mostly he was hoping Sam would buzz off so he could have a

104

smoke in peace. Luke was a pacific soul; it had been the path of least resistance to agree to Sam's suggestions.

A regular piece of luck, Sam said to himself, that he should meet Golightly just as he had got young Luke on board. And he had extracted a promise that a date would be set when they would all meet at Sam's house. Satisfied that he now had the muse if not by the scruff of her neck at least by the hem of her robe, he walked, well pleased with himself, down the lane.

Mr Golightly climbed slowly with Wilfred to his favourite spot on the tor. Making a shade with his hands round his eyes, he watched a pair of buzzards with their stiff stilted wings sail, in a regal mating dance, across the face of the sun. A little way off, stood a group of Dartmoor ponies, two the almost-black brown of their breed and one, larger, hardly a pony at all, a ghostly white. Their manes lifted in the breeze as, begging no favours and enjoining no compunction, they patiently cropped the perpetually renewing vegetable carpet of the Moor.

Mr Golightly gazed for a long while on the scene before him. His was an imagination which, in its time, had fashioned many and diverse things. The imagination is a creator of worlds—and from his had issued gods and kingdoms, peoples and purposes, stables and citadels, deserts and mountain tops, the defeat of principalities, the frail victory of hope. Before him now, the sun was perfecting its own creation, sprinkling the vegetation with a shifting silver sheen. Out of the cool earth, through the sun's unflagging warmth, sprang herbs and grasses and trees. And deep within the earth's fiery centre its power formed the ores of precious metals, silver and gold—emblems of human nobility. But where was that nobility realised on the earth?

Not, to be sure, among the population of Great Calne. It seemed that such virtues had faded from the world, leaving behind only a rusty stain. Perhaps the failure lay in him? Maybe his creative powers, on which so much of his identity had been based, had all been a sham, and the world which had once seemed so various, so beautiful, so new was nothing more than a darkling plain, swept with confused alarms of struggle and flight . . .

If Martha were here she would probably advise a short course of Seroxat. The visit from Wolford had depressed him. He had come away for a rest, a holiday, yet he found he was tired: tired of trying to dodge people who wanted something incalculable from him, tired of trying to master the tricks of a world which seemed to have shot ahead of him, tired of his efforts to weave the lives of those he had created into his idea for a soap opera. Tired, in short, of the memorials of his own inadequate vocation. It was a footling, foolhardy, crack-brained scheme—he'd do best to abandon it, return to his former privacy and allow the slow seepage of his fame to continue unarrested. Who would miss him, after all?

He turned to make his way back down towards Great Calne and found that he was no longer alone. The boy, Johnny Spence, had followed him to the tor.

CHAPTER TWO

When Ellen Thomas, lying on the sofa in her sitting room in the expectation of death, had found that nothing happened, she had felt at first let-down, then affronted. She had steeled herself for the promised end—and then nothing . . .

After a while she got up and went towards the kitchen. The door was ajar and the light from the open fridge lent a sepulchral glow to the face which turned to hers. It looked startled; not the awe-inspiring aspect one hopes for in the Angel of Death. Across her mind flitted the notion that perhaps she should offer him something—a cup of tea, a dry sherry . . .

The face had melted into fearfulness. It's not the Angel of Death, she thought, regretfully. It's a body in need.

A man stood there, a shabby shape, blinking as she switched on the light. 'Shut the fridge door,' said Ellen. It was all she could think of to say. Then she added, remembering what she had considered offering the putative angel, 'Would you like a drink—a cup of tea?'

Later, when she thought about Jos Bainbridge, Ellen realised that he had trembled when she found him, that it was he and not she who had been afraid. Not registering this at the time, she had gone to the kettle and filled it with water, busying herself setting it to boil so that he could compose himself. He had simply stood there, his face pale, sweating gawkily.

'So,' she had said, her back turned to him, no

longer bothered whether he had come to stab it, 'what can I do for you?'

The words laid down an invisible marker.

'I need help.'

In losing her husband, Ellen had lost those everyday occasions to give help which remain unregistered until they are gone. Helping others, she had gathered, was no longer considered a respectable—or even acceptable—element in loving them; but the impulse had not died with Robert.

'Of course,' she said. 'Come into the other room, won't you, and let's have some tea and we'll talk about it . . .'

*   *   *

The sight of Johnny Spence's fearful face appearing over the rocks of the tor also pressed a spring in Mr Golightly's breast.

'John?' he asked, and waited.

Johnny hadn't planned what he was going to say. Muddled in a nightmarish mix in his mind was the image of his stepdad, Wolford and the prospect of Dartmoor prison.

'Please, sir,' he said, fear summoning words he knew from some dim past to be impressive, 'I'm sore afraid.'

Like Ellen Thomas, Mr Golightly was not immune to the pleasures of helping others. The boy had already formed associations in his mind, painful yet affectionate, and the combination was a potent one.

'What's up?' asked Mr Golightly. He found his heart was skipping slightly.

'Please, sir,' said Johnny, reverting to a more familiar idiom, 'I'm fucked!'

*   *   *

Watching the boy skulk off up the high street, Wolford had felt a sense of loss. He stood contemplating the boy's back and thin shoulders before deciding to follow him. The brief start the boy had meant that the athletic Wolford reached the tor only a fraction behind Johnny just as Wilfred began to bark.

'Excuse me,' he called, appearing, ginger and burly, over the rocks.

Johnny had had no time to explain his fix to the man he had instinctively followed. He stood, head drooped in resignation, waiting for the beans to be spilled. God alone knew why he had made up that fuckwit story about the hymn book.

'Yes?' Mr Golightly spoke shortly. His sense of privacy was strong; to be tracked by the very man who had driven him out to the place where he most enjoyed his solitude was an abomination.

'Sorry to trouble you again, sir,' Wolford's voice bore a patina of servility. 'Only it's this young lad here.'

'Yes?' Mr Golightly repeated. A perceptive listener might have detected a thread of menace in the voice.

'He work for you, does he?'

Mr Golightly was watching a crowd of starlings fall for cover like a shower of stones from the sky and disappear from sight beneath the feet of the sheep who grazed the common land. Like as not that meant there was a sparrowhawk about.

109

Shepherds of old, who lived close to nature and spent long months alone on the moor with only their flock and their dog and the realm of the invisible for company, felt a special fondness for starlings on account of their association with sheep.

Mr Golightly, who shared something of the shepherds' faith in the unseen, shared also their affection for the gregarious birds. He shaded his eyes, looking for the neat hunting hawk whose habit was to bite off the starling's head, fastidiously leaving the beak beside the body.

'Yes.'

Wolford's smile, which had begun by being insolent, faded, and the cheeks beneath the pale ginger fuzz turned a darker red.

'Pardon me, sir?'

'I said "Yes", he does work for me.'

Wolford, a habitual juggler with the truth, had a nose for when it was being played with. 'Mind telling me what he does exactly, sir?'

'I don't, though I might ask in return, Mr Wolford, what that has to do with you. I am a writer, as you know. John has been helping me with my research.'

It would have been hard to say who was the more surprised at these words, Wolford or Johnny. The prison officer, trying to hold on to his temper, stared at a white horse with a flowing mane which was cropping the grass just beneath them.

'I see.'

Mr Golightly said nothing. He had finally spotted the elegant outline of the sparrowhawk and appeared to be watching it intently.

'Good,' said Wolford. It was plain his emotion ran on other lines.

'Yes?' said Mr Golightly again, turning back, and the two men, with the boy between them, stood in silence on the tor top till Wilfred began to yap.

'Well,' said Wolford, 'I'll be off, then.'

'Good,' said Mr Golightly, watching the thwarted hawk's outline wheel away across the bright dome of the sky.

CHAPTER THREE

Even those who have never visited Dartmoor may have heard of Widecombe because of the famous fair, and the song in which Tom Pearce loaned his grey mare so that Bill Brewer, Jan Stewer, Peter Gurney, Peter Davy, Dan'l Whiddon, Harry Hawk, Old Uncle Tom Cobleigh and all could ride there. Although the village itself is set in a basin within surrounding heights, the ways up to Widecombe-in-the-Moor are notoriously steep, which is why Tom Pearce's overburdened mare gave up the ghost before the party reached their destination. In those days, the horse was the chief form of Dartmoor's transport; today most travellers go by car or, if they are on holiday, and health or leisure minded, on foot.

Johnny Spence's mother, Rosie, was not on holiday but she owned no car and had grown up with a thorough knowledge of the paths across the moor. She set off for Widecombe by the ancient Abbot's Way—irregularly marked by tipsily leaning stone crosses, whose wise, or foolish, legends are too worn by wind and weather to be easily deciphered. The Way, now also somewhat

111

indecipherable, once formed one of the principal routes across the breadth of the moor, from the imposing Buckfast Abbey to the rival one at Tavistock.

Rosie didn't walk far along the medieval trail but soon branched up and crossed one of the surviving clapper bridges, built about the time that the monks' sandalled feet regularly trod the heather corridor of their Way. Rosie stopped in the middle of the flat bridge, made of huge slabs of unquarried moorland stone; beneath it the brawling East Dart ran boisterously to meet its parent. She was remembering her grandfather, who had been old enough to stable the packhorses for which the cyclopic bridges were built to cross the tracery of rivers seeping from the wide sponge of the Dartmoor peat.

Grandad was the first to call her 'Rosie', after *Rosamundi*, one of the old roses he grew in his garden, where he also grew sweet peas and runner beans which embraced in a pretty tangle around bamboo wigwams. It seemed to Rosie that it had been a more appealing world then. Few people, these days, knew what 'clapper' bridges were, or why they had come into being; or had heard any of the stories her grandad used to tell her, in his greenhouse, while he gently pushed, with big, cracked thumbs, the seedlings into shallow wooden boxes of peaty earth. You never saw those boxes now.

Or heard the tales—like the one about the man who salted his dad, because the weather was too foul for the undertaker to visit to his lonely place on the Moor; or the great storm, when the Devil rode into Widecombe and snatched a member of

112

the congregation playing cards at the back of the church. On the way to Widecombe, the Devil had stopped to demand drink from an innkeeper's wife, who reported afterwards that she heard the liquor sizzle in the diabolic throat.

Johnny had loved that story when he was little— not that you could call him 'big' now. But he had a grown-up way with him for all he was so hard to handle. Even as a bab he had looked at her with those slow hazel eyes which scared her almost. An old soul, her grandma had said.

Her grandma had died right after her grandad, a shrewd, bony woman. 'I've not a moment's peace thinking of the muddle that man'll get into without me,' she had declared, crossly, when a neighbour called to condole. She was dead herself a month after her husband.

Their only son, Rosie's father—Rosie had wondered how he had come to be conceived for she never saw the old couple touch, but then, sex was strange and there were no rules—had become a local tenant farmer. Rosie had gone with him to Widecombe Fair, where the ruddled sheep—whose red markings looked like a child's poster paint— were sold in the days when people still bought English mutton and wool. What they did nowadays Rosie didn't know and her dad wasn't likely to tell her. They hadn't spoken in years. Please God it wouldn't be like that with her and Johnny!

But it might be. History repeated. Grandma had often said so and Rosie'd lived long enough to tell the truth of it. Patterns got into your brain, someone else who'd also loved her once said, and then got into your life and played hell with it. You always hurt the ones you love, the song said. She didn't want to hurt Johnny. But then what about her now, leaving him with Phil, who was capable of hitting Johnny so hard he could easily land up in hospital.

As Rosie walked on she began to make out in the distance the shape of one of Dartmoor's most noted attractions. Widecombe Church, dedicated to St Pancras (famed for the railway station), is called the 'Cathedral of the Moor' on account of its lofty tower. A hundred years or so after the church's conception, those who worked the tin mines were numerous enough to make a fair-sized congregation and it was these 'tinners' who provided the funds to put up, as a thanksgiving for their prosperity, the Perpendicular tower.

The less prosperous holders of the ancient forest tenements, from the valleys of the East Dart, also resorted to the church, 'forest' on Dartmoor being those historic areas where animals once roamed wild and tenants could take 'everything that may do them good save vert and venison'. 'Vert', Rosie's grandad had explained to her, was the green wood of the growing tree. The red deer whose flesh provided the forbidden venison—the cause of many hangings—had been hunted out long before hanging for poaching, and then, finally, hanging itself, was abolished. There were legendary Dartmoor hunters her grandad told her of: Childe the Hunter, for instance, whose tomb lay near the mire, where, as a 'child' herself, in flight from her father, she had half hunted death. It was her nightmare now that Johnny might hunt it there too.

It was no accident that Rosie's mind was fixed on death because it was to visit the graves of her grandparents that she was walking to Widecombe.

Her grandmother had died in the month of April, and, in recent years, Rosie had evolved a ritual in which she paid her respects on that date to the man and woman who had been her steadiest examples of affection. She missed them—the way you missed people you had taken for granted, the way you missed anything you took for granted when it disappeared.

The heather caught at her long skirt and her swinging stride started up birds before her. Maybe she would see a lark. She took it for a lucky sign when she saw her grandad's favourite bird on her way to visit him and Grandma. When she was Johnny's age, she'd won a prize at school in a competition, when she'd been the only one to know the name for a collection of larks—her grandad taught her the word for that too, but she couldn't remember it now.

*　　*　　*

It was Paula's day off and she had an appointment at 'Georgina's' in Oakburton for a bikini wax. There was a purpose to this. It was time, she reckoned, to move in on Jackson. He'd been sidestepping her with stories of 'work', which you'd have to be off your head if you believed, and having hung on so long she was buggered if she was letting him get away. But before she could move in with Jackson there was her mum to deal with.

Her mum had been giving her a hard time lately, moaning on about how she'd bust the washing machine dying her bedspread purple, which was a joke when you considered how they'd had the machine since her mum's boyfriend was around—

at least fifteen years—and it had made a sound like it had a ball and chain round it then! She knew that, 'cos she'd used to lay in her bed hearing the sound of the ball and chain, hoping that her mum's boyfriend would end up with one round him too, if he whacked her mum one more time. Not that she didn't often feel like whacking her mum herself these days . . .

However, she didn't want her mum out of pocket, so she needed to get that Luke Weatherall into her room for a lodger; which meant she was going to have to see to getting him there. She didn't expect too many problems, even though that silly cow Mary Simms was getting nowhere with him fast.

Mary had tried her best with Luke, but it is well known that love is blind—which, in practice, will often mean that young men, who turn out later to have been in love, will remain quite ignorant of this happy truth until it has been revealed to them. Mary had worn her sweetest smile and had tried her hardest with poetry. She had dropped, for Luke's benefit, several lines from 'The Lady of Shalott' while serving up his bitter at the Stag. But Tennyson seemed to be lost on Luke—he only wanted to talk to Mr Golightly. It had crossed Mary's mind to offer to 'do' for the tenant of Spring Cottage as a way of maybe bumping into Luke; but Mr Golightly seemed to be one of those self-sufficient men who liked to 'do' for himself, which was baffling to Mary, who clung to old-fashioned gender ideals.

Paula, however, had brought up her mum single-handed and had methods of getting her way unknown to Mary Simms. Reaching Oakburton car park, she examined her face closely in the mirror of her mum's Micra and decided, in preparation for the seduction of Luke, to have an eyelash dye and her eyebrows tidied.

By the bottle bank, she met Sam Noble, who was calling by the surgery to collect a prescription from Dr Rhys.

Sam had not been sleeping well. His plans for the tearooms to be owned by the village, collectively, had fallen on apathetic ears. Morning Claxon had been making energetic use of her verve with the women and her figure with the men to advance the cause of the alternative health centre, and there were those, of both sexes, who had been seduced by the prospect of massage with essential oils without thought to the likely consequences. In Sam's eyes, these could only be a nasty crop of houses outside his bedroom window and the lowered value of his own. The thought played havoc with his sleep.

Paula, who regarded Sam with the kind of contempt she reserved for her Auntie Edna's incontinent poodle, lowered her glance. This was practice for her proposed encounter with Luke, but Sam was not to know this. Not since the Maltese air hostess had any woman lowered her eyes at him.

'Hi there,' said Paula, 'where you off to then?' She swayed her pelvis just a fraction.

'Oh, just to the doctor's,' said Sam, and flushed.

'Yeah?' said Paula, assuming an indifference which concealed the real thing. 'Not feeling too good?'

'Nothing serious,' said Sam, torn between a wish for feminine sympathy and a desire to be seen as manly. 'A touch of insomnia.' He frowned, trying to look as if he was a man weighed down by grave worldly concerns.

'Oh dear,' said Paula. Her flat, compunctionless face staring unblinkingly at his.

'Would you like a cup of coffee at Green Gables when you've finished your errands?'

'Errands!' thought Paula. Stupid git spoke like someone in an old film. 'Yeah, all right, then.'

Paula, in her short skirt, with Sam looking after her, stepped briskly in her platforms up the street to Georgina's.

'Georgina' was in fact called Di, but she'd bought the franchise as a going concern from the previous beautician who had bestowed her name upon the business. When Paula said she had come for a bikini wax, Di suggested she might like to try a 'Brazilian'.

'Really, they're all doing it in London. A nice neat line down the front. Some people go all the way and have it all off—it's called a "Hollywood", I believe, but first time round I would recommend the "Brazilian". I promise you, it's getting really popular.'

Paula owned a couple of thongs which she'd relegated to the back of her drawer after she'd landed Jackson. She'd thought, in fact, to dig them out as part of the next phase in her campaign to move in with him. The 'Brazilian' fitted in with her plans.

'I suggest we do the wax first,' Di proposed. 'The old eyes tend to water a bit when we're working downstairs . . .'

Sam, temazepam in his pocket, was waiting in Green Gables when Paula arrived, walking slightly

118

gingerly. She sat down, crossing and uncrossing her legs to get the feel of the depilations below. 'A coffee, ta,' she requested. 'Black, I'm on a diet.'

'Surely there's no need for that?'

Sam was looking at her in a way which provoked in Paula extreme disgust. Now she'd got him all worked up she was landed with the bother of getting rid of the old idiot.

'Have to watch me figure, don't I?' Paula was mentally trying on each of the two thongs; one, a kind of lilacky mauve, with little rosettes, was the prettier, while the other, black and pink, matched her bra.

'You have a very nice figure,' said Sam, staring at Paula's chest.

'S'a Wonderbra,' said Paula, deciding that the moment to wean Sam had arrived.

But a swallowed bait is not so readily regurgitated and Paula had done no more than stir up the sludge of fantasy which lies at the bottom of the sanest human heart; Sam was already picturing a welcoming Paula spread out on the bed, in her underwear.

'Well, you look *wonder*ful in it.'

Jesus, give us a break! Paula thought. With the Brazilian wax and her eyebrows plucked to a dangerous pitch, she could afford no more time on this old fart.

'Yeah, well, I must be off, I'm 'fraid . . .'

'Oh, don't go . . .' The words were out before he could hold them back. Conscious that he might have betrayed too much, Sam tried to rescue the situation. 'I was wondering about the tearooms . . .'

'Yeah?' Paula turned a face of vague interest. She had heard from her mum about the tearoom

119

saga.

'You'd be the perfect person to run them, with all your pub experience . . .'

In Sam's imagination there was Paula greeting him in a frilly white apron over a very short black dress.

'Oh, right, yeah!'

'So—' said Sam, rushing on possessed by an impossible idea '—if I were to buy the tearooms, how about it if you were to come and run them? Say you will . . . ?'

Brian Wolford's mum, Cherie, was fond of the expression: There's no fool like an old fool.

'Yeah, well, I'll think about it.' No harm in agreeing and it got the old twit off her back. Paula was itching to get home and try out the results of Di's handiwork under the mauve thong, which would go nicely, she'd decided, with her purple sequinned T-shirt.

CHAPTER FOUR

The graveyard at Widecombe extends courteously towards the surrounding fields which, in turn, almost spill on to the encompassing moor. Rosie's grandparents, who lived all their lives within ten miles of the village, had married, at eighteen, in Widecombe's church.

As a girl, Rosie had kept in a box of treasures, along with a jay's feather and the skull of a weasel, the crimson velvet rose her grandma had stitched into her chemise for her grandad to find on their wedding night when he first undressed her. In

120

memory of this she had planted, on their joined graves, a deep red rose, whose scent in summer brought to her mind Grandma's favourite hymn, 'Summer suns are glowing'.

Rosie had brought with her some of the green garden twine she also associated with her grandad and a dibble, with which she planned to clear her grandparents' graveyard plot of weeds. Beneath the rose she had planted daffodils, which she saw had outgrown their strength and required binding. The granite gravestone read: 'William and Evelyn Coaker, 1899–1986' and beneath this 'In death they were not divided'.

As she worked Rosie sang to herself. 'Summer suns are glowing / Over land and sea.' They were almost twins, her grandparents—born just a month apart and sweethearts since school, which they'd left together at fourteen, he to go to the stables at Oakburton, she to go into service at Buckfast. 'Happy light is flowing / Bountiful and free.' Nowadays people would say by having only each other they had missed out on experience, but when you thought what 'experience' could bring, you might say you went through life more happily without it.

When she had cleared the weeds to her satisfaction, Rosie crossed the road from the church to one of the cafés which promised 'Full Cream Devon Teas', where she ordered a coffee and a ham sandwich. The sun was unexpectedly strong and it was warm enough to sit outside. She lit a cigarette and watched a woman dragging a child across the green yelling, 'Look what you've done to your trousers, for Christ's sake!' and wondered what Christ would have said on the subject. The things people did and said in his name. As if Jesus gave a stuff about mud on some poor kid's trousers.

The weeping, raging boy reminded her of Johnny. He never cried now, but when they first moved in with Phil it was every night, till the threat of Phil's hand dried up those fierce tears. Though it hurt her then to hear her boy's sobbing cries, she almost wished he would cry again. Something had shut down in the candid hazel eyes. But she knew her son—she knew he knew she was unhappy; and he knew, very likely, that it was all her own fault.

*   *   *

As Rosie sat in Widecombe reviewing her past, Paula was engaged in furthering future plans. She inspected her naked body in the bathroom mirror. Satisfied with her new denuded look, she set out for Lavinia's barn in her second-tightest pair of jeans. The encounter with Sam had merely confirmed her view that sex was the way to get a man to do what you wanted.

Luke, innocent of the treat in store for him, was surprised to find Paula when he answered the bell. His preoccupation with the myth of Creation had left him uncertain of his visitor's identity. Confused, but polite, he invited her upstairs. Paula negotiated the stairs with some difficulty: Luke's loft was some way up, and the tightness of the jeans, in concert with the effects of the Brazilian, produced unusual caution.

Gaining the upper floor first, Luke hurriedly pushed some clothes under the Indian bedspread and shoved a dirty plate of cigarette ends under the bed with his bare foot. 'Coffee?' he enquired, as Paula, rather breathy from the jeans and the unaccustomed exercise, emerged.

'Yeah, thanks.' Paula lowered the freshly dyed lashes, but Luke had his back to her and was filling the kettle with a good deal of noisy splashing so the effect was wasted.

Luke's conversation was limited. Like many artists, writers in particular, he was not much interested in flesh-and-blood human beings. When he had established Paula worked at the pub and run the short course of the weather there was only his own narrative poem—over which he was still stuck, he explained to Paula—or *Hiawatha* to fall back on. But here at least he was on familiar ground. And a trapped audience was an opportunity not to be passed up. 'Listen,' he said, 'you'll see the problem if I read you a couple stanzas . . .'

*   *   *

There is a network of letter boxes across Dartmoor. By tradition, visitors to these hidden sites stamp postcards or sign, or write verses in, the books hidden inside the concealed metal boxes. But this strange system grew from a much older tradition, through which lovers and friends communicated across the moor's inhospitable geography and the even greater inhospitality of economic circumstance.

Years back, Rosie's grandad had shown her the private place he had fashioned so that he and her grandma could keep in touch when he was a stable lad and she in service, and they could not hope for many of their days off to coincide. Later, as a girl, Rosie had shown the secret to one other person, and in time, as a young mother, she had also shown his great-grandad's postbox to Johnny. They had played, when he was small, at leaving notes to the Dartmoor spirits, who must be appeased lest they lead you astray and into the mire. Once she had said, 'If you ever run away from home you must promise to leave me a message here,' and wise-eyed Johnny had said, 'You too, Mum . . .'

Rosie walked back from Widecombe towards Buckland Beacon. Around her lay the tranquil Moor, discreet and unjudging. All at once the name for a collection of larks flew back to her—an 'exaltation'! Her grandad would be pleased she'd remembered. She pictured him, getting up out of his bed of earth at Widecombe, bored with inactivity, and wandering up here in his nightshirt. For all its wildness, there was a safety in the Moor you could never be sure of with people. If she left a note in Grandad's postbox Johnny might find it. He was quick, Johnny. He rarely forgot anything. To ring and maybe get Phil, or leave a message that he could get his hands on, was too risky. It was best for her and Johnny if she was out of the way for the time being.

*   *   *

Paula had nodded off.

'. . .Till from Hiawatha's wigwam
Kahgahgee, the King of Ravens,
Screamed and quivered in his anger,
And from all the neighbouring tree-tops

124

Cawed and croaked the black marauders.
"Ugh!" the old men all responded,
From their seats beneath the pine-trees!'

'See what I mean,' Luke said, pausing at last.
'You can't get away from Longfellow's rhythm.'

Paula, coming to with a start, was inclined to fall
in with the old men's responses. 'Yeah, well, I'd
better be going, then.' A kind of respect, forced by
a single-mindedness superior to her own, made her
unusually polite. Before Luke's absolute absorption
in his poetry, sexual allure had no chance.

'Did you call about anything special?' asked
Luke, showing her down the stairs again.

'Oh, yeah,' said Paula, driven by the unfamiliar
experience to explicitness. 'I was wondering if you
fancied taking over me room at me mum's. You
could have it on the money you get from the social.'

'Oh, right,' said Luke, ever polite. 'Yeah, ta. This
is OK for now but thanks for the offer.'

'Jesus, she's welcome to him!' Paula said aloud,
as she picked her heels warily over the bars of the
cattle grid. She could almost feel sorry for that
stupid Mary Simms.

CHAPTER FIVE

The gardener promised by Nicky Pope had never
shown up, so Mr Golightly had fallen into the habit
of keeping Spring Cottage's garden tidy himself.
This, in part, was to ensure that the Reverend
Fisher, or Keith, would not visit with offers of
Christian aid. But it also gave a chance to return to

125

an old pastime. The apple tree by the parlour window, for example, looked as if it hadn't been tended to in years.

Long ago, Mr Golightly had been something of an arborealist and had made quite a name for himself through a rare breed of tree, heralded for its ability to resist disease. But there had been problems with marketing it and in the end he had abandoned his interest in that part of the business, which was nowadays overseen by the industrious Bill and Mike.

It was many years since he had had anything to do with horticulture. To stroll in an English cottage garden, as he was this morning, was a rare joy. A garden is a gladsome thing, he said to himself, surveying the new translucent lime-green growth on the beech hedge.

Not for the first time it struck him that the life of a country labourer was one which might have suited him: where habits are so ingrained they become like instincts, hard labour from day to day in sun and wind and rain, with the weekly break and rest—a life not unlike his own had once seemed to promise. But a labourer would have a wife and family to provide the staple comfort of kinship. The solitary state was one he had lived in so long it seemed a condition of his very existence. Yet once, he, too, had had a family, of sorts, he was close to.

As is often the case on a holiday, away from quotidian concerns, his mind free from the trammels of time, Mr Golightly found he was tending to brood. The original point of his break with the daily round pressed less urgently on him: with each passing day he found himself letting his thoughts, like an unleashed falcon, circle in wider and wider speculation.

He woke early in the narrow bedroom, but now, instead of starting out of bed, as he had at the beginning of his break, he found he was tending to lie, letting thoughts drift and collect, like the leaves from autumnal trees which make piles of mulch for the garden.

It was as if he was giving space to something he had feared. Was 'feared' the right word? Fear had an object—something tangible, definable, at least, with which one could do combat, strive and hope to overcome. This vague looming inchoate sense was more impalpable. Perhaps it was what he had heard philosophers call—without having much clue as to what they might mean—'existential anxiety'. He seemed to remember that had something to do with the prospect of non-existence. Did he fear that he might not exist? It seemed a strange thing to get into a state about since if you didn't exist how could you possibly mind?

Walking now, past clouds of irrepressible milky-blue forget-me-nots, upright scarlet tulips and extravagant garnet and topaz wallflowers, whose dark-scented velvet was already laden with droning bees, he decided that the philosophers were wrong, and that this insubstantial anxiety they went on about had more to do with a feeling that, however powerful you might be, there were crucial concerns outside your control.

Pain, for example. He had heard it said that time heals all wounds. As to that, he doubted it. Time like an ever rolling stream might bear many things away but not the anguish of losing a child. That lay too deep for cure. If anything, like a ravening creature, made savage through incarceration, the recollection had grown more vicious with the passage of time. Why should a dog, a horse, a rat have life, and thou no breath at all? Mr Golightly felt that if he had once known the answer to this question, his grasp of it—if he had ever truly held it—had slipped.

The wicket gate opened as Johnny Spence came through into the garden and immediately Mr Golightly felt his spirits rise. He looked forward to seeing Johnny whose competence he was coming to rely on. And there was also the pleasure in observing that, rather as the garden, freed from winter's repression, was throwing off caution and showing a different side to its nature, young Johnny Spence was also somewhat changed.

For one thing, while he had not abandoned his perpetual hooded apparel it was now pushed back, showing more of his face. Which today was smiling.

'Hi!'

'Hi there!' said Mr Golightly in return.

'I done it. Here.'

Johnny thrust some papers at Mr Golightly, who glanced through them. 'Very good,' he said. 'Come inside. I was about to make breakfast.'

Breakfast was egg, bacon, tomatoes, and thick slices of toast with butter and Frank Cooper's Oxford marmalade.

'I like this,' said Johnny, helping himself to butter. 'Me mum has some stuff for me dad's heart. Don't like that.' He didn't add that he'd be glad if his stepfather's heart packed up altogether.

'Of course not,' said Mr Golightly, who needed no addendum. Like the king in the rhyme, he too favoured a little bit of butter to his bread. 'Coffee?

Or would you prefer Coke?'

They both drank coffee with creamy unpasteurised milk. The morning sun lit up the boy's head making a halo of the mousy hair. Examples of such benedictions on any spring morning were so prodigal that his recent glum musings seemed absurd. But there was danger here, too. Johnny brought to mind another boy child, and even in the seeming paradise of the English countryside there were unmistakable signs of the ineradicable impulse to despoil.

Mr Golightly's bland assertion to Wolford that Johnny was his researcher had been translated into reality without further discussion on either part. Johnny had wondered about this. The papers he had handed over was the script of a TV soap. Why his benefactor wanted such a thing was a mystery, but while he was getting ten quid a day for downloading stuff off the Internet—which, provided his stepdad was out of the way, was a piece of piss—it was a mystery he was willing to leave unsolved.

Mr Golightly was also inclined to forgo inquisition; he had taken pains that no shade of enquiry, other than that directed to his own work, should make itself felt in his dealings with Johnny Spence. Questions were the enemies of easygoing intercourse. He needed the boy at least as much as the boy needed him. One of the things his son had taught him was that the expression of need was a sign not of weakness but of strength.

As it turned out, Johnny was full of handy hints and helpful information. He put Mr Golightly right on the structure of soap operas. 'Scenes only take two minutes, hardly,' he explained, when Mr

Golightly commented on their extreme pace and brevity. 'Gotta keep them watching. People haven't got it up there for anything longer.'

Conversation with Johnny suggested to Mr Golightly how he might bring his great work up to date—by mixing up the characters, events and time schemes. Trying to get the thing to run on linear, causal lines—he had been slow to latch on to this—was part of the trouble. It was an outmoded technique, not the modern style at all. Johnny had shown him that nowadays you had fast cutting between scenes and characters, who no longer needed lengthy explanations or histories behind them.

The script he had asked Johnny to bring today was for the meeting of the writers' group—he was not looking forward to it—which was booked for that afternoon. Sam had been doggedly persistent and there seemed no way, without blatant rudeness—something Mr Golightly preferred to avoid—to get out of it. His plan was to bring along, as a decoy for discussion, one of the scripts Johnny had downloaded.

*   *   *

Sam had, in fact, been suffering over the writers' group the anxieties of all those who initiate on the basis of whim rather than anything really substantial. Three people, when he thought about it, seemed inadequate. He decided to drop over to Backen and sound out—what was the woman's name?—Nadia Something, with the hennaed hair, who ran the antiques shop. Nicky Pope had mentioned that the woman had had a novel published by a small press in Dartington.

Sam rang Nicky, who said she had a copy of the book which she'd been meaning to put among those in Spring Cottage. It didn't strike her as Mr Golightly's cup of tea, so she was happy to drop it by to Sam's.

The novel, a story about a middle-aged woman who travels through time and finds love at the court of King Arthur, had not found its commercial feet; but it had been sympathetically reviewed, in the local paper, by a friend of Nadia's who had described the book as 'sensitive'. It was the same friend who had insisted—after Nadia's husband had gone off with a woman to whom he had sold a grandmother clock—that it was this sensitivity of Nadia's which would ensure that men would 'flock' to her.

Sam, getting his spot of exercise, biked over to Backen just before lunch and stopped off at the Stannary Arms. The journey entailed some stiff uphill pedalling and, once he had reached his goal, he felt in need of something to help him recover his puff. Barty Clarke was in the bar when Sam called in. The latest *Backbiter* had just been put to bed, but Barty was an opportunist and—who could tell?—Sam might provide the very touch needed for the next edition.

Sam knew in his bones that Barty was not to be trusted, but what we know in our bones doesn't always translate well to our heads. The editor of the *Backbiter* listened politely while Sam explained about the writers' group and why he had come to Backen. Barty knew Nadia, on whom, in his capacity as auctioneer, he offloaded the junk you couldn't pay people to take away. He offered Sam

131

a second gin and tonic. The novel the woman had written, Sam confided, looked to him like utter garbage, but beggars couldn't be choosers!

One swallow doesn't make a summer nor a single sheep a flock, but Nadia had been agreeably surprised to find Sam at her door. He accepted a Cinzano Bianco, the remnants of a bottle brought by the manager of a branch of the Victoria wine stores down in Sidmouth, who had been invited to the launch of *A Knight In Her Arms* but had not followed through with any further offerings. Nadia became quite sprightly when asked to join the writers' group and showed Sam her press clippings (luckily not very extensive).

*   *   *

Luke had forgotten all about the meeting. He had slept late, and was about to hurry out to meet Mary Simms, who had rung with another query, this time about Keats. When the phone rang again, and it was Sam on the other end of the line, reminding him that he was expected shortly at the meeting, Luke had called Mary back to explain he had unfortunately double-booked. But she had sounded so offhand about his going round in the first place he couldn't imagine she would mind.

Such misunderstandings are the common currency of human intercourse, especially between men and women. Mary Simms had had many false stabs, picking up the phone and putting it down again, before she held her nerve sufficiently to keep on ringing till Luke answered. Even then she had only kept the wobble out of her voice by forcing herself to sound offhand. 'Yes, I *think* I

132

could be in on Saturday afternoon,' she had fibbed when Luke had offered, if it was any use, to come by to help her arrange her thoughts about 'The Eve of St Agnes'. As if she wasn't willing to rearrange her entire life for him!

And so it was that Mr Golightly, taking a detour by the upper meadows to avoid being early at Sam's, met Mary Simms. On previous occasions he had seen her in her barmaid role, her hair swept back in its velvet band, her dress neat, her make-up immaculate. Now she presented a very different picture—eyes streaked with mascara, her hair wild, and wearing long earrings and a longer dress, chosen to evoke St Agnes and improbably elaborate for a country walk.

'Hello there,' said Mr Golightly. He had not forgotten how the sun had shone on Mary Simms's hair.

Mary stopped. Though her heart was breaking she could not be impolite.

'Hello,' she said, bravely. But her voice faltered.

'What's up?' asked Mr Golightly. The words had slipped out—but he was glad they had, as on hearing them Mary Simms began to cry.

In her long, somewhat old-fashioned frock, her hair tousled into random ringlets, her pearl earrings echoing the tears which ran down her cheeks and her small fingers pleated together and pulling apart in anguish, Mary Simms was a sight for an angel.

'Hey,' said Mr Golightly, mentally resigning Sam and the writers' group to perdition, 'come on, let's go for a walk.'

It will be a young man, sure as eggs, Mr Golightly thought. He had observed Mary Simms's

133

eyes stray towards Luke. Mr Golightly was not an advocate of idle words. He tucked Mary's hand through the crook of his elbow so that as they descended through the fields to the river she leaned her slight weight upon him. It was an agreeable feeling, the pressure of the girl on his arm and beneath them the River Dart, a bright serpent, coiling through woods of oak and ash and hawthorn, as old as England.

The oak leaves were already robustly pushing ahead but the slower ash was biding its time. A tear from Mary Simms's chin dripped on to his wrist. *If the oak is out before the ash then the summer will be a splash.* Without turning to look her in the face, he sensed more where that had come from. *If the ash is out before the oak then the summer will be a soak.*

They were down, now, upon the flat and the river was bibbling around flat grey stones, like the plates dropped by giants. Her face shining with tears, Mary Simms asked, 'Oh, please, why doesn't he want me?'

Goodness knows, child, thought Mr Golightly. Any man in his right mind would want you. But not all men are in their right mind, indeed, few enough are, if it comes to that . . .

Mary was standing by a hawthorn tree. Above her head its knotty thorned branches held out the promise of green-white mayflowers. Looking at her, Mr Golightly saw the likeness of someone he remembered . . .

*　　　*　　　*

The meeting of the writers' group was not a success. For a start, the absence of Mr Golightly set

134

things off on the wrong foot. Sam Noble insisted they wait for a full house and that meant that the other two became disaffected. By the time it was clear that Mr Golightly wasn't going to show up, Luke had begun to read *Hiawatha* aloud. Neither Nadia Fawns nor Sam had been able to endure this and it had led to the two of them drinking gin in a conspiratorial fashion. Luke had gone home to a sorrowful message from Mary Simms and had smoked a joint too many as a consequence, which had led, in turn, to his going off to bed leaving the bath running. The bath, which had been put in by Jackson, and therefore had no overflow fitted, had dripped through Lavinia Galsworthy's ceiling on to the Afghan rug her father had brought back from the days he travelled in the East. Lavinia had been her father's favourite. This was not the first of such incidents—but it was to be the last, and Luke, to the satisfaction of Paula, turned up the next morning in Rabbit Row, with a copy of Longfellow under his arm, sheepishly asking after a room to rent, proving, perhaps, that it is an ill wind that blows nobody any good.

CHAPTER SIX

Jackson was wrong-footed by the arrival of Paula in her mum's Micra, loaded to the gunnels and complete with electric keyboard. The latter showed she meant business. He screwed up his little truculent eyes, 'Wass this, then?'

'Moving in, en't I?'

'Who says . . . ?'

But the defeat of man before the enterprise of woman sounded in his voice. Paula, single-handed, could have controlled an empire or started a worldwide movement. She marched inside and commandeered the sitting room, rapidly whisking away empty beer glasses, full of fag ends, to the dirty kitchen and shuffling into order strewn sheets of the *News of the World*—except for those pages which carried pictures of girls in states of nudity which she screwed furiously into balls and dumped in a bin liner.

Jackson nipped upstairs and kicked a packet of condoms and some mags under the bed. The writing was on the wall—he'd have to find a safer place to hide his stash in future.

'Right,' said Paula, who had brought with her a roll of heavy-duty rubbish sacks and had already filled two with crumpled nudes, beer packs, crisp bags and empty packets of Lambert and Butler. 'That's got that started. I'm off to the Stag, but when I get back we'll give the place a proper tidy.' She smiled, very terribly, at Jackson.

Jackson, who was not lily-livered through and through, said he had to go and see someone about a job and might not be in when she returned.

'Who's that, then?'

One reason men choose to live without the company of women is to avoid just such questions which no reasonable man ever asks. 'That Mrs Thomas,' said Jackson, grabbing at an answer. Ellen had telephoned the day before and left a message on his phone that she wanted some urgent work done.

'Oh, her,' said Paula, scornful. 'She's barking, en't she?' It was a rhetorical question; she was quite happy for Jackson to see Ellen Thomas, who had no tits to speak of and had long seen the back of fifty. And she, Paula, was going to see to it, anyway, that the lazy bastard got down to some work!

It was thanks to Paula, then, that Ellen Thomas received a visit later that same afternoon. She invited an unusually subdued Jackson into the sitting room.

'Thank you for coming so promptly, Mr Jackson,' said Ellen, whose retiring habits had left her ignorant of Jackson's reputation. If she was surprised to receive a visit from a British workman on a Sunday afternoon she didn't say so. 'Will you have a cup of tea?'

Her caller said he didn't mind if he did. They sat on opposite sofas, Jackson very awkward, drinking tea and looking out to the River Dart.

'It's this, you see, Mr Jackson,' said Ellen, getting up to top up his cup from a white china teapot. 'I find I need more space and I was wondering what it would take for you to make the area over the flat roof into another room for me?' And she smiled the smile which had charmed Mr Golightly.

Jackson, who generally drank his tea from a beer mug, was unaccustomed to being received with such civility and was taken aback. As a rule people addressed him simply as 'Jackson'—his rudeness and lazy ways producing in them a tone equally abrasive. Strictly speaking, he wasn't a builder anyway. His two occupations, getting the knickers off girls and baiting badgers, took up the best part of his creative energy. He could hack a spot of plumbing and minor electrics, but large-scale stuff

137

was beyond him. Like many disagreeable people, Jackson was a realist: part of the reason he didn't turn up for jobs was that he knew he wasn't up to them.

Perhaps it was the shock of the arrival of Paula, or perhaps it was Ellen Thomas's disarming smile but, against all previous experience, Jackson found himself wanting to oblige.

'Take a butcher's, will I?' he suggested. No harm in having a look at the job.

Jackson went outside and stared at the roof. He returned and asked if he could have a ladder. There was a bit of bother getting this from the tool shed, where he was told to mind the nesting robin, but once he'd set it against the wall he mounted it and got up on to the flat roof over the kitchen.

The bungalow had been built for himself by a builder who, late in life, gave up building works to become one of the Plymouth Brethren. Perhaps for this reason it was laid out on unusual lines. Planning permission had been applied for, and granted, before the builder's own spiritual conversion had distracted him from the material conversion of his home; but the 'bungalow' had been built, and sold, to include an upper extension.

Jackson spent some time on the roof peering through a window into the hallway, before clambering down and pronouncing that so far as he could see there was 'no problem'.

'Good,' said Ellen Thomas. 'So when do you think you could let me have an estimate?'

Jackson, who had never before supplied such a thing in his life, said he would ring with an estimate without fail tomorrow.

'Very good,' said Ellen Thomas. 'And provided I

accept your estimate, when do you think you could start?'

*   *   *

The news, a few days later, that Jackson was working on Ellen Thomas's house created some unrest in Great Calne. Despite Jackson's reputation for poor workmanship, it was felt by some as a slight that Ellen Thomas should be favoured ahead of a long and patient queue. Sam Noble in particular was offended.

'He promised to come to me next—I've been waiting for years!' he exclaimed to Mr Golightly. 'Of course, he's very lower class.'

Mr Golightly, whose own origins were obscure, made no comment. Rather late in the day, he had called at Sam's to apologise for his absence at the writers' group. 'I am sorry, something came up, but I'm sure you got along famously without me.'

'We certainly missed you, I can't pretend otherwise,' said Sam, unwilling to relinquish the chance to be affronted.

'I'm sorry,' Mr Golightly repeated, mendaciously: he was perfectly ready to have let the world go hang for the walk by the river with Mary Simms.

'I don't know if there will be another. One of the party just hogged the time—went quite over the top!' Sam was certainly not referring to himself; nor to that pleasant Nadia Fawns, who had thoughtfully invited him for lunch on Easter Sunday.

It might have surprised those who knew something of Mr Golightly's enterprises to learn that he was quite forgetful of church festivals. As a rule, he was kept informed of such events by his efficient office, so that the news of the Easter bank holiday, pinned to the door of the Post Office Stores in Steve's green biro—SHOP CLOSED EASTER MONDAY—caught him off guard.

Living so close by, Mr Golightly could hardly help casting an eye over the exterior of the church, but so far he had not set foot inside. Possibly the reminder of the coming festival jogged his curiosity, for, on the way back from Sam's, he turned through the moss-packed gate and up the path past the gravestones, which stood at angles, like the crooked, unruly teeth of some huge earth-dwelling hobgoblin.

Nowadays, with so much crime abroad, many church doors are kept locked, but the Reverend Fisher was much against this habit, believing it showed an unchristian mistrust. Mr Golightly negotiated the large latch and stepped across the stone threshold into the narrow interior, with its barrel ceiling, its painted roof bosses, its threadbare flags and jugs of bright flowers— narcissi, primroses, daffodils, grape hyacinths— echoing the instructive windows of coloured glass.

The air was old and musty, with the peculiar mix of dust and damp which scent the houses of the Lord. Distributed on a wooden table at the entrance were piles of hymn books and copies of the modern Prayer Book, one of which Mr Golightly picked up and leafed through and then put down again with an expression of mild disgust. He was not a one for favourites, but he'd a soft spot for Thomas Cranmer. Cranmer's prose was to die for.

140

It was shocking that the austere and plangent language had been allowed to die instead, but was this not just the problem with his own work, its failure to keep abreast of changing times? Drifting up the side aisle, he stopped to inspect the plaque which bore the name of the men of Great Calne who had died in the Great War—and those in the even greater one which had followed it—and the rood screen carving of Noah, drunk and exposing himself, while his sons cast furtive wooden glances—and garments—at their father's immodesty. There was another carving, of the prodigal son, but this story of paternal loyalty affected Mr Golightly unhappily and he turned back, past the old banner of the Lion and the Unicorn, dating back to Queen Victoria's jubilee, to the table with the guides and postcards, slightly the worse for damp, and the box in the wall which invited him to be honest and place in it any money he might choose to spend on purchases.

Mr Golightly dropped in a pound coin for a guide to the church and a damp-curled black-and-white postcard to send to Martha. She would enjoy smoothing it out.

Writing the postcard back at the cottage reminded him that there were office matters to attend to. But he had only bought one postcard and had already used up the limited space allowed for correspondence, describing two of the carved roof bosses: the pelican-in-its-piety, feeding its young from the blood of its own breast; and the leaping, altogether impious-looking hare, whose sole purpose seemed to be to celebrate its own abundant life.

Intending to e-mail Mike, he opened up his

laptop:

> canst thou bind the unicorn?
> who hath begotten the drops of dew?

Two new messages had arrived.

Since his grievous loss Mr Golightly's disposition to take offence had much abated. From time to time it crossed his mind to question this longanimity, since those who discovered his willingness to let bygones be bygones seemed so ready to take advantage of his new latitude. In times past, when he had been quick to anger and quicker still to take vengeance, there was no doubt he commanded more respect. Nowadays, there was a tendency to treat him as a busted flush, a toothless tiger. The series of e-mails was a case in point: it looked as if he had become the ignominious butt of a taunter.

The annoying questions were goads, the latest seeming to point mockingly at the difficulty Mr Golightly felt himself labouring under. 'Unicorns' were the stuff of fiction—a medium in which he was stuck fast.

But the question provoked another: was a unicorn less 'real' for being fabulous? There were those—poets and artists—who had 'bound' the unicorn, rendering the imaginal creature as distinct and palpable as if they had seen and conversed with it. Some might say—his son had been one—that it was in the artefact of the 'impossible' that reality showed its true reach.

Looking outside he saw a spider's web, one of many whose delicate dentations decked the cottage windows. The spider spun its web simply to trap flies—but what was designed by nature for a natural function may take on more than nature's ends. The fragile structure had caught, in its subtle mesh, the drops of rain from a morning shower and the diamond beads shone in the sun, fragments of some larger, profounder, more luminous light, reflecting the mysterious power of creation to recreate, from its own forms, an infinite scintillation of possibilities; possibilities which gestured at realms far beyond the demands of immediate survival.

Why should that wholly practical, sticky emanation, devised by evolution to trap the food to fill the hungry spider's belly, be able also to catch the human imagination and draw in the impressionable heart? The power of the universe to create and ascend beyond itself was also part of the reality of things—every bit as 'real' as the dead fly in the spider's maw.

And had not his son, his own dearest creation, been just such a spinner of spells, a weaver of stories to catch human hearts?

CHAPTER SEVEN

From her position on the sofa, Ellen Thomas was observing the brilliant orange bills of the white geese picking at the plantains, the plants said to have sprung up, from the prints of his feet, wherever Christ walked. It was Good Friday and the bells from the church tower were ringing for the respectable, and the God-fearing, to make their way to church. Ellen Thomas was neither. If we are quiet and still, she thought, the world turns through us, and what we know turns with it, which is truly to repent.

Mr Golightly also had no thoughts of church that morning. His mood was pensive when Johnny Spence came by to see if there was any work for him.

'Do you know,' said Mr Golightly, 'I think what I'd like is to visit the mire.'

Johnny had told his employer about the mire, which was a place, Mr Golightly gathered, where it was still unsafe to walk at night, or under the frequent fickle Dartmoor mists. Johnny had been warned about its dangers by his mother when he had run away for the first time. Research on future escapes had revealed its whereabouts. He had been punished regularly by his stepdad for his absences, but this upbringing in the hard school of disappointment meant that he never took for granted a right to his own desires, and it was partly this feature of his character which endeared him to Mr Golightly.

Under Johnny's directions, Mr Golightly drove up past the cattle grid and then, taking a bridle path, into the heartland of the moor. The old half-timbered van traversed the rough ground like some shifting creaking house on wheels from Stratford-upon-Avon, but soon they were well out of sight of those who had chosen to celebrate the festival by worshipping with bare arms and knees and quantities of suntan oil.

After a while, Johnny brought them to a halt and they got out and stood at the edge of a patch of land where, to the innocent eye, there was nothing to be seen but grass.

'Here y'are,' said Johnny. He had once watched a sheep struggle to death in the mire and nursed a hope that he might one day witness the dispatch of a human being.

Mr Golightly examined the verdant treacherous vegetation, over which hovered hoards of tiny primeval insects. This example of unredeemed nature suited his mood. There was something about it which seemed to mirror his resiling sadness.

His choice of companion was well founded: Johnny had also wandered in the caves of despair. He told Mr Golightly about the sheep.

'It weren't half struggling, an' making this wicked screeching and its eyes all rolled back and its teeth, and then it went down and you could see this bubbling. They didn't find nothing of it, after.'

This grisly account was offered up through Johnny's implicit sense of the other's mood. Mr Golightly acknowledged the gift sombrely.

'Yes,' he agreed. 'Death is not a pretty sight but people seem to like it, provided, of course, it is not their own or doesn't touch them too nearly.'

'Yeah,' said Johnny, whose pitiless education had freed him of sentimentality. 'Wouldn't mind if me stepdad dropped dead.'

Mr Golightly, who was no sentimentalist either, was still looking at the deceiving surface of the mire. 'Yes,' he agreed. 'Death improves some people.'

The tragedy was these were so rarely the ones who were chosen.

*　　　*　　　*

Ellen Thomas lay on her sofa watching the Holy Spirit bend back the grasses with its irrefragable force. The sound of Jackson hammering overhead didn't bother her. Nor when he dismounted the ladder and came past the window did his soft swearing, for Jackson, miraculously, had continued to exempt Ellen Thomas from his general misogyny and was demonstrating this by keeping his language under his breath.

Jackson had astonished even himself by his fidelity to Ellen Thomas's roof. He had turned up on the dot of nine, wearing workmen's boots and the old baseball cap which showed he meant business. At twelve noon he appeared at the glass door and asked if he might be excused.

'Oh, certainly, Mr Jackson, how rude of me not to say, of course you may use the lavatory any time.'

Jackson, who had been taking a leak from the roof—at best behind the mahonia bush—went puce. The word 'lavatory' from the mouth of Mrs Thomas sounded indecent.

'I mean get me dinner,' he explained.

'Oh, how silly of me, Mr Jackson, of course you must eat. Would you like to eat in here or are you happier outside?'

Jackson had planned to nip up to the Stag and Badge for a couple of quick ones. Paula had the day off and was back at Rabbit Row getting her things from the loft. These, Jackson had been informed, included her collection of True Life Romances, a prospect which struck a chord of foreboding in Jackson's heart. He sensed the days of dodging his own true-life romance were drawing to a close, if the door had not already been slammed shut. The prospect was a bleak one.

'Yeah, like to, yeah,' he mumbled. There was something about Mrs Thomas which soothed his anxiety over Paula. This meant, though, he had to go to the shop for a sandwich. 'Get you anythink?' he asked.

Ellen gave him a five-pound note and said she'd be grateful for half a pound of tomatoes.

'Getting your leg over the widow, are you?' asked Steve, up at the shop. He was quite scared when Jackson, flushing furiously, told him to shut his fucking mouth or he'd find his teeth up his arse.

Ellen Thomas was mildly surprised when Jackson returned with a bunch of stiff white daisies, along with the tomatoes, a sandwich and a can of Red Bull. He returned the five-pound note, refusing to take any money for the tomatoes, and offered the flowers awkwardly. 'F'r Easter.'

'How terribly kind, Mr Jackson,' said Ellen, who liked most flowers. That she did not much like these made her arrange them the more carefully in the cut-glass vase Robert had bought her.

Jackson ate a tuna sandwich on the sofa, wiping his mouth with the back of his hand until Ellen supplied a napkin. 'I'm so sorry, Mr Jackson. Let me get you a glass for your pop. It looks exciting.'

Jackson was all but illiterate and not having drunk a soft drink for many years had chosen this because 'Red' was one of the few words he could read. He poured most of the content on the carpet trying to get it into a glass.

'How silly of me,' said Ellen. 'I can see now it's supposed to be drunk from the can.'

Jackson went the colour of the name of his drink and said he'd best be getting back to work. It was the first time in years he had worked for more than a single hour at a time and he found himself strangely agitated by the process.

*   *   *

There was a problem in starting the Traveller when Johnny and Mr Golightly came to leave the mire. Johnny poked about under the bonnet and wriggled under the carriage but was forced, rather unwillingly, to admit he didn't know what was wrong. In the end, with Johnny steering and Mr Golightly lending his weight, they got the van going. Johnny was keen to stay at the wheel but Mr Golightly considered it prudent to take over once they reached the cattle grid at the moor's edge.

Perhaps it was the temperamental behaviour of the Traveller but Mr Golightly had even less conversation than usual as he drove back down the hill towards Great Calne. He turned on the radio, and when Johnny asked about the music he was told it was by someone called 'Bark'.

'The *Matthew Passion*, John. Extraordinary, wouldn't you say? One could almost imagine the man was there to witness it!'

Johnny, uncertain what event was being referred to, said that he agreed it made 'a fair sound'. He was pleased to be asked in to Spring Cottage and spent the rest of the afternoon listening to a pianist called Solomon whom Mr Golightly said he admired.

'The Jews were always a musical people, John. Look at David. He was a great little scrapper, too. Fighting and music, it's in their blood!'

Later that evening, the sombre mood still upon

148

him, Mr Golightly walked up the hill to the Stag and Badger. Barty Clarke and Sam Noble were drinking together in the bar and discussing the escaped prisoner.

'I promise you he's from hereabouts,' said Barty, whose researches into local history were, for different reasons, as thoroughgoing as Johnny's.

'But shouldn't the police be giving us special protection, then?' asked Sam, nodding coolly in Mr Golightly's direction. He had not forgiven the lamentable dereliction over the writers' group. 'Surely we're all under threat!'

'That's right,' said Barty. 'I expect we'll all be murdered in our beds. Still, look on the bright side, it'll make a good item in the *Backenbridge*!' He laughed heartily.

'Jesus wept!' said Sam, for whom his own safety was no laughing matter.

At that point the sky broke apparently in two with a resounding crack of thunder, so deafening that George said it might have woken his poor wife, Anna, from her comfortable graveyard bed. As for the lightning which sizzled to the ground, barely missing the pub, everyone agreed it must have been visible all the way to Land's End. Mr Golightly, who had ordered a pint of best, was evidently so perturbed by the violence of the storm that he left the inn altogether, with his beer undrunk on the bar counter. Colin Drover, who had seen that it was untouched by any human hand but his own, drank it himself because, as he remarked to his wife, to waste good bitter was a crime worse than rape—a comment which got a sharp retort from Kath, who informed him he was dissing women in saying so.

But this exchange was lost among the general excitement over the weather, which, everyone agreed, even in the unpredictable South-West, was extraordinary.

CHAPTER EIGHT

Jackson's new willingness to work had put Paula in a good temper. He was up and off out of the house without her even having to try. The success with Jackson made Paula uncharacteristically charitable to Mary Simms and now she'd got Jackson in line, Paula's energy needed a new target.

Paula had been back to Rabbit Row regularly and had seen Luke's pathetically few possessions installed there. Mary was soft in the head and would make a perfect match with Luke, who was also a few pence short of the pound. If Mary Simms moved in with Luke her mum could charge double!

Up at the Stag and Badger's kitchen she remarked, casually, 'Know what, if you lay in a man's bed and say his name forty times forty, he's the one you'll marry.' This old wives' tale had been freshly minted by Paula's inventive brain, but it is a rare soul unhappily in love who can resist superstition, particularly a palliative one.

'Is that true?' asked Mary, whose nights had been tearful over Luke.

'Yeah.' Paula busied herself chopping off the heads of the plaice they were deep-frying. She liked looking into their dull dead eyes. 'D'you want the key to me mum's house, then?' Time someone sorted out Mary Simms.

Mary didn't grasp the point of this suggestion at first. She was no gossip herself and knew nothing of Paula's changed circumstances.

'That Luke's staying in me old room now I'm up at Jackson's.'

Light dawned on Mary Simms. 'Oh, d'you think I should though?'

'Yeah, give it a go, why not. It worked with me and Jackson.' Paula, unused to employing her fictional powers, was enjoying herself.

'What if he comes back? What would I say?' But faced with this heaven-sent opportunity, she was ready to throw caution to the winds.

'S'all right,' said Paula. 'I'll keep him chatting here.'

Her plan was to pack Luke off smartly to her mum's before Mary Simms had time to leave. Paula's own previous failure to master Luke was no discouragement—having spent time with him, she was more confident of getting him to leave her company than getting him into bed; and if Luke found Mary actually in his bed surely even he wouldn't be so daft as to pass up the opportunity.

'D'you want the key or not?' she asked, expertly slicing down the backbone of a plaice. 'Me mum's at me Auntie Edna's over Easter so there'll be no one in the house but you. Here's what we do—you go off early and I'll tell old Colic you've come on with your period and had to go home to lie down. Then I'll think up something to say to that Luke. Won't be hard—trust, me!'—to send him off to Rabbit Row, she added mentally.

* * *

Mr Golightly had his own reasons for retiring from the pub when the great storm broke on Friday night. Whatever the cause, his disquiet had been increased by the arrival of another disturbing e-mail.

have the gates of death been opened unto thee?

was the question which had faced him when he returned to the cottage that evening.

Death was a subject Mr Golightly had had occasion to contemplate. It was apparent that men and women feared it—the latter perhaps less so; and yet, he couldn't help thinking, without death life was hardly possible. How to spend one's time if 'time' became eternal was a question he was used to pondering.

Among the tried and trusted books he had brought with him was a rival to his own best-seller, which he planned to make a part of his holiday reading. He had slipped out, before his departure, and bought it from W.H. Smith, where he couldn't help sneaking a look for his own work, placed in a rather out-of-the-way corner of the store and inconveniently low on the shelves. In contrast, *A Brief History of Time* by Stephen Hawking was prominently displayed.

Mr Golightly hoped that it was not a result of professional jealousy that so far he had not managed to get beyond the introduction. There were issues he found he wanted to take up with the eminent scientist—he felt sure they could learn from discussion with each other.

But no scientist, however up to the minute, had successfully tackled the vexed question of death.

The philosopher Wittgenstein had suggested that death was, by nature, unknowable, since, in the absence of life, it could not be experienced. There had been those who had challenged that proposition; Mr Golightly wasn't one of them—there were things about the human condition he himself could never fully understand.

It was this sense of isolation which prompted a call, late on Friday night, to the office, ostensibly over the question of the Traveller, which was still failing to start. Early on Saturday morning Bill drove up on his motorbike. It was his usual day off, so it was a pleasant surprise when he roared into the front garden of Spring Cottage.

'Bill,' said Mr Golightly, going out to greet him, 'You angel! I'm uncommonly glad to see you . . .'

Bill had brought his tool kit and was soon stripped down to his jeans and singlet, flat on his back and tinkering about under the van. Mary Simms, on her way to work, passed Spring Cottage as he was taking a rest from his labours with a cheese-and-pickle sandwich made by Mr Golightly—eaten leaning over the gate, getting the sun on his shoulders. Mary stopped in answer to a question and gave him the name of the local pub—she was just off to work there herself, she explained to the stranger with the impressive biceps.

Work on the Traveller took up the best part of the day. Bill said he might take in a quick pint before he set off back. Mr Golightly directed him to the Stag and Badger. 'There's a young fellow, name of Luke, you might come across there. Give him my regards.'

* * *

153

Luke had been sorry to miss his fellow writer the previous evening. He had stayed in, up at Paula's mum's, waiting for the storm to pass before making his way to the pub where he found Mr Golightly conspicuous by his absence. And tonight there was no sign of his friend either. They were all discussing the storm which had done some serious damage to the Calne roofs and had brought down several lofty trees. Barty Clarke said he knew for a fact it was the most severe in these parts since the great hurricane of 1638.

Missing his crossword companion, Luke filled in as much as he could—which still left a few blank—and sat on his bar stool at something of a loss.

'Go on then,' Paula said to Mary, smacking her on the back and nearly knocking her down. 'I'll tell old Colic you've come on sudden and you've gone home.'

But even the plans of womankind will sometimes go awry. When the tall good-looking young man, with the long fair hair and the motorbike leathers, approached Luke with good wishes from his boss, Luke became hospitable and it wasn't long before the two were deep in conversation.

Bill, while no crossword expert, was able to fill in seven across—'In all fairness, he could be confused with an Englishman (5)'—and, encouraged by this, Luke went on to explain, to his new and sympathetic acquaintance, his problems with the fatally contagious rhythms of *Hiawatha*.

Bill was a good listener. After commiserating with Luke he put it to him that while no writer himself, he had an idea, one he had long felt might have some commercial appeal which—he tentatively suggested—might supplant the American Indians and put paid to Longfellow's dangerous pull. Luke became excited. His poetic account of the Creation had made scant progress—well, he had to say, none at all, really—and Bill had an air about him, enhanced no doubt by the quantities of lager Luke had drunk, which was inspiring.

Paula—who had popped out from the back earlier to tell Luke that her mum had telephoned in a panic about having left the gas on; would he please run back to Rabbit Row and check it out at once?—was furious to hear from Colin Drover, when she came out again to be sure Luke was on his way, that Luke had left five minutes earlier, talking animatedly to 'a bloke in biking gear'.

The two young men had walked up the road to the cattle grid before Luke—his mind quite empty of Paula's mum's, luckily fictional, fears—remembered that this was no longer where he lived. He said if Bill didn't mind he might walk a while on the moor to clear his head, which, thanks to Bill, was buzzing with ideas.

Maybe it was the lateness of the hour, or the lager, though, as to that, he had drunk less than a pint, but Bill accepted an invitation to spend the night at Luke's place, where the landlady was fortunately absent. Luke said when inspiration took him he often went without sleep, so he gave Bill the door key to Paula's mum's. 'You have my bed,' he suggested, directing his guest to Rabbit Row. 'Times like this I often watch the sun come up—I could be out for hours.'

Mary Simms lying in her petticoat, counted to forty. And then another forty. Forty times forty times forty, she would stay there, to be on the safe side . . .

* * *

It was early, the sun had barely risen, and Mary Simms was walking by the river. She had woken bemused, not in her own bed. After a while she remembered that she had gone to Paula's house to think of Luke Weatherall. But all thoughts of Luke had vanished, as the dew which washed her ankles would vanish before the midday sun.

She must have fallen asleep in the strange bed, and in a dream—or state of half-wakefulness—a pencil of light, sweet and precise, had seemed to search clean through her, to her hidden self, grateful and receptive. A vast unstintingness, which she felt first with the stunning force of a violent blow, and which had abated and dissolved into an enveloping and mighty tenderness, had surrounded and enfolded her, lifting her, bearing her, suffusing her utterly, till she woke to a sense, graceful and profound, of an unremitting excellence drenching her whole being, and leaving her for ever changed.

If it was a dream, then it was a dream so absolute and vital that it seemed to Mary more real than the ground she was walking on.

At Caddy's Rock, where history related how many years back a girl had tried to drown her baby and been hanged for the crime, she found Mr Golightly. He was sitting, with his back to her, towards the quick-flowing river, watching a grey wagtail, in a dimple of sunlight, elegantly balancing its long yellow tail. But he must have sensed her presence for he turned as she approached.

156

'Mary?' he said, and in his eyes there was a glimmer of what might have been apprehension.

'Hello,' said Mary Simms. In her state of bedazement she recognised him. 'Happy Easter.'

'You're out early.'

'I could say the same to you!' said Mary Simms, and she laughed, quite disrespectfully, given his age and obvious seniority.

Mr Golightly, however, showed no signs of standing on his dignity. Instead, he looked relieved. 'I'm glad to see you happy,' he said. 'Shall we walk?' And for a second time he offered his arm.

They walked together up through the fields of damp grass, where Mr Golightly rejoiced at finding mushrooms for his breakfast, and along the footpath where the wild garlic gave off a peppery scent, provocative and heady. They parted by the church gate. Mr Golightly did not invite Mary to join him in the breakfast mushrooms; she had, she said, to get home anyway, there were things she needed to organise.

The bells from the tower were ringing, a trifle unevenly, to welcome Christ back into this world; but neither Mr Golightly nor Mary were to be found among the Easter Sunday congregation a little later that morning. However, the spirits of the Reverend Meredith were given a boost by the presence of a fair young man in leathers, one of the holiday bikers, who, doubtless through diffidence, remained at the back of the church and did not join the line to take communion.

Maybe the young man belonged to some other denomination, or perhaps he had not been confirmed. He slipped away afterwards, before the Reverend Fisher had the chance to inquire. Still, it was heartening to see the face of modern youth among them in Great Calne.

CHAPTER NINE

Lady vicar speaks frankly of gay sex experience was the headline which met the thrilled gaze of the *Backbiter* readers on Easter Monday.

Sam Noble read the piece to Nadia Fawns over the phone that morning. The paschal lamb is part of an ancient tradition of ceremonial sacrifice and Nadia had cooked Sam an Easter lunch at which she had worn a silk blouse, rather low-cut, her best black trousers and quantities of gold chain.

Sam drank several gin and tonics (the Cinzano had been ditched and a large bottle of Gordon's Gin had been substituted), helped himself liberally to cashew nuts, and enjoyed the lamb roast with rosemary and garlic. He found Nadia sympathetic over the fate of *Nice Girl*. She looked properly concerned when he described how the film had been jostled from its place of victory at the eleventh hour. And she spoke, not too much, about her own publishing misfortunes.

The two had not met since the fiasco over the writers' group and the talk turned naturally to Golightly's treacherous behaviour. Over this, Nadia was equally reassuring. 'Don't worry, I checked him out on Amazon. He's a nobody!'

Sam was torn between his desire for disgruntlement and a wish to rub shoulders with celebrity. 'Perhaps he uses a pen name?'

'In that case he would have told you. Writers

never hide their lights under bushels—except the really modest ones . . .' Nadia smiled demurely. 'Believe me, he's nothing, my friends all tell me my intuitive side is very strong.'

The lunch had been lingering, Nadia had done all the washing up and Sam had returned to Great Calne with a replenished sense of his own importance, a tonic even during the palmiest days.

So it was only manners to ring to thank his hostess the following day.

Nadia quickly fetched her copy of the *Backbiter* and read it in company with Sam over the phone. The Reverend Fisher, the paper alleged, had frankly owned that the sexual practices she preached about sprang straight, so to speak, from the nag's mouth. She had to put her money where her mouth was ('Not a pretty thought in the circumstances,' Sam wittily remarked) and come out openly in favour of gay priests, of both genders.

'So she condones buggery,' said Sam.

'Oh, don't,' said Nadia, 'such an ugly word!' Her writing career had made her especially sensitive to language.

Paula's mum, back from her visit to her sister in Somerset, also read the paper, over a bowl of Bran Flakes and cup of Nescafé with Luke.

Luke had found a new lease of life for his writing. Paula's bedroom was too small for a desk, and there were still a number of furry animals which took up space, so he had set up his office at the kitchen table where the steady drip-feed of chatter and local gossip from Paula's mum was soothing rather than distracting. It was as if some weak-voiced bird, depleted of its natural drive after years of captivity, was constantly trilling, mindlessly

159

and softly, in his ear.

'Right!' he said, when Paula's mum said that she felt, personally, that what people did in the privacy of their own homes was their own affair and that the lady vicar had been ever so kind to Edna after Ron had passed over, when she and her sister bumped into her at Tesco's. And 'Right!' again, when Paula's mum found, on the other hand, she couldn't help wondering how the Reverend Malcolm, who, as he knew, had had Parkinson's, would have taken the news . . .

Just how the Reverend Malcolm would have taken the allegation that his successor had a homosexual history remained a matter for a psychic medium, since he had joined Paula's mum's sister's Ron on the Other Side. But there were other, more accessible, opinions voiced on the topic that day in Great Calne.

For one thing, the allegations revived the Tessa Pope and Patsy scandal, which, by association, reintroduced the tearooms as a hot subject of local concern.

The great thing about scandal is that while it can die it is always susceptible of resurrection.

'I think it's horrible,' Nadia Fawns said. She had invited Sam over for a drink and he had stayed on, since it seemed she had just thrown together a lasagne.

'Can't say I care for diesel dykes myself,' said Sam, 'particularly not wearing dog collars!'

'I hate anything unfeminine, don't you?' Nadia jingled her gold bracelets, but Sam was unaware that the exchange was one of the first steps on the foothills of a relationship. Nadia's words were simply a signal to him to renew his efforts towards

160

the tearooms.

Mr Golightly was no devil's advocate but neither was he one for taking sides.

'Some might say tolerance was a religious requirement,' he suggested, when Sam, meeting the writer in the street, hotly aired his views.

'I doubt Our Lord had that kind of cheek in mind when he told us to turn the other one!'

Mr Golightly looked suitably rebuked. Who was he to say? Although it had once been something of a thorn in his side, these days he had no special views on sexual behaviour. If he considered sex at all it seemed to him a topic which had taken on a significance too cumbersome for so quixotic a human activity. Nevertheless, he could hardly help becoming aware, not least from his soap opera researches, that sex today was a subject which resembled a series of educational, and social, hurdles: something onerous and definitely to be grappled with.

While 'grappling' was a skill Mr Golightly felt he had lost the knack of, Sam had not. 'Few people stop to consider the destabilising effects of too much liberal thinking.'

'Quite,' said Mr Golightly, whose sympathies were all with the thoughtless majority.

The truth was that Sam had spent rather a lot of time thinking about the shortness of Paula's skirts, which had greatly fuelled his outrage. He wandered now, seemingly idly, up the street towards Jackson's in the hope of catching sight of his tearoom goddess.

Paula was outside with a J-cloth, wiping the leaves of some primulas she'd rammed in on either side of the concrete path. The violence of the

161

storm had washed earth everywhere and the leaves were unsightly with dirt. To see to the borders Paula was wearing her high-cut faded denim shorts, a mauve strappy vest-top which revealed a couple of tattoos—a rose on the left shoulder and a leopard on the right—her platforms and a 'ruby' nose stud. Sam stared in admiration.

'Oh, hi,' said Paula, unenthusiastically.

'You look great,' said Sam, who was sweating slightly.

'Yeah?' said Paula. Even if she had fancied Sam, she was not the type to be won by compliments.

'I was wondering—' Sam faltered over the gate which only that morning had been given a fresh lick of paint by the zealous goddess—'if we could have a word about the tearooms?'

'Sure,' said Paula. 'You'd better come in anyway—you've got paint all over you.'

White spirit was fetched from the garage and Sam sat, like a small child, home from playschool, having the paint vigorously removed from his hands.

'What did you want, then?' asked Paula. Under her instructions, Sam rinsed his hands in the kitchen sink and wiped them on the two sheets of kitchen roll provided, while Paula ran over the sink area with an antibacterial spray.

'I'm going to have a word with the bank—it's all quite feasible—I can buy them myself and it would keep the tearooms open in the village. You mentioned, very sweetly, once—' Sam blinked and looked across to Jackson's chipped but gleaming cooker—what a regular little homemaker Paula was!—'you said once you might think of managing the tearooms . . .'

'Yeah, all right, then,' said Paula. It didn't sound a bad plan. Give her something to do—a break from Jackson and a chance to stick it to old Colic and his stupid wife at the Stag.

'You mean you will?' Sam couldn't believe his ship had come home so swiftly and laden with the hoped-for cargo.

'Don't see why not. The key's round at me mum's. Go and have a look at them if you like.'

The tearooms, since the departure of Joanne and Patsy, and the subsequent refusal by Paula's mum to see to them, had not been touched by any living creature, save the rats. Rats cut no ice with Paula. To her, the tearooms looked most desirable—plenty for her to get her hands on and get a nice little business going. Her mind which moved at the pace of an express train began to itemise the necessary steps required to lick it into shape.

Sam, on the other hand, faced with the reality of his prospective investment, felt disheartened. The place of his fantasy was a paradise of soft-porn gentility, not a toppling, rain-sodden, outbuilding, full of vermin droppings and doubtless grossly overpriced.

'What do you think?' With the innate fickleness of the human heart, he angled for a negative response.

'I think it's lovely,' was Paula's emphatic answer. Her head was already full of schemes for the curtains—baby pink, or blue, she thought, with tiny, lacy bows.

*   *   *

163

At Nicky Pope's, as with almost all the households of Great Calne, the vicar's sexual leanings were being thoroughly analysed, with Nicky giving it as her opinion to Cherie Wolford that the whole thing was 'disgusting!' The conversation was conducted in lowered tones and out of Tessa's hearing. The poor child had had that nasty experience while helping out at the tearooms. But the sound of a lowered voice, especially a parental one, is a sure way of attracting attention. The vision of the Virgin having faded with repetition, Tessa Pope's imagination was in need of refurbishment. It wasn't long before she was in the lounge on her knees and crying, while her mother tactfully extracted the story of how the lady vicar had touched her 'round the bra area' when she was helping her with the flowers up at the church.

Tessa Pope's revelation was a piece of luck for Barty Clarke, whose phone hadn't stopped ringing since the latest edition of the *Backbiter* had appeared. Although he was practised at sailing near the wind, even Barty was alarmed by the boldness of the piece when he saw it in print and was planning to consult his solicitor the following day when the Tessa Pope story broke. It reached him via Nadia Fawns, who had run low on tonic and had dropped by the Stannary Arms to buy a couple of bottles for an impending visit by Sam.

Barty, greatly relieved to hear how his insinuations had been rewarded by fate with this surprise witness, offered to buy Nadia a drink. Nadia accepted a Campari and soda and described, in some detail, the Arthurian novel which Barty had already heard about from Sam in the very same pub. But this Barty kept to himself. There was another edition of the *Backbiter* due out in a couple of months and he had a reputation to live up to now.

*   *   *

All this while the Reverend Fisher was ignorant of the downturn in her personal fortunes. She had taken the occasion of the Bank Holiday Monday to visit her sister, Mandy, in Weston. Mandy kept a sweetshop, specialising in seaside rock and sugar confections. Bank holidays were prime time for pink sugar legs and false teeth and she couldn't herself get away. Meredith returned late in the evening to find Keith in a lather.

Keith had stayed away from the pink sugar legs with a fabricated headache in order to watch the 2.30 run at Epsom. On a sure-fire inside tip from the man who ran the chip shop down at Oakburton—whose cousin's sister was dating one of the lads at a racing stables—he had extracted two hundred quid from the joint savings account to put on 'Mother's Ruin', and had been anxious over the consequences. 'Mother's Ruin' had cantered home last but one, which coloured the mood with which he met Meredith when she arrived back from Weston with a bag of sugar pebbles. He shoved a copy of the *Backbiter* at her. 'See! That's where bloody feminism gets you! I won't be able to show my face!'

The Reverend Fisher, however, was not one to flinch under fire. She wasn't bothered about her husband's sexual reputation; nor, very much, her own. To be pilloried and jeered at was, after all, the fate of her leader. True, he had not been a woman,

165

but, as the man in the film had said, 'No one is perfect!' She grabbed the *Backbiter* and read the item thoroughly and then went straight for the telephone.

'What are you doing?' asked an astonished Keith.

'Ringing Mr Clarke,' said Meredith with cold calm. She asked Directory Enquiries for the number.

CHAPTER TEN

Jackson had made strides with Ellen Thomas's new room. It was hard to credit, but he was off in the morning with a flask of tea and a pack of sandwiches he even got for himself. True, he left the bread knife (nicked by Paula from the Stag and Badge) smeared with jam and peanut butter, but, as Cherie Wolford observed, when Paula, dropping by her mum's, spoke a little roughly on this theme, Rome wasn't built in a day! Cherie, who had come by to lend Paula's mum a book on irritable bowel syndrome she'd been given by Morning Claxon, had also opined that it took a good woman to turn a man round.

There was no question that Jackson had been turned in some direction, but the key to his conversion was only indirectly Paula; his double-dyed shiftlessness had been given a jolt by the event which sets even the steadiest person awry: Jackson had fallen in love.

Jackson had loved only once before—Trixie, a Jack Russell who had bled to death in his owner's

166

twelve-year-old arms after losing a fight with a bull terrier. Since that time the badgers had borne the brunt of Jackson's subliminal erotic drive.

Falling in love is a brutal business. Jackson had managed to slide by, for over thirty adult years, under the cover of lust—often a false security. Getting the knickers off girls like Paula was a hobby—one he was seriously committed to; but it had not prepared him for the tormenting, strickening, taloned attacks of real live love.

Among love's hidden terrors is its capacity to knock away old crutches and breathe on fiercely, and arouse, comfortably slumbering life. Ellen Thomas's sympathetic manner had reached in and quickened faculties in Jackson he didn't know he possessed. It was a painful revolution.

For one thing, he was forever running up and down the ladder to check out with Mrs Thomas that he was doing 'the right thing', where in the old days, had there been any fuss, he would have enquired if she was confusing him with someone who gave a fuck? There were times when he woke in the night, agonised that he might, inadvertently, have used *that* word with Mrs Thomas—the thought of using it now made him sweat with anxiety.

No badger could have been more painfully baited than Jackson. He found himself victim of a desire to please which ran altogether counter to his customary form. The loss of his old devil-may-care self left him helpless before a new, and minatory, inner character, one which, as with most despots, was constructed on unstable lines.

Mr Golightly observed Jackson one morning, sitting on an upturned barrel in Ellen Thomas's

167

garden, surrounded by geese and dolefully eating his breakfast of peanut butter sandwiches, and recognised a man in a crisis. Mr Golightly's own experiences had made him indulgent towards the retarded. He knew how it was when the hard rind, which has forbidden the incursion of emotion, drops away from the swelling heart leaving it exposed. At such moments a man needed company.

'Hello there!' he called across the barbed wire. Jackson, sunk in a gloom at his predicament, started, and the geese, startled, hissed maniacally. Jackson was in secret fear of the geese; but he was in more fear of Paula and his first reaction was to believe that she had arrived with some fresh and harrowing demand. He was relieved to see it was only the writer chap from next door. Gratitude made him expansive.

' 'Lo!'

'Nice bit of work you're doing,' said Mr Golightly, who knew the value of encouragement.

Jackson perked up. 'Like it?' he enquired. Love had inspired a shaky-looking, boat-shaped construction on the bungalow's flat Plymouth Brethren roof.

'An old friend of mine once built something on those lines,' said Mr Golightly, nodding in the direction of Jackson's work.

*   *   *

On Mondays and Thursdays, Mr Golightly got in sausages and chops from the travelling butcher, who had once been a special needs teacher. On Fridays, there were kippers and smoked haddock from the travelling fishmonger, who had been lead guitar in a band called Rock Salmon. The name, the fishmonger said, had given him the clue for his change in employment.

Johnny Spence arrived just as Mr Golightly was cooking sausages, so it was nothing to throw a few more into the pan.

'Do you happen to know why a raven is like a writing desk, John?'

'Ravens them big black birds up the Moor, aren't they?' Unlike the fledgling raven, Johnny didn't refuse breakfast.

'It's a riddle from a book but the author never gives the answer. It's been plaguing me.'

'It'll be on the Internet,' said Johnny, his eye on the sausages. 'Do a search if you like.'

Johnny waited till his mouth was full to speak again. 'Anything else you want doing?' he asked. Wolford had not been round yet, but with his mum away life with his stepdad was dicey.

Although he was of a mind to avoid questions, Mr Golightly couldn't help wondering about the whereabouts of Johnny's mother. His own parenting had been so deficient he hardly felt he was in any position to judge. Johnny's mother may be under pressures—or, like him, believe she was, because, it was clear to him now that, with his own son he had been negligent. He was aware that, with Johnny, he was making up for some of that neglect. But it was hard to know how to occupy the boy. There were only so many soap opera scripts he could ask him to download from the Internet.

'What does your mother think about you being here all the time?'

Johnny flushed and Mr Golightly turned away and busied himself mixing mustard. He liked the

169

English variety which he had bought in bright yellow powder in a tin from the Post Office Stores. He stirred methodically—it took patience in the mixing to keep out the lumps.

When he looked again at Johnny he was staring at his empty plate.

'Another sausage?' asked Mr Golightly, and then, because he occasionally believed in the virtues of nettle grasping, 'John, where is your mother?'

Johnny and his mum had come with his stepdad to Great Calne when Johnny was five. Before that they'd lived in a caravan near Plymouth and had got the council house in Calne when his stepdad's nan had died. At least since they'd come to Calne he'd had his own bedroom.

'Don't know,' he admitted after a pause. 'She's gone somewhere.'

'Oh dear. What about your stepfather? Does he know where she is?'

Johnny made a face. 'Shouldn't think so. What's he going to know?'

'I don't know,' said Mr Golightly, candidly. He felt that things had not been intended to work out this way. The more he saw of the world, the more it seemed to him that everything had got into a tremendous muddle.

But seeing Jackson sitting on his barrel Mr Golightly had a brainwave. Johnny possessed many more skills than his Internet competencies. He was, he explained to his employer, in the habit of 'multitasking'. At present he was busy replacing the plugs on most of Spring Cottage's ropy appliances. And he had already dealt with the stove so successfully that the smoke went quite docilely up

170

the chimney. Nicky Pope, when she popped by to ask if the gardener had called yet, had suggested that the next time she let the cottage she'd have to raise the rent.

'How about helping out with Mrs Thomas's building works?' Mr Golightly suggested. He observed across the way how Ellen Thomas's geese, sensing Jackson's fear, were hissing at him forbiddingly.

Johnny's response to this was equivocal. He didn't much like the thought of helping anyone but Mr Golightly; but, like Jackson, he had discovered the new, and pain-inducing, desire to please.

'If you want.'

Mr Golightly's sensibilities had quickened. 'It's only next door so you could take your meals with me,' he reassured. 'We could talk the project over together.'

It would keep Johnny busy, but he also had a neighbourly concern for Ellen Thomas—and for Jackson. Having, with his weather eye, appraised the construction on the bungalow roof, Mr Golightly sensed that the building works could do with a hand.

CHAPTER ELEVEN

The Reverend Fisher was a brave fighter, but, like many martyrs, she was fighting with her hands tied. Sex and religion, separately, are high-calorie foodstuffs for fancies hungry for sustenance and the Reverend Fisher combined the two, and made an exceptionally juicy bone. The Tessa Pope story,

171

with all its opportunities for shock and sympathy, was too tasty for the village of Great Calne to bury too soon.

It was the Easter break and the Plymouth College was closed, so the vicar didn't even have the empathic support of her counselling colleagues to fall back on. Like many people who end up in the countryside, Meredith was secretly afraid of nature and had barely explored beyond the immediate surroundings of the village. But faced with notoriety, and the triumphant sneers of Keith (who had seized the occasion to deflect attention from the depleted joint account), Meredith began to ramble abroad. She didn't venture up on to the moor, which, in her imaginings, was filled with women-hating rapists, but she made her way down to the more approachable reaches of the river.

She was walking there early one morning when she encountered Mr Golightly, sitting on Caddy's Rock, where he had met with Mary Simms. This time he was watching a dipper immersing its white throat and bitter chocolate body in the spangling brown waters.

Mr Golightly was alive to the scandal which had scorched Meredith Fisher. He didn't, as in past days he might have done, join in the vicar's husband's jibes that she was reaping the rewards of her own mistakes. Mr Golightly wasn't at one with the Reverend's outlook but he knew how sorrow is an architect as well as a demolition expert and maybe even now was laying down, in the vicar, the foundations of a wider view.

'Hi!' he said, instinctively—and without any counselling training—adopting the idiom of the person he hailed.

Meredith looked alarmed. Unlike Mary Simms she didn't recognise him. Closer scrutiny revealed the writer from over the road.

'Oh, hi there.' Unusually, for Meredith, she found herself hoping she would be able to get away.

It might be that Mr Golightly was getting a bit of his own back, because if he was aware of the vicar's wish for privacy he ignored it. 'You're out early.'

It was the same remark as he had made to Mary Simms but Meredith heard it as a charge. 'I'm always up before six!'

'Ah,' said Mr Golightly. If he felt put in his place he didn't show it. Experience had taught him that, when in a hole, what is needed is a sense of comradeship. 'Me too,' he agreed. 'No one about— that's the best part.'

'It's when I pray,' said Meredith.

This was not quite the full tale. Meredith used the early-morning hours to write up her counselling case studies and practise her Swahili. Praying was an activity to which she paid lip-service, but in her mind it was mere sponge cake and flummery, which didn't merit the energetic application of real-life demands.

Mr Golightly was not one for praying himself and didn't probe too far into the vicar's story. Instead, he proposed a walk. He didn't offer, as he had with Mary Simms, his arm. No doubt he felt decorum, or the vicar's principles, would lead her to refuse it.

They walked along the narrow path beside the river. Foils of light flashed between branches of the trees; at their feet, stems of penumbrous bluebells were unfolding into flower, the lustrous leaves

173

making an undercarpet of brilliant green. Thread-of-gold catkins swung on hazel bushes, like the downy, muted clappers of small invisible bells, silently pealing alongside the clean voices of the woodland birds. By the river bank, Mr Golightly spotted the skulking form of a rat—but rats also have their place in the scheme of things, he mused; on such a day even a rat was owed toleration.

The Reverend Meredith, however, was blind to these manifestations of regenerate life. She was the victim of injustice—and from one of her own sex—and not all nature's clemency was equal to dispelling that rankling rejection. She walked in the shade of human degeneracy, deaf to the birds which jubilantly warbled a spirit superior to the soiling contacts of the mortal world.

Mr Golightly, who knew something about the effects of injustice, knew enough not to counsel the vicar in her dark hour. He whistled a few bars from *Fidelio*, but the revolutionary theme did not have the strengthening impact on the vicar that it had had on Johnny Spence. Meredith was not musical; indeed she was tone deaf, a fact which had been mutteringly noted by the old bell-ringers of Great Calne.

After a while they came to a place where the river made a wide bend and Meredith stopped and stood, apparently inspecting a grey heron. The heron, hunched and indifferent, was watching the waters for passing fish. 'Why me?' she asked. 'Why me?'

She was speaking to no one in particular—unless it was the heron she addressed. Mr Golightly, in the absence of any visible other, spoke.

'I sometimes ask myself the same question.'

'Oh,' said Meredith, turning upon him a face of taut rage. 'You men! You turn every damn thing to your bloody self-centred selves!'

Mr Golightly liked to think of himself as pretty much equal to any display of emotion but even he, schooled under Martha's tongue, was taken aback. 'Hey,' he said, 'steady on!' He might have added 'old girl'—thinking of a mettlesome jade he had once used to ride—but stopped himself in time.

But his response had an effect. Meredith's face began to soften and fold. She took off her specs and wiped her eyes. 'Sorry,' she said, and blew her nose on a tissue which had dwindled to a small, damp twist in her hand.

'Here,' said Mr Golightly, offering his handkerchief. A red-spotted one—a point of disagreement with Martha. He was taken to task over his refusal to give up cotton handkerchiefs which, besides being unhygienic, were, she contended, adding to the laundry load, which was ecologically unsound.

The otiose handkerchief, however, was a success with the Reverend Fisher, who brightened. 'Like Benjamin Bunny's!'

'Peter Rabbit's in fact, I think you'll find.' Mr Golightly explained he was a Potter fan. 'Beatrix rather than Harry—I'm afraid I've not got round to him yet. It's her prose I like—a wonderful cadence, and you can't help admiring a woman who farmed her own sheep.'

He described to the vicar how the celebrated children's writer had once met a tramp who had taken the sack on her head, worn as protection against the rain, as a sign that she was a fellow-traveller. 'Weather's nowt so good for the likes of thee and me,' he had companionably commented.

A lively exchange followed over the merits of *The Tale of Mr Tod* over *Two Bad Mice*, Mr Golightly favouring the former, the vicar the latter. He was too tactful to say so, but he couldn't help thinking it boded well for the vicar, and perhaps less so for Tessa Pope, that in both books the principal characters were of a vicious turn of temper.

CHAPTER TWELVE

The evening fell soft and unobtrusive as a nightjar. In the feathery, receding light, Ellen Thomas waited for the stars, shreds of holiness, to appear. It was now many nights she had waited like this, staring into the gathering dusk.

Her mind, limber and detached, flew effortlessly, a silent owl, to where she could see the lights of a car, creeping along the crest of the hill opposite. She pictured some prowling Martian, or other alien invader, inspecting the strangeness of the twilit human world.

She, too, had felt a stranger here. But she was no longer bound upon an axle of torment. Looking across at the blank shapes of the hills and the rims of trees, black against the sky, and beyond, and higher still, the evanescing stars, the grubbiness, the meanness and the pain seemed to dissolve into a larger vision: obdurate and fatal, but also splendid and possible and glorious. The little flickering world was there still, but behind it there lay a greater power.

A sense of peace and assurance filled her. The fear and the worry, the snagging tenseness, had shifted and settled to an equanimity and repose. The sting had been taken out of things, leaving her free to be comfortable.

She checked her watch. Looking towards the field, she saw the horse had come, the horse which never showed till the stars, white as he was, gave the sign.

Quiet as a moth, she moved across the room and into the hallway, opening the door of the bedroom where the man stood waiting for her, as he waited every night. He had in his hand the bucket which he used to urinate in.

She took the bucket from him and emptied it herself into the lavatory. He had protested when she first did this but now he acquiesced, tacitly acknowledging that there was something in the action which satisfied her need to have thrown off any barrier to his being there.

He moved behind her, silent, in his socks, to the sitting room where the glass door was open to the night. He stood back while she looked out and then beckoned to him to come.

'All clear. You could risk going out, if you wanted.'

But he shook his head. He had been out a couple of times but more to please her. For himself, for the moment, he was happier inside.

She returned from the kitchen with the bottle of wine and the plate of sandwiches which had become their daily shared meal. For some reason the sandwiches fitted her sense of the need for stealth—but also something careless and free, a picnic at the races, perhaps. Anyway, there was an air of insouciance about the sandwiches; she spent time thinking up new piquant fillings.

What she didn't know was that the man had become used to routine and was alarmed by variety. Much as he had craved change, it was the regularity of his life here that he clung to. Each day he slept, in the spare room, concealed by bedclothes in case of some chance intrusion. Only at night did he emerge from his cover, stretch his legs and share a meal with her.

Ellen had heard about the prisoner on the run from the young man with the unfortunate beard at the Post Office Stores. And Jackson had mumbled to her, as he left one evening, 'You look out for yourself, now, mind,' and she understood that he was urging she be watchful.

'My builder, Mr Jackson, thinks I might be murdered in my bed by you.'

Jos Bainbridge blinked. After the days in semi-darkness, his eyes were sensitive. 'I don't have to stay . . .'

'Don't be silly, I was joking . . .' Her smile was braver than his.

'They're bound to find me sometime.'

'But why?' Ellen said. 'Why should they look here? I never go out anyway. And there's nothing to link you with me.'

And it was true—there was nothing: not history, background, age, sex, experience, social habits, inclinations—nothing. The absolute purity of their association filled her with an exuberant joy. It flew in the face of nature and yet . . . and yet it was utterly natural.

'They'll never look here,' she repeated. 'Why would they? I've never seen you before, never heard of you—you're a complete stranger! Why in God's name would I harbour you?' She relished the thought of their little cabal, the two of them, her and Bainbridge.

His story unfolded—through many silences and bites of sandwich—with him saying more when he saw he was not disbelieved. She didn't know why she believed him except that there was no reason not to—she didn't care what he'd done, she didn't care if he raped her in her bed, she had hoped he had come to kill her. But she knew he wouldn't. She knew she was right because she didn't care.

He told her that his parents had died in a plane crash when he was two years old; he had been brought up, in Plymouth, by his mother's sister, who late in life had married a member of her Methodist church. When he was ten years old, he had had a fit—and had been diagnosed epileptic. Perhaps because of this he had never been any use at school—his 'uncle' called him soft in the head.

At that she was concerned. 'Should you be on medication?' Dr Rhys was charming; she could always brave the surgery at Oakburton and ask him.

He shrugged. 'They put me on phenytoin inside. But I've not had a fit since the day I was taken. I doubt I will again. There's something there in place, you see.'

He'd left his aunt's house, he said, as soon as he could leave school. He'd been forbidden a pet at home but always had a love of animals and offered himself for hire with a local farmer, who took him on as a shepherd. As a result he grew to know the Moor, like a friend, he said, and he hadn't so many of those.

179

He fell in love with the farmer's daughter—younger than him she was, a wild one . . . she had loved to dance, and they had gone dancing together, to clubs down Plymouth way, coming home all hours—he had had to watch himself to be up in time for the sheep . . . she was a dazzler, a star above him, he had known he would lose her . . . Ah, yes, he said, when Ellen made a demurring protest, he was a loser, he had always known he would.

She was a tease as well as beautiful: she'd mocked him, implying he was impotent—not man enough, anyway, to possess her. His upbringing had made him fearful over sex and he hung back. There were times she left him altogether, and went off and didn't come home for weeks, when he would wander on the Moor and want and want her. She didn't get on too well with her father, they quarrelled frequently so it was partly that—but partly, too, he knew, that he, Jos Bainbridge, wasn't enough for her.

One day, she'd come home, after months away, and had been angry in a way he didn't understand, had picked a fight, saying he was to blame, what did he expect, did he think she was going to wait for him for ever? In desperation at his own timidity, he'd drunk the best part of a bottle of whisky. They'd gone to a place on the Moor he thought of as theirs, and she had lain on the grass, laughing, her skirts pulled up showing her lovely legs—and, suddenly, something in him snapped, and he'd taken her and entered her roughly.

She had moaned and cried out as he came inside her and he had been visited by the most appalling feeling—that he was evil, that he would be damned

180

for ever, that he was noxious, vile, hideous, that he had tainted his darling, that he was the worst of men, that he would suffer for all eternity, that he was riddled, as his aunt had told him often, with mortal sin.

He had wandered off in horror, aghast at his own filth and ugliness, drunk the rest of the whisky and, still beside himself, returned to where he had left her to find another man there.

He stopped there and she had said, more to help than a wish to probe, 'Who was he?'

'I don't know. I'd never seen him before. He was beating her up. I tried to stop him—I was stronger then, and drunk with it, but he flattened me. Knocked me out. When I came to there was a mist down and I was still hung over. In fact, I didn't know what had happened. People say "it was like a dream" but—'

'Sometimes reality *is* like a dream?' she interrupted.

'Yes.'

Of course she knew that. 'Don't say more than you want to.'

'Maybe another time . . .'

*　　　*　　　*

Ellen Thomas, when first she heard Jos Bainbridge tell his story, had been conscious of the strangest feeling. She followed the account, in the glimmering dimness in which he told it—which added to a sense of its being part of some taboo, or mythic story, told in the crepuscular conditions of a tribal ritual—as raptly as if it were being etched before her by some fiery comet on the night sky.

181

The words, faltering, passionate, yet altogether credible, sprang something deep within her, trapped till now, clogged in the wheels of her own desperation, which, shaken free, infused her suddenly with intense and staggering life. The starkness of the story, its violence and tenderness, the love he felt for his childish sweetheart, the horror of the outcome, declaimed by a man who spoke without artifice, revealed him—the depth and breadth and heart of him—more vividly than anyone she had ever known. The brevity of their acquaintance, and the circumstance of their meeting, illumined an intimacy so incontrovertible it was as if they had known each other since beyond the back of time.

Whatever there might still be to learn of his history, it would only be peripheral, a sop to curiosity; there was nothing of himself, the man's own sheer and vital self, withheld. No crannies of concealment. Not even Robert had bared his soul so frankly before her. It filled her with awe, and then with wonder, that another living being should trust her enough to come so close. Seeing him eating her sandwiches, she remembered a winter when the weather had been harsh so that robins had fed from her outstretched palm and thought: he, too, takes bread from my hand!

She looked, from where he sat—palely eating on her sofa—then across to the sheep, also pale in the gloaming.

'Funny you being a shepherd. I used to lie here looking at the sheep. I had a fancy they were runes which spelled out some mystery.'

'Maybe they did. They've sense in them, sheep.'

'I've always seen them as rather silly animals.'

' "Silly" comes from "sely" '—her look was an enquiry—' "holy" it means, in the old speech. Sheep are clever, though. You know about the leer, do you?'

'Tell me.'

'It's where they graze on the Moor. But there's no boundaries marked, you see. No walls or fences keeps them in. They learn it—where to go safe.'

'How?'

'The dams teach it to the lambs. That's why foot-and-mouth's so feared—if a whole flock's slaughtered you lose not just the flock but the knowledge of the leer. There's none left to teach it, you see.'

Later, she was touched with pity, and then with sadness, but when she heard this, Ellen Thomas felt exultant. The moorland space which bore no visible definition, unbounded save by the sheep's implicit knowledge, answered something in her. She was like a sheep which had lost its leer, and now she had found it again—a terrain where she was free to wander when she had lost all sense of where she might safely go.

She knew, as she listened, long before he reached the end of all he told her, that she would do almost anything to help this man. The tale she was audience to seemed to infiltrate her bloodstream, her lymph, her nervous system and was circulating round her, informing her responses, knocking against her retired heart. The knocking beat up the blood in her. She had always thought her own thoughts, but they had come and gone lamely, without conviction.

As he spoke, through the pressure of the intimacy and the candour of the telling, she felt her thoughts root and expand. Out of the dark he had come to her—his darkness cancelling hers. It was as if under sentence of death she had been given to drink a fatal poison; and found it instead the elixir of life.

MAY

CHAPTER ONE

Paula was at a loose end. She had scoured and scrubbed, bleached and polished, swept and vacuumed every available surface of Jackson's shambolic house, bagged up years of rubbish, domestic and garden, and had even penetrated the garage where, amid impressive filth, she found Jackson's pornographic magazines. Jackson had been toying with setting fire to them. To return home to a curt comment from Paula, that she'd 'binned his comics', was a double blow: it deprived him of the chance to express nobility towards his secret love and left him more than ever at the mercy of Paula's jibes.

Paula had perceived that her plan with Mary Simms and Luke had not borne fruit. Luke was hardly ever at the pub these days. And God knew what had got into Mary! The silly cow seemed to have spent the whole night in Luke's bed with nothing at all to show for it and was now mooning around with a daft expression on her face and rushing off to the toilet every five minutes. As for that Luke . . . Paula was mightily pissed off, when she had called round to Rabbit Row to pick up her *Lord of the Rings* collection of figures, to find her mum ironing his shirt.

Paula had done her own ironing since the age of eight; that—and the constant absence of Jackson, whose reformation in the matter of work, like many reforms, seemed to have gone over the top— prompted her, on her evening off, to call in at the church where the vicar was giving one of her classes on 'Woman as God'.

Numbers, never high, had fallen since the vicar's own fall from grace. Tessa Pope had been one of the few regular attendees, but she was currently expending all her religious zeal trying to keep out of the vicar's way. The vicar, however, whose walk by the river with Mr Golightly had restored some of her vim, was determined not to be cramped by recent events which she was preparing to discuss with the bishop, who had sent a handwritten note suggesting the two of them have 'a quiet chat'. To jettison any professional commitment was to imply guilt; in defiance of Keith, she refused to cancel the class on 'Judith and Holofernes', which that evening consisted of herself, and Paula.

Paula was not familiar with the Bible but she became quite engaged when it was explained to her that Judith had, single-handedly, cut off Holofernes's head—an action for which the biblical heroine was apparently applauded by the Almighty. It struck Paula that there was maybe more to Him—or Her—than met the eye. It also struck her that the vicar looked more than usually bedraggled. On an impulse, Paula invited her back for a drink. Jackson, she knew from experience, would not be back till well after closing time.

Despite her bold public stand, Meredith was feeling the effects of being a social pariah. All she had to go home to was carping reproaches from Keith; Paula's was the first offer of friendship she had received since the allegations began to circulate—indeed, since she came to the village at all.

Paula was the sort of girl the vicar had, in the past, been secretly afraid of—the kind at school who stole your lunch and stuffed it down the toilet and then shouted obscene things at you on your way home. It was an honour to be the invited guest of such a person. Meredith accepted gratefully, and she and Paula walked up the village together, passing a rather red-faced Sam Noble on the way.

Back in Jackson's, now spanking clean, kitchen, Paula opened two of the bottles of scrumpy she'd found jammed away in a corner of the garage along with a leaky car battery, a broken hedge trimmer and the pornographic magazines. From her Stag and Badger stash, she produced peanuts and a catholic assortment of flavoured crisps.

'Cheers!' she said toasting the air with her bottle. 'Here's to women!'

Meredith was unused to drink and scrumpy is best left to those with strong heads. Intending to say nothing—often a prelude to sudden loquaciousness—it wasn't long before the unaccustomed alcohol, and the novelty of an attentive audience, led to the whole Tessa Pope story pouring out.

In no time at all Paula had ingested the relevant information. The vicar's predicament provided fuel for the mental furnace whose heat had been so wasted on Mary Simms. The discussion of Judith and Holofernes had not fallen on stony ground: Paula had been gratified to learn, from such a source, of violence being put to educational ends.

'Listen,' she said, leaning across to offer a beef crisp to Meredith, 'here's how it goes.'

By this time the vicar had polished off her first bottle of scrumpy and was well on with the next. Shards of crisps flew wildly as she started on a heated account of the process of female

189

circumcision. Privately, Paula's withers were unwrung. Any girl mad enough to allow *that* to be done to her deserved all she got! However, this evening she was prepared to indulge the vicar and allowed her to rabbit on.

From time to time, as the vicar expounded her theme, Paula leaned across the table and swept some of the crisp crumbs into a little pile and then into the palm of her hand. Her guest was showing signs of moving down to another topic on her long list of cruelties perpetrated on the female sex, when Paula decided it was time to draw a line. Her organised mind preferred to deal with the present atrocity which, as she pointed out 'weren't done by a man but by that nutty girl'.

She sent the vicar up to the bathroom to wash her face before packing her off back to her husband. Time enough to settle his hash when the Pope kid was sorted. Having steered the vicar, her hair rather wild, through the front door, Paula settled to indexing her collection of True Life Romances.

The True Life Romances didn't take long to knock into shape and Paula looked about for other employment. Finding nothing amiss in the already pristine surroundings, and seeing the evening was fine, she went out for a breath of air. She didn't fancy going up the Stag, where it was too like work, but she fancied she might walk round to her mum's for the Micra and maybe run over to Backen to see what was on at the Stannary Arms.

Mr Golightly was returning from an evening stroll by the Dart when he met Paula. Although they had never been introduced, by this time he knew by sight most of the residents of Great Calne and he grasped the occasion to extend his acquaintance. He greeted her, describing where he had been walking.

'Don't go down to the river much meself, it's ruin for the shoes,' Paula explained.

Mr Golightly glanced down at Paula's feet which, perched on four inches of heel, were magnificently adorned in thin straps of baby blue with a floppy blue flower at the toe. 'Yes,' he agreed, 'I can see those wouldn't suit the path of dalliance. My own I choose so they will take me on all terrains.'

They walked down the hill together towards Rabbit Row. Mr Golightly, who had been missing Luke's company, asked for news of his friend.

'Doing his stupid scribbling night and day, so far as I can see,' said Paula shortly. She was privately livid that her mum seemed to have taken to the new lodger with so little apparent regret for the departed.

Mr Golightly also felt something like jealousy. It sounded as if Luke had got up fresh steam with his writing just as he himself had begun to despair of making any headway at all. A silence led to his asking Paula, 'Do you watch a TV soap yourself?'

'Yeah, course,' said Paula. She watched them all, when she had the chance. '*EastEnders* I like best.'

At Johnny's advice, Mr Golightly had sampled *EastEnders*. 'I prefer *Neighbours*, myself. It has an upbeat note.' *EastEnders* had more of the tragic impulse, a style he was keen to avoid.

'They're all the same.'

'You'd say so?'

'Yeah, course,' said Paula. 'That's the point.'

'Is it?'

191

'Oh, yeah. They're all about sex and money—that's what people want . . .'

'And not love?'

'Yeah, I s'pose,' said Paula, grudgingly. 'But what people call "love", en't real.'

'Would you say there was such a thing?' asked Mr Golightly. Paula struck him as unusually clear-sighted.

'Search me,' said Paula. 'If there is, I en't met it. Mostly what people call "love" is wanting their own way.'

They had reached Rabbit Row but Paula stayed talking to Mr Golightly, leaning on her mum's Micra in the benign impartial rays of the late evening sun. Her companion's attention made her confiding—the writer seemed less of a wanker than most men and she found herself discussing with him the vicar's plight.

'What's done her head in most is it was this girl done it to her.'

Mr Golightly nodded. 'Yes, I feel for the vicar. Betrayal is hard to come to terms with. Dante placed it in the central circle of hell. He had a point. But perhaps we are all traitors somewhere?'

Paula had not heard of the great Italian poet. She said she, personally, wanted to help the vicar who, if she knew anything about it, had no interest in sex. To Paula's mind, the vicar's obsession with female circumcision didn't qualify—that was the kind of stuff you got on BBC4—not proper sex at all.

Mr Golightly had a thought. 'Maybe that's the problem?' he suggested. 'Perhaps we shouldn't be altogether innocent about things like sex. What's ignored takes its revenge, you know?'

192

Paula said that in her view the person who had the 'problem' was that stupid kid, Tessa Pope, and if there was any revenge to be taken it should be taken on her.

Mr Golightly agreed. 'It's the child, clearly, who has the hang-up, not the poor vicar. It puts me in mind of the Witches of Salem. There's an excellent play on the theme.' He sketched the plot of Arthur Miller's *The Crucible*.

Paula listened attentively to the story of the sexually repressed adolescent girls who turn a Puritan community upside down with hysterical allegations of witchcraft and Satanism.

'There you go,' she said. 'Sex, like I said.'

'Or power?' suggested Mr Golightly.

'Same thing,' said Paula, sagely. 'Sex 'n' power—getting your own way—that's how life is.'

CHAPTER TWO

The very early morning lies at the ragged edge of consciousness, and while the curtain of the waking world is still half pulled, it is possible to steal among revenants of other worlds and not disturb their influence.

Ellen Thomas had woken to the soft insistent sound of cawing birds and the knowledge she was going to paint. It was as if the secret between her and Bainbridge piped into her veins fresh reserves of energy. The few hours she had slept were not, as before, fitful and wary, but peaceful and profound.

Ellen, in her nightdress, took her easel, her sketch pad and her box of pastels to the garden and began to make swift arcs across the page. She knew that she had to capture the long bands of mist, which racked the hilltops, and the scattering black birds which flew in between.

Crimson and powerful, the sun slid upwards, gashing the embers of the sky and leisurely raking it out to a tawny trenchant rose. Away across the hillside, the wind in the growing grain was making teasing, fluid whirls—like swirling, dancing petticoats, or the fluent signs and characters of magic writings. And the birds . . . how perfectly full of soaring life they were as they swooped and bowed and tumbled in the cold dawn . . .

During the days of misery and fearfulness Ellen had taken down her watercolour paintings from the sitting-room walls. They had come to seem mere tinsel, hiding an incompleteness they could never cure. One day, she had found in a cupboard a framed print of Robert's, stowed away and forgotten, Van Gogh's last painting, the cornfield, where the black crows presage the artist's suicide.

Ellen, in her own darkness, had understood the artist's torment. She had put the print up on the wall and studied it. The flying crows seemed to point to an escape from her own precariousness. She longed to take flight with them, away from a world which menaced and negated her. And it was birds, black and flocking, she had heard when she had woken to the sense of penetrating freshness infusing her being and propelling her outside.

The birds in Van Gogh's cornfield were crows. The birds which summoned her now were rooks, the crows' gregarious cousins, who resembled their carrion relatives as sleep resembles death—a likeness which hides the essential difference. It was

194

as if through the fine-meshed net of despair, which had covered all events and people, and had hidden from her the meaning of things, had flown these exuberant birds. Their harsh clarion signalled something dim but potent, of which she herself could only sense the stirrings, but which the arrival of her secret guest seemed also to portend. The birds had broken through the veil of dismay, pecking holes in it in their quest for the protected content which it was their nature to devour. It was as if they were picking out her soul's vital secrets, tiny, yet filled with mysterious promise—seeds plucked from the fruit of her consumed heart.

*   *   *

Mr Golightly had also woken early that morning and he took himself off to his place of contemplation on High Tor. The last time he had visited he had spotted ravens. And there was one now, beak laden, its powerful wing-beats making nothing of the wind.

Mr Golightly sat on the flat, table-shaped rock and tried to remember why a raven was like a writing desk. He watched the anxious parent ravens and their brood, three puffed-up, sooty young thugs, almost ready to fly.

One of the adult ravens arrived and tried to stuff a morsel of live stuff into the bill of one of the young. But the young raven turned its head, the wriggling meal was not to its liking. Was it full? Anorexic? Or plain rebellious? Apparently, not even ravens were immune to concerns about their offspring. This notion that a creator had influence over the objects of its creation—where on earth did that idea come from? A parent, even a raven parent could tell you it was nonsense . . .

The conversation with Paula had made him pensive. Was she right that 'love' was, for most human beings, nothing but a cover for their own desire? The events of Great Calne, as he had witnessed them, certainly bore out Paula's cynical view. Yet, for all her unblinkeredness, Paula's wasn't the whole truth—if such a thing was anyway discernible.

Over the years, Mr Golightly had come to place more confidence in truths than 'truth', a concept he looked on with suspicion ever since a man who might have saved his son had asked a specious, damn fool question about it. But, especially since embarking on his new recreation, he found his mind kept returning to an idea his son had been fond of.

His son had insisted as a fundamental truth that love was always creative. But conversation with Paula had raised another problem. It seemed to Mr Golightly, watching the ravens feed their fledglings in the ubiquitous, levelling illumination of the sun, that love was very much like light—a thing that everybody imagined they knew but whose nature was very hard to define.

Yet from time to time—particularly since taking his holiday—he had felt he was on the brink of penetrating that enormous mystery. There was a law of the sun. Was there also a 'law' of love? Rapture, wonder, compassion, tenderness—the great emotions ranged to the pull of it—yet for all its supposed gentleness there seemed also to be something very reckless about love. His son had been called 'meek'; yet he had been, above all,

196

passionate, eager, impulsive, recalcitrant—given to risk of the highest order. It was that risk-taking ability which, he was coming to see, was so remarkable. For when the terrible had joined with the true, the sacrifice had been ruthless and the law of his son's nature had become one with providence . . .

*   *   *

Ellen Thomas, in her nightdress, stood at her easel in the garden, painting birds in the flowing, dappling light. In her mind, they flew upward . . . ever onward and upward, into unimagined stratospheres, where time and space dissolved into the limitless aether beyond. She had thrown down the burden and now the birds lifted her, out of the little doom of irrelevance, the awful terror, the state of huddle which had cramped and hurt her. Never had she felt so clear, so free of polluting distractions.

As she painted, she found that whatever jarred she could at once paint out—and this too, this editing process, this disencumbering, peaceable eliding, which she did without thought but without regret either—it was remarkable how it seemed to be cutting the strings which had entangled and bound her, loosed her free to be whatever it was she was to be. With no sense of where she was going, or what was proper to this enterprise, she followed her inclination, which was, mostly, to remove and excise, to take out.

Yes, she was softly rubbing things out as she stood there, her needs, her desperations, her inclinations, all were disappearing—till she was left, footless and featureless, bodiless, almost, with only the strange divinations of the birds to speak for her. The ancient soothsayers looked to birds for auguries—the birds upon the wing were the flexion of her soul.

Mr Golightly, returning from his walk, and come to talk to Samson, spied Ellen across the barbed-wire fence. He quickly moved away but she must have felt his presence, as she turned round to greet him.

'Hello,' she said, 'I am painting.'

'Yes,' said Mr Golightly, 'I see.'

'Mostly, said Ellen, pausing from work as she spoke, 'I am painting things out.'

'It is vain to do with more what can be done with less?'

'Exactly,' said Ellen. 'I'm glad you understand.' She returned her gaze to a rook disappearing into the sky.

As the birds flew in and out of the deliquescence which had become her person, so too did the words of Jos Bainbridge, mingling with the flitting birds with the impalpable authority of a dream. They seemed to come from the same abode of otherness and darkness, the black birds and Bainbridge, flocking through the transparent envelope which surrounded her, alighting on the branches of her growing thoughts, gathering together in mysterious conjunctions, and then, as suddenly, arising and departing, leaving her in a solitude which had once incarcerated her and had now become the purest peace.

The gates of mercy had clanged shut against her, and here had come the harbingers, carrying in their bills the key to her release. They were her

198

guardians, the birds and Bainbridge, her shady sentinels, her allies, the coordinates of her release.

CHAPTER THREE

The Easter holidays had passed miserably for Tessa Pope. Her story about the vicar had brought her attention: condolences and queries had been forthcoming, but she was learning that fame also brings privations. Tessa had never been popular in the village but now the local children laughed after her and called her rude names. And she was mortally afraid of meeting the vicar, which meant she spent the best part of her days watching TV inside.

Back at school—the private one in Newton Abbot which Nicky Pope thought less rowdy than the local primary—Tessa felt safer. But she was plagued by nightmares—one, in particular, about a fox which got under the bedclothes and terrifyingly snapped at her private parts.

In the past, if she was going up the village, Tessa took the short cut through the graveyard. But now, to avoid notice, if she went out at all, she had been using the route which went round along Rabbit Row. Paula, who had gone over to her mum's to ferry more soft animals to Jackson's, met Tessa face to face outside.

'Hi there,' said Paula, and grinned.

Tessa's recent history had made her more than usually apprehensive; detecting something sinister in Paula's address she tried to walk on round her. She knew who Paula was, and admired the several

199

studs in her nose and the extreme shortness of her skirts. But until today Paula had never shown the slightest reciprocal interest in Tessa Pope.

Paula, who had been loading toys into the Micra, still had her Orinoco Womble in one hand. She gripped Tessa's wrist with her other. 'Come inside,' she suggested, still grinning.

Tessa was about to protest when Paula clapped Orinoco across her mouth and pushed her down the garden path. Once inside the house, she shoved Tessa along the passage, past the kitchen—using her knee in the small of her captive's back when she became resistant—and into Paula's own old room where, to make a firmer gag, she wrapped her scarf round Orinoco and tied Tessa to the bed's leg with Luke's dressing-gown cord.

'Don't try anything,' she warned, 'or . . .' and she delivered a snappy excerpt from the vicar's talk on female circumcision.

Paula returned to the kitchen where Luke was busy writing. He looked up politely and offered her a Nescafé.

'No, ta,' said Paula, furious that this was her mum's coffee he was offering. 'Have you got the time?'

'Sure,' said Luke, consulting his watch. 'Ten forty-five.'

'Oh, right,' said Paula, 'I'd better be off. I just come by to get some more of me things but I've got an appointment to have me legs waxed at eleven.' She whipped back to the bedroom.

'Now,' she hissed into Tessa's ear, 'hear this. You're going to write how you made a mistake when you said what you said about the vicar.' And then, recalling her walk with Mr Golightly and his account of the Witches of Salem, 'You can say the Devil done it, if you like. Yeah, that's it, say Satan appeared to you and told you to say what you said . . .'

Tessa, released from Orinoco, and too distraught to cry, obediently wrote her 'confession' with the blue biro and plain sheet of paper which Paula, covering all eventualities, had taken the precaution to supply. Grabbing the paper, Paula used the knee to shove Tessa back ahead of her and out down the path into Rabbit Row. 'Now, listen, kiddo,' she said. 'If you ever open your gob about this . . .' and she concluded the lecture on female circumcision.

Morning Claxon, on her way back from a workshop on crystals, dropped by Nicky Pope's to find out the date when Spring Cottage was coming free. She had met a tarot reader who was looking for a six-month rental, 'somewhere not too pricey, but with good vibes'.

Tessa had scuttled home from Rabbit Row and was in the throes of explaining how she had come to have been misled about the vicar. A strange man, darkly garbed, who spoke in sepulchral tones had accosted her early one evening in the graveyard and forced words down her throat and into her stomach, which she had been commanded to expel with the story she now knew to be false. She'd been scared to look too close but now she came to think about it she was almost sure there had been something long and scaly, possibly a tail . . .

Nicky Pope said, when Morning called back with a remedy against the powers of Satan—made of the ground teeth of neutered dogs and with a provenance which went back to Druid times—that it wasn't like Tessa. The child had been so upset that she hadn't shed a single tear. All she wanted—it broke your heart to hear it—was to put things right for the vicar, who had been so sympathetic over the Virgin.

Paula was a natural General and knew instinctively the calibre of men and women. After her leg wax, she rang the vicar on her mobile. Running her hands down her calves, she invited the vicar to join her for a hot chocolate with whipped cream at Green Gables. She had a suggestion to put to her, now that Tessa Pope was dealt with and the amended story was in the bag.

CHAPTER FOUR

'Mister Spence, how nice.' Ruddy-cheeked and booming, Wolford straddled Johnny's path blocking out the sun.

'What you want?' asked Johnny, unconsciously rubbing his shoulder where the memory of Wolford's handling lingered.

'Touchy, are we? So what has Mister Spence been up to?'

'Helping down there.'

'What's that, then?'

'Helping Mrs Thomas with her new room, aren't I?' said Johnny, who would have preferred to tell Wolford nothing.

'Oh yes? What she want with you there?'

'Mr Golightly said to,' Johnny averred. Here at least he was on strong ground.

'Shouldn't you be at school?' Wolford asked.

'Shouldn't you be screwing them poor bastards up at the jail?'

'I've got my eye on you, Spence,' Wolford yelled as Johnny ducked past him up the street. 'I'll be round to have a word with your dad any day, don't you worry your sweet life!'

*   *   *

Jackson's pride in his project and his new-found capability, had been eroded by his increasing awareness of Johnny's superior cleverness. Ellen had made sure to address all her business communications to Jackson, but, once Johnny had arrived on the scene, it was obviously he who solved the problems. Jackson was illiterate but he was not a fool. He was crushed when Johnny rattled off some complicated calculation to demonstrate how a basin in the new bathroom could fit; and humiliated when the boy worked out, on the back of his hand in biro, the flow to the new drainpipe.

Johnny also mended an ancient lawnmower which had defeated Jackson, who had advised the purchase of a Flymo. The lawnmower had been Robert's and Ellen was reluctant to discard it. She cautioned Johnny, when he went to inspect the mower, about the nesting swallows, down in the lower shed. 'It's the swallows' loft—they're keeping it warm for me . . .'

If there is a specific against jealousy it is as hard to find as the disease is to endure. The boy had infiltrated Jackson's empire, and had gained the trust of the object of his worship. Once it was he she had told to mind the nesting birds. Jackson had a growing suspicion that when he left in the evening Mrs Thomas got the boy to check over the work.

As a measure against this, Jackson had taken to working later and later. He had put away his tools and was replacing the ladder in the long grass, when Wolford, hands in pockets, sauntered by.

Wolford had never spoken two words to Jackson on the occasions they had coincided up at the Stag, but he stopped and greeted him now before strolling through into the garden and introducing himself to Mrs Thomas who was sitting in the garden with her sketchbook.

Wolford stood chatting and looking over her shoulder. Jackson, feeling protective, went across himself and, for want of any other means of expressing devotion, offered her the remaining tea from his flask. She refused the tea—nicely of course, she was always polite—and he had seen a sketch of the boy on her sketch pad.

The arrival of Paula had dramatically altered Jackson's nightly routine. Where in the past he would come back from the Stag and Badge and fall down senseless, often missing the bed by a mile, sometimes not even making it to the bedroom at all, these days he was expected to bathe and shave before he came to bed. But even smooth-faced, Jackson proved a problem. His silent passion for Ellen Thomas bred insomnia. With all the twisting and turning, Paula had decreed that he'd better sleep on the floor; he was 'driving her mental', she said.

That evening, locked in the bathroom, examining his bulging belly in the mirror Paula had installed, and thinking about the boy's face he had seen in Mrs Thomas's sketchbook, Jackson felt quite 'mental' himself. Worn to distraction by unbearable longing, on the bedroom floor, with a cushion for a pillow, he tried, unsuccessfully, not to imagine Ellen Thomas's bony hips pressed into his own, and her long legs twined around his waist and her white hands delicately cupping his scrotum. At least on the floor he was spared the bevy of animals which formed a furry citadel around Paula. With the crowd of creatures in the bed there was barely room for a grown man.

Close by, in her elevated position in what had once been the bed of which Jackson was sole custodian, Paula made little grunts, her retinue of freshly washed Wombles guarding her Sleeping Beauty form. Jackson, wondering how the fuck this could have happened to him, got up and went downstairs and looked dismally at the drawing Paula had prepared for the True Life Romance bookshelf. It was designed, he noticed, to fit the space where once he had kept his beer crates. Under Paula's regime, Jackson had shifted his stock to a high cupboard, but he had no secure hopes of it remaining there long.

Jackson climbed on a stool and extracted four bottles of Newcastle Brown. In an effort to get his beer gut down he had been trying to drink less— but what was the fucking point? Ellen's sketch of Johnny Spence had set off a train of misery which only strong drink could arrest.

Love is the great binder and looser, and drink the great defrayer of embarrassment. A while later, without quite knowing how he got there, Jackson found himself outside Ellen Thomas's house.

The stars were still out and the slopes of the moor glowed with an eerie light. A barn owl veered out of the darkness, shrieking; and a badger lumbered by, maybe sensing a new-found safety from this torturer turned victim. In his state of agitation the night sounds were terrifying to Jackson. He stood, heart palpitating, staring at a white horse across the way in the field.

Inside was his beloved, Ellen of the White Hands—the only woman who had ever treated him with kindness. Weeks of tongue-tied passion had eroded Jackson's inherently shaky self-control. A tidal wave of emotion swelled up within him, and without any formed plan he began to climb the ladder to his ark. Up there, at least Ellen Thomas was beneath him, and not unassailably above him, like the white stars . . .

*   *   *

'If it weren't for her I wouldn't have bothered—not so near the end of my time.'

Between bites of sandwich, Bainbridge spoke in his strange rustling whisper, so that Ellen had to stretch her ears to hear him.

'I was so glad to be back on the Moor again, when I was put on resettlement and working outside in the peat and heather and water, I never thought about escape. I never felt the need, you see.'

She nodded, understanding the resignation which was not indifference.

'I was in a work party clearing a leat. That evening, I stopped to watch some rooks worrying a harrier—they do, you know, birds of prey don't get

206

much past rooks. When I looked back, the rest of them were hanging about having a smoke before getting into the van. The screws are quite easygoing with the resettlement bunch. I was known to be no trouble and I suppose so near the end of my stretch they didn't think to mind out for me. I always knew where I was on the Moor, better than they did, but this time we were near where I used to go with her, and suddenly I had this feeling . . .

'I wanted to tell her that whatever had happened had to happen, that I loved her, that she wasn't to think I blamed her . . . I know it sounds crazy . . .'

'No,' she said, 'not crazy—not crazy at all.'

'I just started walking and after I'd gone a way I thought: they haven't noticed—so I ducked down and wriggled along till I got to more cover. I wasn't scared at first about them coming after me, but some protective thing must have kicked in because I made for the mire—that was part of her and me too—she used to dance across it as a child. I knew the dogs would lose my scent there, you see.'

'Do they still use dogs?'

'There's no scientific substitute for a dog's nose, thank God!'

'And then . . . ?'

'I gave them the slip. I waded down river from the mire, the Swincombe, I knew it well, you see. It would have taken time to get the dogs and by then I'd drowned my tracks. There was something I suddenly thought of—'

Her look said: say it only if you want to.

'She gave me something she'd had since she was a girl. I hid it, when she'd gone off and left me, in a place she showed me—she said only I knew it—but

207

who knows?—with a message, saying I loved her—I suppose I hoped she might find it there. I never asked her if she did because—well, I suppose because I never saw her again after they took me. I was walking downriver and it came to me: if it's still there it's a sign you'll find her. You know how you do?'

'Yes, I know.'

'Mad, really, because it would have been ten years, near enough.'

'And was it there? Did you find it?'

He said nothing; and she felt in her eagerness she had intruded. Light was filtering through from the garden and it was time he returned to his daytime bed. She got up ready to say good night—and saw he was crying.

'That was the amazing thing—' in the faint dawn light she caught the tears. 'After all this time—it was there. Stuffed in behind a stone where I'd put it. I've got it with me,' he said.

*   *   *

Jackson had brought with him the last of the Newcastle Browns and he opened the bottle with his teeth, spitting out the cap. It fell into the recess that had formed on the oddly constructed bungalow roof. With a drunk's fastidiousness, he lurched perilously across the roof to retrieve it. The movement brought him face up against the internal window which looked across the hallway to the spare bedroom. Reaching down to find the bottle top, he made out the pale form of Ellen Thomas, with a man in her arms.

CHAPTER FIVE

Mr Golightly found another communication when he opened up his laptop:

who hath given understanding to the heart?

If anyone did, Mr Golightly knew that the universe was constructed on no plan or theory and that its riddles couldn't be answered by neat phrases or easy solutions. But the e-mailer's questions followed a trend which he had a dim and perturbing sense he ought to recognise.

The questions provoked further questions. Take his characters, for example. If anyone had given them 'understanding' it had to have been himself, their author. But that was just to push the question back a stage—where, if he had any, had his own understanding come from?

The truth was, though it was one he had not fully faced till now, any real understanding had sprung from the shock of losing his son. Until that event he had been remote, reserved, intolerant of human folly. The pain of loss had altered all that. But it was not till he had come here, to Great Calne, and tried to live a life of anonymity, that he had become more conscious of the trials which beset an ordinary person.

Had he ever before had any real comprehension of what was asked of human beings? Even the patient husbanding of ordinary steady affection, he thought to himself, is as rare as the red-throated pipit, as hard to find as the eyrie of the golden eagle. The fact was—he was in a better position to see it now—people were lonely. In his elevated position, and with constant claims to distract him, he had kept that knowledge from himself. Only here, in Great Calne, had he felt—or allowed himself to feel—the ache of chronic loneliness. And yet, wasn't it that same loneliness which had fostered understanding in his heart . . . ?

He was climbing, as he pondered, the steep incline to Buckland Beacon where, he had been told by Colin Drover, at the Stag, some religious-minded philanthropist had had the Ten Commandments inscribed in stone.

'An eccentric idea, but no doubt well intended,' Mr Golightly had commented; and Kath Drover had observed that there was still much to be said for the Commandments; to which her husband had added that it was well known that it was dangerous to fancy your neighbour's wife's ass, which earned him an old-fashioned look from Kath.

Mr Golightly stopped to catch his breath and watch a family of buzzards, the babies like small old-fashioned planes buzzing soundlessly above. Starting up again towards the beacon, he saw a young woman approaching from the lee side. He hoped she might walk on; but she stopped and kneeled down.

Mr Golightly's vision tended to long sight and focusing on the woman's face and expression he found it was familiar. After further observation, he was as sure as he could be that this was the mother of Johnny Spence, the woman who had been so elusive.

'Forgive me,' he said, walking up behind her with his usual quiet tread. 'It's Mrs Spence, isn't it?'

The woman, still kneeling, swivelled round sharply. 'My God,' she said, 'you gave me a fright!'

'I'm sorry.' He hadn't meant to alarm her. 'You were looking for something?'

Rosie Spence laughed uncertainly. 'Oh, nothing. Just seeing what was there.' She crumpled a piece of paper in her hand.

Mr Golightly felt awkward. He realised that he had caught her unawares. 'I'm sorry,' he said. 'I should have explained—I'm a friend of Johnny's. You look so like him . . .'

Rosie Spence's skin had the transparency of her son's. She flushed. 'You know Johnny?'

'Very well. A bright boy. He works for me.'

'Really?' She sounded relieved. 'That's kind of you.'

'No,' said Mr Golightly. 'Not "kind". He has been what I can only describe as a godsend.'

'I'm so pleased.'

'The pleasure is mine.'

'He's not much of a one for school.'

'I shouldn't worry. In my view it's overrated. My own son never attended school—nor did the Queen, I believe,' he added hastily. He didn't want to sound sexist. 'But you are anxious over Johnny?'

Rosie looked at her questioner. She didn't see a man of late-middle age, of medium height and unremarkable features. She saw a pair of eyes which seemed to penetrate to the bone.

'Look,' she said, and Mr Golightly, whose joints were not as supple as he would have liked, bent down, rather stiffly, and peered where she was pointing into a hollow in the rocks. It appeared empty of anything but heather. 'It's an old postbox. The moor people used them to send messages to

211

each other—this was my grandad's—he and my grandma used to leave each other messages when they were courting. I left this here for Johnny . . .' She held out the crumpled piece of paper.

'He didn't get it, then?'

'No. I didn't know how to get in touch with him any other way. It was stupid of me, but I didn't know what else to do.'

'You're worried.' It was a statement rather than a question.

'I'm worried sick.'

'I can give him a message.'

Rosie hesitated.

'I believe I can be trusted to keep my mouth shut.'

'Thank you,' said Rosie. 'Would you say I'm fine and I'll be here today week? Next Sunday, about this time.'

'Consider it done.'

'And give him my love?'

'Of course.'

'Oh God,' Rosie said, sitting down suddenly on a rock. 'It's all such a bloody mess. I don't know what to do.'

Phil Spence had been working the shooting gallery of a fairground in Plymouth when Rosie met him. She had levelled the rifle at the mechanical bear, which had reared up on its hind legs and growled, rather sexily, when her shot hit home. This had excited Rosie, and being the only woman customer to have achieved this superior marksmanship, the shot sent a corresponding bull's-eye into Phil Spence's heart.

Admiration for the spunky young woman had spawned first lust and then a certain weak

212

affection, but the effort of sustaining any emotion was too much for a constitution brought up on alcohol and beatings, and soon Rosie and her son became the target of Phil Spence's own hopelessness.

In a bid to inculcate affection for her son, Johnny's mother had his name changed by deed poll to his stepfather's, but the ploy never worked. The name stuck, but not the obligations that she had hoped would attend it.

'Perhaps,' said Mr Golightly, lowering himself carefully on to a massy boulder, 'there isn't anything you can.' Beside him, carved on two flat stones, he observed, along with the injunctions not to kill, steal, covet, or commit adultery, the exhortation to 'honour thy father and thy mother'. There should have been, he thought, a commandment to honour children, too.

'Anything I can . . . ?'

'Do. There may be nothing to be done.' The Commandments had a certain magisterial impressiveness but as a prescription for human behaviour he couldn't help finding them a little bald.

'I know but . . .'

'But of course that doesn't help much, does it?'

The eyes had lost their penetration and now looked merely kind.

'Not much.'

'It's like this,' said Mr Golightly, and he spread his hands and contemplated them—they were broad hands, muscular and workmanlike, the hands of a sculptor, or a pianist. 'You create something, a child, a book, a world, whatever, and if it is a true creation then it doesn't stay yours—it takes on its

213

own life and independence.'

'But a child—'

'Even a child,' said Mr Golightly, interrupting, 'has authority. Sometimes a superior authority.' He was remembering how his own son had given his parents the slip when he was no more than a slip of a thing himself and had run off to talk to those who were considered his elders and betters. 'We have to respect it,' he said, 'even if what the child does seems to us impossibly rash.'

It came to him, thinking of the young raven disdaining its parent's well-intended food, that the unique power of each individual makes up the slow pulse of destiny. How could there be a blueprint, since no one could bargain for the maverick impact of any contributing part?

'It's not anything Johnny's done—it's me; I keep thinking how I'm to blame.'

'Well, of course you do,' said Mr Golightly, sounding almost cheerful. 'And in a sense you are. It is rank folly, if not a kind of madness, to embark on a creation. Any author will tell you the same!'

'You're a writer?' She remembered now, before she'd left Calne, she'd heard that a writer had moved into Spring Cottage.

'Among other occupations—writing's more of a hobby.'

'It must take your mind off things.'

'In a sense it puts them on it. As I said, I had a son, too, so I know how you feel . . .'

'Responsible?'

'Horribly!'

'I'm sorry,' said Rosie Spence, who had a sympathetic nature and knew when not to probe.

At the end of the Ten Commandments the

philanthropist had tacked on another one: *A new commandment I give unto you: that ye love one another.*

'You see,' said Mr Golightly, not quite noticing what had prompted him to continue, 'when you love you give a hostage to fortune. A real love, and I'm coming to see that is a rare enough thing, exposes you, because what happens to the loved one is not yours to command. People imagine they can control their fate, or that somewhere there is someone, or something, a being which can control it for them. But fate is made up of so many varied parts that at best you can only bear it, your own or anyone else's—and that is, or can be, dreadful.'

A single magpie flew past. One for sorrow.

'Especially,' he added, 'if what happens feels as if it might have been prevented.'

'Maybe,' said Rosie, ' "preventing" things might be wrong, anyway. Even if you could. They might be the wrong things you prevented.' She wasn't quite sure herself what she meant by this.

Mr Golightly, however, looked cheered. 'You're right,' he said. 'The old meaning of "prevent" meant to anticipate—it would be putting the cart before the horse, then, "preventing" things, instead of letting events unfold. Sorry, I'm a crossword fanatic,' he explained.

'My dad liked crosswords,' said Rosie. She looked sad. 'I'm no good at them—women usually aren't.'

'Well,' said Mr Golightly, 'I doubt if it's the case that there's anything women are "no good" at, if they've a mind to it and it's always valuable to have the feminine angle.' Many years ago, there had been a woman he had hoped might help him, but

215

he believed she had betrayed him with his business rival. He had made a fuss over this at the time—the recollection made him feel foolish now.

Rosie Spence looked down to where a gang of Dartmoor ponies were close-cropping the grass—as they had been when she lay on the moor as a girl, before she had given away for ever her chance of love. Nowadays the ponies were bought and slaughtered wholesale and hacked into chunks of bleeding flesh and parcelled up and sold for dog food. 'I was a prostitute for a while.'

'Many distinguished people have followed that profession,' said Mr Golightly, tactfully.

'I wouldn't say I was "distinguished". I was into drugs and things, and there was this man . . .'

'Naturally.'

One of the ponies, a skewbald, skittered suddenly sideways on tiny legs. There were so many things she could hardly bear if she thought about them. 'I was a mad thing, took drugs, quarrelled with my father. I only stayed home because of someone who was kind to me . . . Anyway, I was one of those who got hooked on drugs and this man—' after all these years she couldn't bring herself to say his name—'used the habit to hook girls like me in further.'

'One of my son's best friends was in your line of work,' said Mr Golightly. 'I didn't know her myself but I gather he thought highly of her. I imagine her sexual expertise was useful to him—helped him to see other matters more clearly.'

'It's funny, you know, people go on all the time about sex these days but they really haven't a clue what's going on.'

'It's not a subject I know much about,' said Mr

216

Golightly, apologetically.

'I didn't for sure. Now I know more than I want to. I didn't know, for example, people have sex for all sorts of reasons which have nothing to do with sex.'

'I should imagine so.' That was the problem with evolution—adaptability was a sound principle in theory but it allowed for so much bewildering complication.

'They have sex like they take exercise, for instance, because they think they should.'

'Oh dear—that doesn't sound much fun!'

'Or because they are full of something they can't get rid of—mostly hate in our case,' said Rosie. She sounded tired.

'Fear, as well, I guess?'

'For sure. Fear of being alone, mostly. I married my husband to get away from the other man. And so's not to be alone.'

'It's not an uncommon attempt at solving loneliness—marriage.'

'It doesn't work.'

'No,' said Mr Golightly. 'It wouldn't.' There was no need to beat about the bush.

'Johnny was someone else's child. The person who was kind to me. I treated him very terribly. Oh God, what a mess!'

'I often think so myself. I expect you did your best in what seemed an impossible situation.'

Rosie Spence looked down at the carefree River Dart where, as a girl, she had contemplated drowning herself. She wanted to do so still. 'That's nice of you but I don't think so—I was just trying to save my own skin. It hasn't helped me and it's harmed Johnny. His stepfather loathes him, loathes

217

me too, but that doesn't matter.'

'It might to John.'

'Oh God, you're right!' Her skin, so like her son's, surged red again.

'I'm not always right.'

Rosie Spence lit a cigarette. 'I used to come here sometimes with the man who was kind. He loved me—at least I think now he did. I didn't see that then—but I didn't see then how I could matter to anyone. D'you understand?'

'I think I do.' He hadn't known how he had 'mattered' to his son—and on that account his son had apparently sacrificed himself.

'Do you think anyone ever has enough love?'

'I don't know,' said Mr Golightly. 'To be frank, I've been wondering how much I do know these days.'

Once he had prided himself on knowing everything.

CHAPTER SIX

Nadia Fawns was rereading her novel, *A Knight In Her Arms*. It seemed to her that there was wisdom in it, a wisdom which she was failing to apply to her own life. Despite her friends' reassuring claims, no troop of men had so far beaten a path to her door. Melissa Swan, the heroine of her novel, had not hung about waiting for action. She had courageously swallowed a potion of wolf's claw and mistletoe and travelled through time to find her own true knight.

Sam Noble lacked some of the finer points of the

chivalry of Sir Elidor, but, making the best of things, Nadia decided the moment was ripe to give him a nudge.

The kitchen facilities of the Backen cottage were limited. Sam had been round regularly for dinners which Nadia cooked painstakingly from her Delia Smith recipe books. Before the meal he drank gin and tonic—never fewer than two—and ate the pricier kind of nuts.

It had always been Nadia's idea to improve matters with the installation of a fitted kitchen, one in which she and Delia could better parade their range. With Sam to be got on the boil, there was no time like the present.

And nothing like a fait accompli either. Katy's Kitchens in Exeter had a 'Special Offer'—one which included a double fan oven and an automatic spit. With this in mind, Nadia booked a carpenter—recommended by Barty Clarke—to start work on the renovations.

'This will be our last supper—for a while,' she said to Sam, spooning juice over duck breasts.

'Oh, why?' Sam was spreading the gravy over the mash. He was specially fond of mashed potato which he had never got around to learning the trick of since the split with Irene.

Nadia explained about the kitchen. 'I'll have no facilities here for some time, I'm afraid.'

Sam, who had become unconsciously dependent on the regular free feeds, felt suddenly abandoned.

'You can always come over to my place.'

The average human heart is a nervous organ and by visiting Nadia on her own territory Sam had left open a means of escape. If she turned nasty he could always go home. Women could turn nasty—

there had been an embarrassing scene, in a hotel near Reading, when the Maltese air hostess had locked herself in the bathroom. Hearing himself voice these rash words to Nadia, Sam wanted to summon them back; but she was already thanking him fulsomely.

'Oh, that is kind. Perhaps I could bring over some of my china. He's starting on Monday and I have been bothered where to store it to keep it safe.'

Nadia arrived on Sunday in casual cords, and a good deal of lipstick, and unloaded a quantity of boxes from the boot of her Volvo. Sam felt dismay mount as the stack mounted in his kitchen.

'Would you like to help? Be careful the dog doesn't knock over the soup plates, they belonged to my grandmother—the one who came from Normandy. People say I have a sort of a French look about me. It's the cheekbones, I expect. The bay tree would go well here, what do you think?'

There was a lot of clutter accumulated at the back of Sam's cupboards which Nadia suggested should be chucked out. Sam dug his heels in a couple of times—once over a pan for poaching eggs and then over a mincing machine—but the protest came more from principle than conviction. As Nadia pointed out, the egg pan was made of aluminium, which led to brain damage—he didn't want that, she supposed. And not even Delia demanded hand-minced meat from her devotees— the mincer was practically an antique—perhaps he would like her to sell it for him in her shop?

Having substituted her own extensive collection of crockery and cooking implements, which thoroughly colonised the emptied kitchen

220

cupboards, she drove off in the Volvo to ferry over another load.

Mr Golightly walked back from Buckland Beacon deep in thought. The encounter with Johnny's mother, and her heartfelt admissions, had moved him. And it was sustaining to find a kindred spirit also challenged by the ruthless test of parenting. He was coming down the high street, contemplating the solaces of companionship, when he encountered Sam Noble, standing outside his house staring moodily at a small 'bronze-effect' statue of Cupid, naked, and astride a dolphin, which Nadia had felt it safest to fetch over from Backen, too.

Daphne rushed down the path and began to rub herself amorously against Mr Golightly's leg as Sam, still nursing a grudge over the writers' group but in more pressing need of moral support, hailed his neighbour.

'Don't think you've been in my house, have you?' he asked, magnanimously overlooking the previous discourtesy. Mr Golightly agreed that this was the case and Sam invited him in and offered Earl Grey from one of the tins of assorted teas which were newly ranged along his kitchen counter.

'Thank you, no,' said Mr Golightly, who had a particular horror of bergamot. He turned down an offer of an espresso made from Nadia's state-of-the-art Italian machine, which had been installed next to the teas, but accepted a cup of ordinary coffee and admired the bay tree.

Sam became embarrassed. 'It belongs to a friend. I'm just looking after it,' he explained.

'The wicked flourish like them, I've heard tell,' said Mr Golightly, affably.

221

                              *   *   *

The 'quiet chat' between the Reverend Fisher and the bishop had taken place and it had been agreed that recent events merited a break from the usual claims of duty on the vicar. She had suffered, and withstood, a crisis, and the bishop, a man of pacific tendencies, was keen that the flap die down before she resumed her pastoral round. So she was not at her familiar post in church that Sunday morning but was walking, in her sunhat, when Morning Claxon, out on her run, almost crashed into her.

'I beg your pardon,' Morning apologised. She took another look at the vicar. Events had wrought changes in her. Behind a pair of smart new sunspecs, chosen from the Giorgio Armani collection at Oakburton's optician, she was sporting eyeshadow—a vivid blue, perhaps unconsciously inspired by the bluebells she had passed on her riverside walk with Mr Golightly.

Morning had recently become a disciple of a guru living near Penzance—an ex-tax inspector, who taught that the spiritual path was most fully embraced by exploring all love's byways. In this spirit of amity, Morning took the vicar's arm. 'Fancy a walk?' she enquired.

The vicar and Morning walked up the lane to the sun-spangled, earthy-smelling moor. They made their way along the bridle path, where Mr Golightly had walked with Wilfred, and Ellen Thomas had met the presence in the gorse bush. On the same clump of brimming, scented gold, a wheatear was lustily exercising its distinctive voice, a mellifluous warble mingled with a strange harsh

                                   222

creaking rattle—for, unlike humankind, nature doesn't pretend to consistency.

Morning remarked that when the gorse flower was out kissing was in season, a saying she had recently learned from Mary Simms, who had called round looking for a natural remedy for nausea. Mary didn't like to trouble Dr Rhys, she said, who, poor man, looked worn out with all his work at the surgery. She had not gone on to explain to Morning—who had been brought up on a high-rise estate—that the gorse flower blooms in all seasons, which is why, as all country people know, kissing never does go out of fashion. So perhaps it was with a misplaced sense of seizing the moment that Morning turned and suddenly embraced the vicar, kissing her full on the lips.

The vicar, who had not been kissed so passionately since the night when Keith was drunk and had mistaken her for the girl from Hove library—which had led, in time, to he and Meredith becoming engaged—was too taken aback to protest. Morning's bosom was bountiful and yielding and after so many rejections Meredith found it soothing to be clasped there. She allowed herself to linger long enough for Morning to pat her on the shoulder blade and remark, 'Love is Everywhere' (one of the ex-tax inspector's more popular wisdoms).

Buoyed up by her walk, and filled, indirectly, with the tax inspector's enthusiasm, the vicar had returned home and embarked on a programme of clearing. Keith was out and Paula, in response to a call on her mobile, came over to lend a hand. The two had almost completed the task when Mr Golightly, on his way back from Sam's, stopped to say 'Hello'.

Meredith straightened up. 'Clearing things out,' she explained. 'Stripping away.' She beamed at her congregation of one. 'Anything here you fancy?'

Mr Golightly, who had a weakness for second-hand books, poked about in one of the boxes which Paula, stripped down to her vest, and showing her tattooed shoulders, had been shifting outside.

'This one,' he said, picking out a dark blue-bound volume, 'if you really don't—'

'No, take it, take it!' urged Meredith, excitedly. 'I don't want any of them. Love is not possession!'

She invited him in for tea and a slice of lemon sponge, brought by Patsy and Joanne—late of the tearooms—who had been passing through Calne to look up old acquaintances and had called by to congratulate the vicar over her stand on Gay Rights.

Mr Golightly, unwilling to explain his aversion to tea a second time, politely declined. Paula said if Meredith had finished with her she would be off too. Before he left, the vicar kissed Mr Golightly on both cheeks and informed him that 'Love was Everywhere', a sentiment which he felt it was hardly his place to challenge.

Going down the steep concrete ramp which led to the road, Paula, a little unsteady on her heels, grabbed Mr Golightly's arm. Mr Golightly was touched. He had warmed to Paula and admired her taste in shoes. The shoes displayed courage. It took courage to befriend a social outcast in a time of trial. He remarked that he was pleased to find the vicar back on her old form and invited her ally over the road for a Scotch, which, coming from a man, Paula thought an unusually sensible invitation.

224

Inside Spring Cottage, Mr Golightly steered his guest towards one of the floral chairs and poured them each a large measure of whisky. He threw the book he had extracted from Meredith's box of discards down on to the orange sofa.

It is a tricky moment when any author finds a cherished, hard-wrought work in the position of poor relation in a second-hand bookshop. In principle, Mr Golightly was inured to this—it was not news to him that, just as for many years men had died for the right to read his great work, nowadays it had become a staple of cast-off bookstores. But finding his jewel among those books that the vicar—practically a personal friend—was casually jettisoning had been a jolt.

'What's this, then?' Paula asked, picking up the book. Unable to sit still for long, she'd already been round the room on her knees collecting up threads which had moulted from the rag rug, made by Emily Pope in the days when she still had her sight.

'Only an outdated classic in which nobody's much interested,' said Mr Golightly, rather pettishly.

Paula flicked it open. 'S'the Bible, en't it?' Her encounter with the Old Testament heroine, who had cut off her enemy's head, was entwined affectionately in her memory with her own victory over that stupid Tessa Pope.

Mr Golightly, slightly ashamed of his peevish outburst, handed his guest a half-full toothglass. 'Would you care for water? It's not bad from the tap.'

Paula preferred her Scotch neat. She knocked back the content of the toothglass while flicking rapidly through the flimsy pages.

'I went to one of the vicar's classes on the Bible. I liked it meself—it's got style. Here, this bit's good.' She read out: *'Then the Lord answered Job out of the whirlwind, and said, Who is this that darkeneth counsel by words without knowledge? Gird up now thy loins like a man . . .'*

'Good God,' said Mr Golightly, almost spilling his whisky, 'I shall forget my own name next!'

CHAPTER SEVEN

It was Sunday, and Jackson had told him there was no need for him to come to work that day, but his stepdad was home and with nothing better to do Johnny called by Spring Cottage.

'John,' said Mr Golightly, ushering his young friend into the parlour where Paula, giving her feet a rest, was reading on the orange sofa. 'You know Paula?'

Paula was aware of the miasma which surrounded the Spences. Her own fatherless state had encouraged a sensitivity to appearances—her mum was a weakling, but one Paula protected with a natural *noblesse oblige*. In marrying Spence, Rosie Coaker had gone down in the world. Paula, alive to the dangers of social decline, preferred not to risk infection by association with its sufferers.

' 'Lo,' she said, unenthusiastically, not looking up from the book.

Johnny was used to being snubbed. On the other hand, he wanted it to be seen that he was esteemed in Mr Golightly's eyes. 'Come to see if you've got any work for me,' he said, in the hope of impressing

226

Mr Golightly's visitor.

'I might have. When Paula has finished with that book there are some references I'd like you to trace.' Mr Golightly went over to the gateleg table and switched on the laptop. 'I'll be with you in a trice . . .'

There was not the man or boy alive who could hope to impress Paula. Nevertheless, she stopped reading and stared expressionlessly at Johnny Spence. She couldn't stand kids; in fact, she planned to get herself sterilised as soon as she could afford to pay for it. But this was the kid who'd been working down at Mrs Thomas's. She'd been getting a feeling that there was something funny going on there with Jackson. The other night he'd come home crying—pissed out of his head and covered with mud and blood and his front tooth bust. It'd taken an age to get the stains out of his vest.

Jackson had also been off sex—almost seeming to prefer the floor she had relegated him to. Paula had been willing to overlook this on the grounds that having got her foot well in his door her main objective had been achieved. But a girl has her pride.

The Spence kid was pretty. Maybe Jackson was gay? She wouldn't put it past him, and, as her Auntie Edna said, there were more of them about these days than you thought.

Mr Golightly got up from the table where he had been copying something from his laptop and handed Johnny a sheet of paper. 'See if you can find these in that for me, will you?' nodding in the direction of the book.

'Here y'are,' said Paula, suddenly chucking it at

227

Johnny's face.

Johnny caught the blue-bound volume dextrously, but didn't bother to look to see what he had in his hand.

'Yeah, sure.' He shot a look of sly triumph at Paula, but Paula worsted him.

'Walk you back home, shall I?'

Johnny, instinctively, turned to Mr Golightly for help, but for once his patron let him down. He made no saving intercession and Johnny found himself swept up and out of Spring Cottage.

Halfway up the hill, Paula, darting ahead on her heels like a determined stilt, Johnny dragging behind, they met Sam, with Nadia's arm firmly through his. Sam offered a curt 'Hello' and tried to pass off any acquaintance by hurrying by.

But Paula wasn't having this. She shot Sam a smile that Tessa Pope might have recognised. 'How you, then? How's the plans for the tearooms getting on?'

Sam looked sheepish but made no comment, and the couple disappeared into his house.

Johnny, embarrassed by the unaccustomed exposure, was only anxious to get back to his usual obscurity. He was alarmed when, up at the top of the village, which ran up to the stretch of council houses where the Spences lived, they ran into Wolford.

Paula had lived for many years next door to Wolford and his mother—perhaps it was her recent train of thought, but with no extra external evidence a light suddenly went on. Johnny had stepped fractionally backwards away from the prison officer and Paula stepped back too, to stand shoulder to shoulder beside the boy.

'Calling on anyone?' she enquired.

Wolford's motives for visiting the part of the village where the Spences lived were not wholly clear to himself. He vaguely wanted to get a look at Johnny's environment; but he had no serious plan to visit Phil Spence, or anyone in Johnny's family. He was thrown off balance by Paula's armour-plated smile.

'Been to see my mother.'

'Oh, nice,' said Paula, raising her eyebrows. Rabbit Row was the other side of the village. 'My mum there, was she?' In fact, her mother always went across to her sister Edna's on Sundays.

'I'm afraid I didn't see,' said Wolford. He didn't look at all at Johnny, who was staring at his feet. The three of them stood for a while with Paula grinning till Wolford said he'd best be getting back or his mother would be wondering where he'd got to.

'Yeah, mustn't fluster the poor dear,' said Paula, with, to Wolford's ear, abhorrent mateyness.

Paula's prejudice about the Spences was reinforced by the state of the gate to number four, which stood off its hinges leaning on a run-to-wood privet hedge crammed with Coke cans and crisp bags. The front door was in such poor shape that Paula found herself wishing she'd brought along her sandpaper to give it a good rub down. There was no bell, and the knocker had no back plate, so she rapped sharply with her knuckles on the window.

'Yeah, what?' came a voice from somewhere inside.

Paula did not try to explain herself but wrenched the door open. She was met in the hallway by a

229

man wearing a vest and a pair of stained trousers.

'Your flies are undone,' said Paula, smartly taking the offensive. Experience had taught her that few men recover well from this observation.

While Phil Spence fumbled obediently with his zip fastener Paula stalked past him into what she took for the kitchen. It was clear to her that it had had no proper feminine influence for some while.

'Where's your wife?' asked Paula, taking advantage of her lucky strike over the flies. As well as True Life Romances, she was a devotee of True Life Crime and was hopeful that Johnny's mother might be stashed in pieces in the deep-freeze cabinet, which had smears of what might be dried blood over its chipped surface.

Johnny had shot upstairs to get to the computer before getting a smack round the head. He knew better than to hang around and he wanted to get Mr Golightly's stuff done quickly in case the screw turned up to shop him to his stepdad.

To Paula's disappointment, Phil Spence's response to her question was apparently innocent of guile. 'Fucked if I know.' He produced a tin of tobacco and began to roll a joint. 'She done gone off. Bitch,' he added, as if bothered that his reputation might be damaged by too great a show of uxorious concern.

'When she gone, then?' asked Paula. She was sorry that there was to be no murder but a vanishing was almost as good. There was that film she liked, where the girl disappeared in a petrol station and got herself, and her boyfriend, buried alive.

Phil Spence lowered himself on to a chair with most of its back missing. 'Want one?' he asked, offering her a spindly joint.

'Ta, take one for later,' said Paula. She didn't smoke herself, it stained your teeth but, as Cherie Wolford would say, it didn't pay to look a gift horse in the mouth. 'So how long she been gone, then?' she enquired again, sticking the spliff down her Wonderbra.

' 'Bout three four weeks, I reckon,' said Phil, vaguely. His memory was the worse for the increased intake of beer and dope since his wife's disappearance.

'Who's looking after the kid, then?' asked Paula. She got up and filled a kettle after wiping the handle with a mouldy-looking cloth. The sink was filled with soggily disintegrating tea bags. 'Make some tea, will I?'

'Ta. Looks after hisself mostly.'

'Oh, right,' said Paula. 'Where d'you keep your sugar?' Phil Spence nodded in the direction of a cupboard which, when opened, proved to be full of scuddling silverfish. 'How 'bout I take him off your hands till his mum comes back, while you get yourself sorted?' suggested Paula, picking out two tea bags from a split packet with the precision of a neurosurgeon.

CHAPTER EIGHT

Ellen was sitting on the step of the door to the garden, her arms folded round her knees. Bainbridge was inside while she guarded the threshold. She had become a creature of thresholds, like the lares (or was it the penates?);

231

the old gods Robert had told her the Romans worshipped. They were liminal beings both, she and Jos Bainbridge.

Wilfred emerged from the kitchen and padded silently towards where Bainbridge, his big form folded, sat on the sofa.

'It's lucky Wilfred likes you.'

'My aunt used to say I had a black dog on my shoulder when I was in a temper as a little 'un. I wasn't s'posed to get angry, you see, because of the fits. But I thought it was wrong—the image, I mean. I loved dogs and they me, as a rule.'

'People say terrible things to children, don't they? Sometimes I'm glad I couldn't have any. I might have done terrible things too.

'I doubt that.'

'I don't know—I've been thinking we don't know what we might do till we're tested.'

'We had this discussion group,' he said, after a pause. 'They've pretty good education programmes inside and one of the governors got me interested in literature and philosophy. Anyway, we had this group which was supposed to be about "personal ethics" and one of the men, who was in for killing his wife's lover, told us that before it happened, before he killed the guy he was inside for, he used to keep asking his friends this question: If I called you in the middle of the night and asked you to help me be rid of a dead body would you help?'

Ellen thought a moment. 'I suppose for him the "right" answer could only be "Yes".'

'He used to ask us, in the group—you get close, you see—what we would say. I said I couldn't tell him truly what I might do about anything till it happened. There aren't any rules in advance. You

232

don't know who you are till you're there, in it, you see.'

'And then there's no time to think.'

'It's why I like animals. They've no call to think in advance.'

'And they don't have rules of behaviour.'

'They're themselves—which is the hard thing for us. The hardest, I'd say.'

'Especially on your own.' A solitary bat flickered by—the first that year. It was a while since she had been able to hear their high squeak. When Robert was still alive. 'When my husband was away, working in the Middle East, I used to send him my love through the bats,' she told him.

'"The bat that flits at close of eve / Has left the brain that won't believe." A bat's as good a messenger as any.'

'Who's that?'

'Blake. The governor I mentioned put me on to him—he was a poet, himself, the governor. "A robin redbreast in a cage / Puts all heaven in a rage," he used to say.'

'A poet, really?'

'They're not bad people, you know, in the prison service. Some of the screws were some of the most decent men I've known. There's more than one man's family, come from a distance and money tight, had their fares paid for by the prison officers having a whip-round.'

'I suppose we tend to think of it as just a repository of evil.' It looked so menacing, the great granite façade of the prison. Even in the days when she went out and around she tried to avoid driving past.

'There's good and bad there like everywhere

233

else. I've seen murderers treat new inmates, shattered by where they'd fetched up, with the tenderest kindness—though there's plenty of the other sort, of course.'

'What did they think of you there, the others?'

'Oh, they let me be. They knew the truth. You get to in prison, you see.'

CHAPTER NINE

Mr Golightly was making a shepherd's pie when Nadia Fawns called at the back door. He was following a recipe he had torn—slightly furtively—from an out-of-date *Good Housekeeping* magazine he had found up at the Stag and Badger where, deprived of Luke's company over the crossword, he had read about this season's colour for paint and soft furnishings (lilac) and, should he be entertaining ambitions for cosmetic improvement, the pros and cons of Botox and liposuction.

Nadia was dismissive of *Good Housekeeping*. 'Shallots are much more flavoursome than onions—and Delia always adds a tablespoon or two of Worcester sauce. Delia's my bible. Where do you get your meat?'

Mr Golightly, who didn't know who 'Delia' was, but didn't like to seem ignorant of any one's bible, explained he got in the mince from the butcher who came round in a van.

'Is he organic?' asked Nadia. She was very keen on all that.

Mr Golightly had to acknowledge that here was another ignorance. So far as he was concerned, all

234

animal products were organic—an attitude Nadia found hopelessly antediluvian.

'No, no,' said Nadia. 'Most so-called "fresh" produce is full of dangerous toxins. It's essential to buy organic. If you saw what gets into ordinary food—the damage to the nervous system is shocking.'

Having installed her kitchenware at Sam's, Nadia was faced with the more delicate task of installing her own person. She had begun this manoeuvre that day by preparing a Sunday lunch of venison, culled from a local deer farm. To accompany the rich meal of felled stag she had bought two bottles of middle-priced burgundy.

Sam, unused to alcohol in the daytime, had drunk a bottle and a half of a heavy Beaune and felt the need to lie down. 'You go upstairs, why don't you, and have a nap?' suggested Nadia. 'I'll clear away down here.'

Sam had woken in a panic to find Nadia in bed beside him, stripped down to her cream satin 'teddy'. Beneath this garment were further items he supposed must be suspenders. Not that he had anything against suspenders, it was just he had forgotten how the hell to tackle them. He fumbled around helplessly, till Nadia, taking matters into her own hands, gave some purposeful guidance.

The whole thing had gone off briskly, and to Nadia's satisfaction. But the campaign was in its early stages—she knew that commitment was essential to any relationship—especially one started later in life. Like most women she had instincts, ones which told her that developing their liaison was not uppermost in Sam's mind. They'd gone for a stroll and there'd been an encounter with that girl with the very short skirts who worked up at the pub and who'd made some crack about the tearooms. Nadia had heard about Sam's ambitions for the tearooms. Something was needed to establish her own presence in his life. A small party, with one or two other male guests, chosen to put Sam on his mettle—Barty Clarke and Golightly, for instance—would make their alliance more of a fixture. 'I've called to invite you to a little drinks do we're having next Sunday,' she beamed. 'If the weather's kind we'll be able to have it in the garden.'

'Thank you,' said Mr Golightly, non-committally. He was learning to take these social hurdles more in his stride.

His stride might have been thrown, however, by the discovery that he had been selected as a potential romantic rival, or at least someone to sharpen up Sam Noble's intentions. Other than Martha and Muriel, Mr Golightly's recent work had kept him largely out of touch with female company. Left to his own devices he would give Nadia Fawns a wide berth, but it was an unexpectedly pleasant aspect of his holiday, the friendships he had formed with his other women neighbours.

Up the road at Jackson's, one of these was perusing the results of Johnny's research. Never one for seeking permission, Paula had been through every last thing Johnny had brought over from Storey Lane with the intention of binning most of it. The pages he had printed out for Mr Golightly were stuffed into a Sainsbury's bag and while Johnny was in the bath Paula skimmed them through.

Mr Golightly was seeing Nadia out when Paula turned up at the back door. 'Stupid cow thinks she's somebody 'cos she's written a book.' Paula didn't give a monkey's who that old idiot Sam Noble chose to go with, but she knew trash when she met it. Nadia Fawns's book couldn't amount to anything—no one had seen it in Tesco's. 'How's your own writing coming on?' she enquired.

'You know what,' said Mr Golightly, 'I'm thinking of giving it up. I'm not sure I'm cut out for the modern style.'

'Hey, never say die. I brought over the stuff the kid done for you. He says it's research. S'interesting.'

'You think so?'

'Yeah. I read the rest of it in the vicar's book. Here.' She handed back the blue-bound volume.

'What did you think?'

But Paula was wrinkling her nose. 'You got something cooking? I can smell burning.'

'Hell and damnation!' said Mr Golightly, shooting out to the scullery and returning with a pan.

'It's that Nadia Whatsit,' said Paula, taking the pan and examining the blackened contents. 'She'd put anyone off. That's what that sort does. They does your head in so you can't think straight.'

'You may have a point.'

'Still, sorts the women out from the boys.'

'How d'you mean?'

'Put people under pressure and you see what they're made of. Like old thingy, back in the day, you got the kid to print out the stuff about. He took a hammering and a half you'd reckon would drive anyone round the twist, but he stuck it out and it all worked out OK for him in the end.'

'You'd say so?'

'Well, he got all them sheep and goats and she-asses, an' that, didn't he? Mind you, you can stick those friends of his. Friends? Nightmare, if you ask me. That Sam Noble'll get more comfort out of that Nadia Whatsit's fanny than you'd get out of that lot in a month of wet Christmases!' She laughed. 'Well, see you, then. I'd better get on back, make the kid his supper.'

'Just a minute,' said Mr Golightly who had been examining the pages and suddenly remembered he hadn't delivered Rosie's message. 'Where is John?'

Paula jerked her head. 'Staying with me up at Jackson's. Seemed best with his mum away. The place was a pigsty and the kid's running wild. Needs discipline, he does. You and me together, we'll keep him in line.'

'No, Paula,' said Mr Golightly, affectionately. '*You* will keep him in line. Ask him to come over when he has a minute, will you. There's something I forgot to tell him.'

'You come up to ours, why don't you? You know where we are? The row of old council houses up the top of the village. You'll know the one—'s' got one them toadstools they make up at the prison outside.'

*　　　*　　　*

The shepherd's pie was past saving and Mr Golightly made do with bread and cheese for supper. Instead of going up to the Stag and Badger, he took the Spiderman mug outside to the garden bench and sat, cradling his coffee, mulling the

238

results of Johnny's research as the sun slipped down to the other side of the world.

It was simple to be the sun—it just came up and went down, or whatever it was people nowadays thought it did, the theories changed so often he had lost track. But no one, so far, had ever had the temerity to suggest that the sun didn't exist!

Swear by Thyself that at my death Thy Sunne
Shall shine as He shines now, and heretofore . . .

His old friend Jack Donne might have sympathised with his current state of mind. The poet understood the comfortless abyss of perfect loss and the lonely pinnacle of absolute love. And bridging both, the desolate plain of abandonment. But Donne, on his deathbed—lying in the shadow of his own imminent annihilation—in his final, fretful, feverish longing, had begged to be reassured of the continuing recreation of love's constant light, had turned, in his last need, to a Creator for whom 'sun' and 'son' were one.

Who, on earth, had he to turn to?

He went inside and put on Haydn's *Mass in Time of War*, went to the scullery, made another cup of coffee, put some milk in the microwave, spilled it on his hand as he was pouring it, tipped over the Spiderman mug, swore mightily, looked for a J-cloth, found he was out of them, placed a tissue over the pools of milk and coffee which were slowly combining, and walked back to the window, where he stood staring out at the green-and-amber-trailed sky.

A wedge of wild geese flew past—seven black silhouettes, like the seven stars, or the seven angels, who fly in and out before the Holy One.

Stepping across the room he turned up the volume of the music: it was his favourite moment, the point in the Agnus Dei where Haydn has the kettledrums boom out like a roll of cannon fire.

It was easy to be a star, or a goose—or even an angel. What was damnably difficult was being human. There was so little to hang on to—all those impossible questions seemed to offer such scope and largesse until you had to live with them.

The phantom e-mailer had been sending questions he himself had posed centuries ago and which he'd become too abstracted (or raddled in his wits? he'd almost forgotten to give Johnny that message from his mother) to remember. What had he been thinking of allowing patient loyal Job to undergo that torment? He'd even participated in it.

If anyone did, he should know that the universe was not a cheat, or a hoax, or a box of tricks governed by some sleight of hand. What is forgotten, or ignored, will seek retribution. It appeared that someone, or something, was giving him a taste of his own medicine . . .

CHAPTER TEN

For all its squalor, Jackson's place had once been his own, where he could eat his breakfast off the floor—however filthy—if he felt like it. But now his home had become a dungeon, where the gaoler had once been his to command and ignore.

Jackson's labile inner state was pressed still further by nagging thoughts of Ellen Thomas's secret. The castle in the air he had been building with such pride and devotion had been exposed as made of straw. The image of the man he had seen in his beloved's arms worked corrosively through his system, dragging with it haunting thoughts of the boy whose face she had favoured over his own.

Arriving home that evening he heard music, and coming into the lounge saw the object of his jealousy ensconced at the keyboard and wearing one of his own sweaters which Paula had shrunk in an overenthusiastic wash. An unusually pink Johnny—also from enthusiastic washing—had found Paula's keyboard and discovered that he could pick out tunes by ear.

Paula had taken off her shoes and was jiving with a long scarf tied to the door handle. The lights were full on, making sparkles of her glittering toenails, 'Mauve Crazy' courtesy of Georgina's.

'If you can't find a partner take a wooden chair!' Paula yelled, picking up the bar stool she had recently smuggled back from the Stag and swinging it wildly round.

Jackson stared, tried to speak over the music, failed to make himself heard and turned tail. Ellen Thomas, Paula, womankind—they could all go fuck themselves the lot of then for all he fucking cared. He paused on his way down the path to kick a stone-effect toadstool, presided over by a pixie with pointed shoes and a pointed hat which, with Johnny's help, Paula had brought over from her mum's earlier that afternoon.

*   *   *

News travelled fast in Great Calne and, almost as

soon as the event was accomplished, Wolford heard from his mother, who had heard it from Nicky Pope, that Johnny Spence had been taken in by Paula up at Jackson's. Wolford arrived at the Stag and Badger just as Jackson was ordering his fourth pint. Barty Clarke was relating to Paula's mum and Kath Drover details of some case over in Plymouth, where, he claimed, a local man was on trial for immoral earnings. Sam Noble was loudly deploring the sexual mores of the times to Luke Weatherall, who had dropped in to buy cigarette papers and made some remark about throwing—or not throwing?—stones, anyway, he was a poet and the remark was incomprehensible to Sam.

Wolford sat down at the bar next to Jackson, ordered himself an orange juice and asked Jackson if he fancied a chaser.

'Don' mind, yeah,' was the muttered response.

When the beer and a couple of doubles had been downed, Wolford enquired about Johnny. 'Got the kid who was helping you out building up at yours, I hear.'

Jackson belched. 'Little shit.'

'Well, you know women . . .' said Wolford, and waited.

'Bitches, whores and liars!' Jackson pronounced, definitively.

This came close to Wolford's own assessment. 'Yeah, but we love 'em, don't we?' he enquired ambiguously.

'You might,' said Jackson, trying to drain an already empty glass. 'I reckon they're the Devil in disguise.'

'Have another,' suggested Wolford, ordering another orange juice and a double and a pint from

242

the girl who was standing in for Mary Simms, who was still off sick. 'That room you're building. How come you've got the boy helping you, then?'

' 'Twas her done it,' said Jackson, moodily. 'She wanted it.'

'Paula?' asked Wolford.

'Nah—Mrs Thomas,' said Jackson, his rumbling turbulence threatening to erupt into naked rage.

'Really?' said Wolford. 'What she want another room for anyway. All by herself, isn't she?'

Behind them, Barty Clarke was regaling Sam with statistics about prostitution. 'Most of them are under age,' he assured.

'Dunno,' said Jackson, struggling to keep faith with the memory of his Beloved of the White Hands.

But Wolford's feral instincts smelled a secret.

'She got a boyfriend or anything?' he hazarded.

It was a tame enough guess; but to Jackson, in his unhinged state, it seemed like the last straw. Everyone but him had known the truth about Ellen Thomas.

'She got someone, I reckon.'

'Really?' asked Wolford, smoothly ordering another double. 'Anyone we know?'

A voice far down in Jackson whispered that he was about to err, that he had already gone too far, that he had better retreat, that he was about to trespass on a shrine and that the deity who dwelled there was relentless, and merciless, and, once roused, would pursue him for all time.

'Have another, why not?' said Wolford, sliding the glass of whisky towards him. 'You know what, we've got this con still on the loose. No trace of him. Any strange men we have to investigate—

you'd be helping us in our enquiries, in a manner of speaking . . .' He flipped open his wallet and indicated a twenty-pound note.

'Appalling!' reiterated Sam.

The sight of the note set off competing strains in Jackson. He wanted to strike the wallet from Wolford's hand, pick up the bar stool and smash it over the screw's head. He had no need of cash. Ellen Thomas paid him each week on the dot; and while Paula extracted the lion's share, he was not fool enough to let her know the full extent of his earnings. For the first time in his life he was flush. And, in fact, Jackson was not a mercenary man; had he been so he would have been more regular in his habits. Money meant little to him, but he was experiencing that sense of thwarted entitlement which arises when desire and deserts are mismatched. Caught in a conflict, Jackson hesitated.

Wolford took out the twenty-pound note and then, laid on top of it a tenner. He held out the two notes just a little in front of Jackson's sweaty face. 'Between friends,' he remarked. 'We won't say anything to anyone. I've met your good lady.'

Intending to give an impression of moral support, Wolford was referring to Paula, but Jackson supposed it was Ellen the screw meant. To Jackson's drunk-dazed, hope-smashed, frenzied mind, everyone knew his adored one better than him. More to get them out of his sight, and the whole nightmare over with, he grabbed the notes and shoved them into his pocket.

'She's got him staying in her spare room. Don't never see him daytimes,' Jackson said.

As Mr Golightly walked up the garden path at Jackson's, a chorus of voices advised him that they were only twenty-four hours from Tulsa.

Johnny was sitting at the keyboard, a very different boy from the furtive creature Mr Golightly had first seen flattened beneath the Traveller van. And Paula, dancing barefoot, her purple vest showing gleaming tattooed shoulders, resembled some record-breaking, pint-sized javelin thrower.

Jubilation is an expansive emotion. A feeling close to pride began to fill Mr Golightly's breast. 'I'm sorry to break in on the fun,' he said.

Johnny, thrilled at the chance to show off, started up wildly with 'Love Me Do', but Paula checked him. 'Manners! Mr Golightly's come special to see you,'

'Oh, please,' said Mr Golightly, who hated to stand on ceremony.

But Johnny appeared quite at home. 'What's up, chief?'

'I've a message for you,' said Mr Golightly, trying, and failing, not to sound mysterious.

'S'all right,' said Paula. 'I know when to make meself scarce. I'll put the kettle on. Coffee, en't it? Or there's scrumpy, if the vicar's left us any, that is . . .'

*   *   *

Jackson, his skin filled with an inflammable mix of whisky and Newcastle Brown, walked tremblingly back from the Stag. Halfway up the path he paused to piss on the figure on the toadstool. The stream of urine fell short of the pixie which leered cunningly up at Jackson.

'You're out, boyo,' it said. 'Finished, washed up, vamoosed, vanished, neither here nor there, an ex-person, no kind of a man at all.'

'Din know you was Welsh,' said Jackson, beerily.

'Cornish,' said the pixie. 'A piscie, if you want to know. And this is a mushroom, not a toadstool. Not that you're worth telling, hardly.'

It resumed its position of stony aloofness.

Jackson continued his unsteady progress up the path. The front door was wide open and through the lounge door he could see Paula in her purple sequinned strap top. Her skirt had ridden up her thighs and her face was alight with sweat. 'I ain't nothing but a hound dog . . .' she crooned.

'Bitch, more like,' said Jackson. But the pixie— or piscie—had knocked the stuffing out of him, and no one heard him as he made his way on hands and knees up to the bathroom.

CHAPTER ELEVEN

Jackson was wrong about Ellen and Jos Bainbridge: the tableau which had caught his dismayed sight, as he peered through the bungalow's crazy interior window, was not of two lovers. At least not in the way that he supposed.

The night she found him in her kitchen, Ellen had seen Jos Bainbridge, and those we see truly we love—and for all time. They met in the space between worlds, where the rule of quotidian

246

concerns—prudence, common sense, custom, cupidity—like the law of gravity, at a distance from the earth's strong pull, attenuates into airy nothingness, and we are let free to be ourselves; that liberty itself induces love, for who does not secretly long to be released from the cramp of self-obsession and the prison of self-regard? Somewhere in our being the scent of freedom lingers, like the elusive smell of cut grass from a dream of lost summer, or the breeze off fresh and endless oceans. The everyday world is at once too carping and too cautious to admit such recollection, although, if we are lucky, it catches us, fleetingly, as we ride, or run, or paint, or cook, or make love—or music, wine or stories. Only to the blessed does it return in a single quenching shaft, as it did to Ellen Thomas the night she met Jos Bainbridge.

Eros is protean and adopts many shapes, and not all take the forms of amorous attachment. Their nights were spent in a series of picnics, such as children devise away from the peerings of adults, in secret glades or twilit clearings, where the entrance to faeryland might be found and tales are told of rash ones, who have lost their way inside that hidden kingdom and have never been returned.

The night that Jackson had peeped through the window Ellen had been folding Jos Bainbridge in her arms, as a mother might a scared child, or a sister a much-loved brother, off for many years to sea; or a man his sick dog.

'What did happen to put you there?' she had asked. 'Can you say?'

He had told her; and as he spoke his past requisitioned her own memory, so that she knew in

247

future it would never again be entirely hers.

When he woke, he said, his head hurting like hell and fuddled in his mind, he had not gone back to the farm for several days. What disturbed him most was that the man had found out their secret place. Later, he realised that it probably wasn't secret—that the man had known where to come. When he finally returned, the police were called to 'interview' him—he laughed at the word, 'as if,' he said, 'I'd applied for a job with them, or something!' She had explained her state to her father by saying he, Jos, had forced her to have sex and her father had called the police and made her repeat the allegation . . . he saw now it was fear—fear of her father's anger, fear, for all he knew, for her life, from that man, that made her say it . . .

'First time I heard the voice it was in the police cells, waiting to see what they were going to do with me. I'd already "confessed" that I'd been with her, slept with her and told them—they get you to say all kinds of things you don't see the harm in at the time, you see, so I'd said how guilty I felt. But I did. I felt guilty as hell. I didn't force her and it wasn't me who beat her up—but I kept hearing those voices in my head saying I was the Devil, I had done the work of the Devil.'

'But you told them about the man you saw?'

An owl hallooed across the darkening hollow beneath the hills before them.

'I didn't. At first because I didn't know what she'd said, and I wouldn't say anything to get her into trouble with her father. Then, when it became obvious they wanted me to confess to more than having sex with her, I knew there was something going on. But I didn't know what. And there were

248

the voices telling me I was wicked, you see. And I didn't want to say anything to hurt her. So I said nothing and they kept taking me out and putting me back in the cells till I was almost mad—if I wasn't mad already. And then one night there was this other voice that drowned all the others.'

'What did it say?'

'Have you heard a nightingale ever?'

She shook her head.

'Hard to describe unless you've heard a nightingale. It was achingly clear, but also a kind of extraordinary chuckle, a chink into something so deep and so pure and so . . . so lovely, you would die to hear it—like the sweetest bird's song it was, hidden in the dark.'

A bird. She might have guessed. Jos Bainbridge knew what it was to be put in a cage.

'The barrister said I should plead guilty because they'd already got a confession out of me, you see, and my sentence would be lighter. But I wouldn't . . . I can't hear the song of a bird now simply as a sound—it always has that other meaning for me.'

'What is the meaning?' she asked again, and her heart hurt in her ribcage. But it was not the hurt of the tiger's maul—it was the clamour of something wild to be free, like the caged redbreast.

The owl made its faux forlorn call again.

The quiet they sat in was almost too huge to bear. But you sat in darkness and then, if you sat there long enough, you learned to see. Sitting with him like this she was learning to make things out in the dark.

'It's truth,' he said, finally, and she had the sensation that around them the creatures of the night had paused to listen. 'The meaning. A bird can't lie. When I wouldn't plead guilty, the barrister wanted to use the epilepsy with balance of mind disturbed. But it wasn't a fit and I never hurt a scrap of her. I couldn't lie about it, you see.'

Speak the truth and all things vouch for you . . . Yes, thought Ellen Thomas, but that is more likely if there is another on your side.

'But she lied, your girl lied about you?'

He answered so quietly she had to ask him to repeat it. Then, as if addressing not her but some brilliant star chamber, convened far up in the bruised-purple sky, he lifted his chin and spoke—and long afterwards she felt the shadow of the tremor of pity and terror shiver through her.

'She said, in court, I'd raped her and beaten her up. I got ten years, without parole,' he said.

JUNE

CHAPTER ONE

That morning, the spotted flycatchers had come, and had already begun to fashion a nest above the garden door. As Ellen was painting, she heard the gentle whirr of wings as they hovered in the air, plying their beakfuls of building matter, building their nests with impeccable design.

She had been up working for some time, when Wolford called. He walked straight round to the back of the house to where she was standing at her easel. She left off painting at once.

'You're out early, Mr Wolford.'

'The early bird catches the worm.'

'Do you think so? Worms are such unfathomable creatures. When I was a child, boys at my school used to cut them up to watch the separate sections wiggle away. I always thought it so instructive—they seemed to react to injury by taking on quite independent lives. Did you ever do that, Mr Wolford?'

Wolford gave an uncomfortable assent. 'Reckon I did most things when I was a lad. Proper tearaway, I was.'

'Of course, you lived in the village, didn't you? Have you called about anything special? I'm just about to eat breakfast. Would you like some? I'm afraid I have no marmalade.'

Wolford refused breakfast. Side by side, they sat on a garden bench which looked across the fields to the hills as Ellen, very upright, drank coffee from a gold-rimmed china cup. She did not, as she had to Mr Golightly, describe the hermit's congregation of otters in the brook below, but she pointed out a flock of crossbills sitting on the barbed wire at the end of her garden.

'Oh, do look, Mr Wolford, they're rather rare. Do you see the strange bill? It is credited with having been twisted into that shape while attempting to wrest nails from the crucifixion.'

'There's a horse kept in that field, isn't there?' The woman's way of talking made him feel uneasy.

Ellen stared at him. To do this she had to turn her head round. 'What colour horse?'

'A white one, isn't it?' For Christ's sake, what was wrong with that? Wolford had been briefly engaged to a girl who had had a similar effect on him. She had said, once, after they had had sex, 'You weren't thinking of me, were you? You were thinking of we won't say who . . .' and had laughed knowingly.

'How interesting,' said Ellen. 'The white horse. But you've come for something, Mr Wolford . . .?'

Wolford went to the point more quickly than he had intended. 'We've a prisoner out, been missing for some while. You've not seen anyone who might be him?'

Ellen's grey eyes looked dead at his. 'My husband died a while ago and since then I have become rather reclusive. I am sure people will have told you that about me.'

This was true. 'Never pokes her nose out, hardly,' his mother had said.

'So, you haven't seen a man, at all?' said Wolford, uncomfortable, but pushing on none the less.

'Are you asking about my personal life or pursuing an official inquiry?'

254

'I am asking a serious question, Mrs Thompson—'

'Thomas.'

'Excuse me, Thomas. I must tell you that it has been alleged that you have had a man staying here and if his identity is unknown then it's my duty to report the matter to the authorities.'

'Heavens,' said Ellen comfortably, ' "the authorities". Let's see. I'm fifty-four, not entirely beyond repair but no oil painting either, and, unhappily for me, unattached. Someone, in the village—I assume it is—has been kind enough to suggest that a man might still find me passably attractive. Is that what you've come to discuss? My sex life?'

Wolford gave an official note to the clearing of his throat. 'I don't think you've grasped the seriousness of the situation, Mrs Thompson, I beg your pardon, Thomas. This man is dangerous. We have to pursue all avenues of inquiry. He has not been apprehended, unfortunately, and you, and all women, if I may say so, attractive or not, are in danger from him.'

'You know what,' went on Ellen, as if she hadn't heard him, 'it puts me in mind of a wicked story my husband used to tell. About an elderly spinster— are you sure you won't have any coffee?—who rang the police to say there was a man in her bedroom. The police said they were unable to ascertain the nature of her complaint.'

'The man is a serious sex offender,' said Wolford, by now in a cold rage.

'Goodness,' said Ellen, turning suddenly round to him again. 'So you have kindly come to warn or protect me. Is that it?'

'To an extent,' said Wolford, stiffly. 'But also there is the question of this man, it has been suggested—'

'I do wonder who that could be?' said Ellen. 'Isn't it exciting? Would you like some toast? The butter isn't quite rancid. Perhaps it is my neighbour, Mr Golightly. He comes over from time to time. We talk about poetry.'

'Where would that take place?' asked Wolford, thinking of what Jackson had said about the bedroom. He supposed it was possible that the two were having some holiday romance.

'Where do we discuss the poetry, do you mean? Oh dear, Mr Wolford, I think I must draw the line at that. It isn't your business—is it?—to know the circumstances in which a discussion of Robert Frost took place between consenting adults.'

Over the barbed wire, in fact, the very first time she had met him. *Good fences make good neighbours*, he had said, and had asked her no questions.

The sun disappeared behind a cloud and her bare arms gave an excuse to say she must go inside. As she saw Wolford off she wondered what Mr Golightly would make of the roles she had concocted for them—two washed-up, middle-aged people, consoling each other in their enforced solitude.

She waited till she was sure Wolford had gone and then went to the spare bedroom. Lifting the bedcover from his face, she thought: he expunges himself so successfully it's as if he isn't here.

'Someone from the prison,' she mouthed—and he nodded to show he understood. She wondered if it was a relief that something had happened at last.

256

*   *   *

All day she painted in a kind of fervent clarity. Never had she worked as she worked now, allowing the birds to fly from airy otherness into the hidden alembic of her creating source, then out down her arm again, through the brush in her hand. They were strange birds, ravens—almost human in their habits. Long ago, in Gilead, the prophet Isaiah had been fed by ravens—one of many such stories—bizarre when you thought about it—of the hospitality of creatures to humankind. Why ever did they bother? But in the story, it was their Creator who sent the rescuing birds . . .

As their little portion of the earth spun further from the light she went to fetch him. The days were so long now she left it till later. He was out of bed already, waiting, with no shadow of impatience; it crossed her mind that he was waiting to be led away.

'Who was it, from the prison?'

'Brian Wolford. He lives here—or rather his mother does.'

Bainbridge pulled a face. 'That's bad luck—he's got a thing about nonces.'

'Nonces?'

'Sex offenders. You don't get many in Dartmoor because it has no sex offenders treatment programme. Only those like me who insist they're innocent get there—"refuseniks", they call us.'

He had made such light of his time there she had hardly registered it. Ellen had a sudden flash of the reality of what he'd undergone. She pictured the ominous squared entrance with its heavy iron bell and before it the portal arch with its virgilian motto—'Parcere subjectis et debellare superbos': to spare the vanquished and subdue the arrogant—and behind it the anonymous granite, passively forbidding.

Jos Bainbridge had been through hell enough—he must be spared—he must never go back.

'Another "refusenik" I knew told me Wolford turned a blind eye when he was done over by some of the "better" class of inmates. Reckoned Wolford knew who did it but kept quiet about it. He's unpopular with the other screws. They don't like types like Wolford giving them a bad name.'

'He struck me as a mother's boy. Prowls about with a bully's air and a self-satisfied look on his face. He just wandered into the garden one evening, when I was sketching, without so much as a by your leave. Poor Mr Jackson was horrified.'

Outside, the sky was drawn silk across the dying lamp of the sun. About the shadowy garden bats had begun to flitter, mutely petitioning. Her sketchbook was near and for something to do she picked it up and began to pencil the outline of a tree in the fading light.

Bainbridge sat on the sofa, folded down in introspection. I'll miss you, she thought, and mentally shook herself, getting up to fetch their supper tray from the kitchen. When she returned he had taken up the sketchbook and was looking at it.

'Sorry—d'you mind?'

She was surprised that she didn't. 'Go ahead.'

'No, it was rude of me. I should have asked.'

She gestured that it was OK and he flipped back looking at the previous sketches.

'Who's this?'

He had stood up and passed the book to her—the portrait she had done of Johnny.

'The boy who's been helping out here—on your room, actually.'

'Who is he?'

'Johnny Spence. A local boy. Clever—I like him. What is it?'

He was taking the sketch pad over to the door and then out into the garden. It was lighter than inside but he rarely ventured there.

'It's Rosie,' he said, almost stepping on her foot as he pushed the page towards her. His face had gone as pale as the imminent moon.

'Rosie?' From the way her heart was being pressed to death she knew who he must mean.

'The girl I loved. It's her, no question—like as two peas. Where does he live?'

He had never named her. She had never asked. She didn't even know where Johnny lived though it must be somewhere in the village. 'I can find out,' she said, 'My neighbour, Mr Golightly, will know.'

CHAPTER TWO

In the months after her husband's death Ellen had felt she might wither away with loneliness. She had loved Robert physically, emotionally and mentally, and, to her surprise—for she was not a woman who expected much—he had seemed to reciprocate each of these different strands of love. There had only once been a question mark over their happiness—a period of dull agony when he had become sexually withdrawn and generally preoccupied and she had wondered about Dawn Phillips, the smart brunette who was the racing correspondent on the paper for which Robert worked. Eventually, her face flushed and her heart racing, she had raised this with her husband, steeling herself to hear the worst and he had met her timid enquiry with roaring, reassuring laughter. 'Good God, girl,' he had said, 'she's a piranha. D'you think I want my blasted head examining? It's my blasted prostate not Phillips I'm worrying over.'

But it was his heart, not his prostate, which took him from her. Later, she wondered if she had mistaken her fear of the dark-haired girl for some anticipatory fear of that other dark despoiler of partnerships.

Ellen never got over missing Robert. But as the months went by, before her encounter with the gorse bush, she had begun to find, like some wise woman gathering simples in a springtime wood, a few solaces in living alone. One of these was a sense that, left to her own devices, she knew just when to do things. Before, she had been Robert's willing executive. 'Let's go to Vienna!' he would say, and she would, gladly, organise the trip. Or, 'Let's have dinner at the Café Royal' or 'go to the pictures' or 'the races'. Once she had suggested they visit an exhibition, Matisse, in Paris, and she had been a little wounded at how hard it had been to get him to agree. He had loved it when he got there, though. They had stayed in a cheap hotel near St Sulpice, and he had teased her that she was someone he had picked up in the café-bar across the square and taken back to the hotel for a fling. 'Come on,' he had breathed into her ear, in the sexually enticing Paris dark, which smelled of pastries and ambiguous sanitation and the scent of strangers. 'It'll soon be back to the wife, so turn me another trick, will you?' And she had been pleased to oblige.

She had shaped her will to Robert's, and with him gone she'd had to learn to find a way of her own. It had not been easy, but with the loss of other footings she had acquired judgement. So, the evening after Wolford's visit, and seeing the light was on in Spring Cottage, she said to Bainbridge, 'Go back to your room, will you, I'm going out for a while.' And then, as an afterthought, 'I'll leave the house dark.'

*   *   *

Mr Golightly had spent the day reading his own work. It was a long while since he had read it through and there were parts he found he had misremembered, parts he wished he could rewrite, and some he'd forgotten and preferred not to be reminded of. He was still up when Ellen tapped lightly on the window. If he felt surprise at receiving a visit so late from his unsociable neighbour, he didn't betray it but offered Ellen a glass of hock.

'Thank you,' she said, dropping on to the perilous orange sofa.

'I'd value your opinion on this,' said Mr Golightly, setting down the vicar's book and pouring wine into the toothglass. 'I think it's rather good myself. The Germans are at their best with wine and music.'

'But not jokes, or Jews?' suggested Ellen.

261

Mr Golightly made no further comment but merely sipped his hock. The wine was the colour of liquid sovereigns. Ellen had been given a sovereign as a child by a great-uncle who had been in India and claimed to have a scar left by a tiger on his buttock. It had been an abiding childhood fear that he might one day offer to show her the wound.

'Speaking of Jews,' she went on, 'I wondered if you could tell me where your boy is?'

Mr Golightly started at this. For a fraction of a second he misunderstood. Then he recognised she meant Johnny.

'Yes, it is rather a ghetto existence he has led, but I hope we are beginning to change all that.'

'I need to get in touch with him,' said Ellen. 'It's quite urgent.'

Mr Golightly looked at his neighbour. She wasn't an alarmist or a troublemaker. 'I can fetch him now if you wish,' he said.

'Oh, if it's not too late I can go,' said Ellen, not wanting to give trouble herself.

But Mr Golightly insisted. He suspected Johnny would still be up and it was no bother, he assured her. While he may be as old as the hills he had not forgotten his manners. They forbade him, he said, to allow an attractive woman out on her own on a dark night.

It was not, Ellen thought, impossible to imagine Mr Golightly, in a Paris hotel bedroom. She lay back on the uncomfortable sofa, drinking the cool gold wine. The music playing on the cassette recorder was Mozart; 'Don Giovanni,' she thought.

*   *   *

Up at Jackson's, Paula and Johnny were arguing in the kitchen.

'No, you gotta,' Paula was saying.

'I don't do school,' Johnny repeated. 'You don't learn nothing there.' There might have been a point in staying with his stepdad.

'Bollocks,' said Paula. 'You're bright, you are. You got to get on in this world.'

'School's shit. Bet you never did it.'

Paula, who was taking some clothes out of the tumble-dryer she'd recently bought on a scheme which gave you two years' interest-free credit, flicked a shirt at Johnny's head. 'What's that got to do with it, stupid? You stay here, you go to school, right?'

'Mr Golightly never.'

'That's different,' said Paula, smoothing out a towel. 'Artists, writers an' that, they're not normal.'

'Nor his son, didn't, he told me. The Queen never neither.'

'Well, you're not the Queen less I'm very much mistaken. Anyway, what's your mum say?'

Johnny flushed. 'She don't mind.'

'What 'bout your dad, then?'

'He's not my dad.'

'What 'bout your real dad? What's he say?' The flush deepened. 'Or don't you know where he is? Never mind,' Paula relentlessly continued, folding the towels. 'You're the same as me, you are. Neither of us got dads. D'you know your real dad's name?'

Johnny shook his head dumbly. His mum never talked about his real dad.

'Me neither,' said Paula, cheerfully. 'Still, I'm better off than you. I got me mum's name, I en't

263

got no stupid man's.'

*   *   *

Don Giovanni, still defiant, was being dragged
down to Hell when Mr Golightly returned with
Johnny, whose sensation at hearing his employer's
voice at Paula's door had been profound relief. His
first thought on entering the parlour at Spring
Cottage was to see if he could catch the tune of
what he was hearing. Yup—he thought he had it—
definitely the last number, which was easy once
you'd got it in your ear.

'Johnny,' said Ellen, who had risen from the
sofa, 'I'm sorry to trouble you but I wonder, could
you tell me where we can find your mother?'

Gratitude at escaping Paula's inquisition and the
restorative effects of Mozart's harmonies softened
Johnny's usual defences. He shot an enquiring look
at Mr Golightly, who nodded reassuringly.

'Might do. Why?' Johnny said.

*   *   *

The house was dark when Wolford returned to
Foxgloves, but his sixth sense told him it was not
unoccupied. Jackson's ladder was lying along the
wall of the bungalow. If there was any trouble he
could always invent an intruder on the roof.

Wolford, for all his bulk, was a light mover. He
was careful as he mounted the ladder and walked
quietly across the roof to the window which looked
inside. But it was too dark to see anything.

Lights were on next door at Spring Cottage. The
white horse the woman had been so funny about

264

was cantering round the field behind the gardcn. Wolford liked horses. As a child, he had ridden on the moor and he'd had thoughts of joining the mounted police. He stowed away the ladder and stood in Ellen Thomas's garden, beneath the pear tree where the green fruit was beginning to form, watching the horse pass soundlessly before him in the oblique light of the risen moon.

CHAPTER THREE

Bainbridge was in his room when Ellen Thomas returned from Spring Cottage. She sat on the sofa, looking out at the moon, which had etched a bright scimitar into the tarnished-silver sky.

A downy feather of memory drifted back—the day she and Robert married. They had delayed their honeymoon by a couple of days for him to finish an assignment, and she had cooked a special meal for him the evening of their wedding day. The food—she couldn't now remember what it was—had tasted disgusting, and Robert had gone on stoically eating it and saying how it was 'fine' till she had lost her temper and thrown her plate at the wall and rushed from the room screaming, 'It isn't, it isn't, it's bloody awful, you know it is!'

He had come and found her in the bedroom and peeled off all her clothes, except for her stockings (white for the wedding), and made love to her, laughingly, passionately . . . a homecoming.

She looked at the painting on the easel she had finished that day.

'Ravens, aren't they?' He had appeared, so quiet

265

she hadn't heard him in his socks.

'Yes.' It didn't matter who saw the painting now.

'There were ravens used to nest up on High Tor.'

'D'you know why a raven's like a writing desk?' she asked, wanting to delay what she had to tell him.

'No. Is it?'

'It's a riddle—from *Alice*.'

'I never read it—I didn't read much till I was buried,' he apologised.

'It doesn't matter,' Ellen said hastily. She felt strangely shy. 'I think we've found Rosie.'

'No!' he sat down on the sofa. 'How?'

'Someone you'd like, I think. My neighbour, Mr Golightly, knows Johnny. You were right to spot the similarity—she's his mother.'

'My God!'

'Yes.'

'Now,' she said, rather severely, for she was visited by a sudden fear that she might weep, 'we have to be practical. No point in spoiling the ship for a ha'p'orth of tar. Rosie's not here at present—'

'You mean she was? In Calne?'

'Yes, I know. All this time—but she's not actually here now, she's been away, I don't know why and I don't think Johnny does, but he's meeting her next Sunday. He's going to take Mr Golightly with him. Mr Golightly has met Rosie and she seems to trust him.'

'When did they meet?'

'I don't know that either. I'm sorry—I feel I should have been doing more instead of going on with that pointless room.'

It seemed now like the action of a deranged

266

woman. Why had she done it? As a flight from her own want? Because she needed someone to share the anguish which had pent her in?

'It's OK,' he said. 'I couldn't have coped with this till now. You can't hurry the leaves on the trees—things have their own way of happening. I couldn't, I mean, you've been . . . no one could've, really . . .'

She looked at him—and he looked back levelly. In another existence, she thought, you and I would have been partners, cellmates and soulmates.

'The thing is, you see,' he said, 'we'll always have this, here . . . we'll know it, like the sheep and the leer . . .'

And that was true, too. Real love isn't mush, she thought, it isn't spongy sentiment or sanctimonious milk and water—it is knowledge unspoken, subtle and illimitable as the weather: tacit, unassailable, lawless, inviolable. It is difficult precisely because it doesn't—won't—die; it's a power stronger than reason, because it laughs at the neediness of reason.

'I don't know who it is can have seen you,' she said, not needing to answer him directly. 'But we'd better be extra careful. I'll lay Jackson off in the morning. He seems to have laid Johnny off already. And then it's a matter of keeping our nerve.'

CHAPTER FOUR

Mr Golightly was put out to find Nadia Fawns, dressed in startling black lace, when he answered an insistent tap-tapping at the back door the following Sunday morning.

'Hello there. Just called to remind you that you're invited over to ours for drinks.' She didn't want any repetition of the unreliable behaviour over the writers' meeting.

'Ah,' said Mr Golightly, mentally fishing around for a plausible let-out.

'Any time from twelve noon onwards and for one or two special people there's lunch to follow—but keep that under your hat, won't you?'

Mr Golightly promised that if he had a hat the information would remain securely beneath it. The last thing he wanted to do was attend a drinks party, let alone a luncheon. 'I may only be able to look in for a few minutes,' he volunteered.

'Promise you'll come . . .' Nadia smoothed the black lace.

'I have another engagement but I'll put my head round the door.'

*　　　*　　　*

It is a feature of the English summer that it is capable of almost any enormity, and the day which had been promised 'fine and sunny' grew baleful and threatening. A warm front, in from the Bristol Channel, unrolled a thick carpet of clammy mist across the west.

'I was going to have the drinks on the lawn,' Nadia complained to Sam. She'd had the fish pond cleaned specially and took the weather personally.

Sam wasn't bothered what the weather brought so long as it didn't bring Paula. He'd had enough trouble trying to account for that remark about the tearooms she'd made when they'd met so

268

unfortunately last Sunday in the high street. The fateful snooze had brought in its train further episodes of energetic passion with Nadia. Sam was worn out, and exercised over what to do should the two women meet again. It was a blessing to open the door at noon and be met only by Morning Claxon's bosom.

Conversation to start with was a little one-sided. Hugh was undergoing a liver cleanse, which, Morning explained, confined his intake to nothing but apple juice and Epsom salts. He sent his apologies, and Morning. She outlined for their education the philosophy of her guru, Swami Chandraseka Ananda (formerly, Mr Eric Handley of Stevenage). Sam shuffled bowls of nuts, and ashtrays, until Nadia reminded him of the effects of passive smoking and crisply informed him that, the weather not withstanding, anyone who planned to smoke would be asked to do so outside.

Keith arrived without the vicar, but at the same time as Kath Drover from the Stag, who had brought along a couple of bottles of Hungarian red they were trying out from a shipper who was setting up in Exeter. Colin, Kath said, was up at the pub but hoped to be along shortly . . . such a shame that Mary Simms was still sick as they had never felt a scrap of worry leaving the Stag in her hands, the replacement girl was not the same at all and Colin had had to check the till twice, which you never had to do with Mary.

Lavinia Galsworthy, who arrived after Kath, broke the news that Mary Simms was moving into her studio flat, the one once rented by Luke. Lavinia said Mary appeared to be in strapping form. The girl had filled out a lot, lost that peaky look she once had. She felt safer with a woman tenant, Lavinia said. The way young Luke had smoked she'd always been worrying she'd land up burned alive.

Cherie Wolford, who was hoping her son, Brian, might manage to get along to the party later—Sunday was a problem for them up at the prison, with the new governor introducing a whole new rota system—said she'd had high expectations of Mary Simms and Luke. But from what she'd been able to make out from Paula's mum, since Luke had been living in Rabbit Row he'd his nose in his writing from dawn to dusk and never saw a living soul hardly—not even Mr Golightly who'd been such a pal of his. All work and no play, was what Cherie said she felt like telling him!

It was true, Kath Drover said, you never saw young Luke up at the Stag these days, but then Mary had been off work since Easter so, you never knew, maybe that was the reason. At which Morning Claxon announced to the room at large that Love was Everything—a remark which no one knew how to respond to, so it was perhaps fortunate that at that point Mr Golightly arrived . . .

*   *   *

Paula had heard about the drinks party up at the Stag from the Drovers and was fuming that neither she, nor her mum, were invited. She'd been quite taken by the offer of running the tearooms. That stupid old git Sam Noble needn't think he could pick her up and put her down as though she were garbage! Although she was officially due at work, Paula, in her shortest skirt and skimpiest top,

270

dropped by Sam's house just as the vicar was arriving.

The vicar was also dressed to the nines, in silk trousers, a combat jacket and a pair of high-heeled mock-croc ankle boots. She complimented Paula on her outfit and embraced her warmly over the bronze-effect Cupid. 'Come on in,' she urged, taking Paula's arm.

'I en't been invited,' said Paula, meaningfully.

'I shall say I brought you,' said the vicar, whose old personality had reasserted itself.

Giggling, in a manner which Sam, when he answered the door, found unnerving, the two women, ignoring their host, processed arm in arm, to be hailed by Barty Clarke.

'Here come two of my favourite ladies and don't they look gorgeous!' After the unsteady behaviour of the Pope child, Barty was keen that peaceful relations between himself and the vicar be restored.

'No, really,' Mr Golightly was saying. 'I must be off . . .' He found himself jammed into a corner, cut off from a means of escape by a barricade of black lace.

'Oh, not before you've seen my cuttings. We're fellow artists, you and I,' said Nadia emphatically. She had just witnessed the arrival of the vicar, and Paula.

*   *   *

Mr Golightly had adopted the old country habit of leaving his door unlocked so that his house should be available for all comers. Johnny, by now used to popping in and out, was already waiting inside

271

when Wolford came by Spring Cottage.

Johnny had just come out of the bathroom when he saw, from the stairs, the top of Wolford's ginger head. Johnny backed upstairs and into the box bedroom (the repository of the late Emily Pope's tax correspondence), where he stayed still as stone.

Wolford looked around the parlour, coughed and called out, but there was no answering response. The laptop was open on a table by the window and Wolford walked over and idly tapped the key which lit up the messages.

Someone called 'Nemo'. Looked like weird stuff going on there. Maybe Golightly was part of some Internet child porn ring, which would explain his interest in the Spence kid.

Johnny waited till he was sure Wolford had left, counted 'hippopotamus' two hundred times, and then slipped out through the back door and under the wire to Ellen Thomas's. The door from the garden was open and he was looking at her painting when she came through.

'It's good!'

'Thank you. You don't happen to know why a raven is like a writing desk?'

''Cos there's a "b" in both and an "n" in neither?'

'That's clever,' said Ellen, once the penny had dropped.

''Tisn't me, it was on the Internet.' Johnny never took credit which wasn't his due. 'Mr Golightly asked me to find it.'

'Where is he—you should be going.'

'Don't know. Just been over there now but that screw was round.'

'Oh, Lord,' said Ellen Thomas, 'did he see you?'

272

'No, I was upstairs. He don't like me.'

'I don't think he likes anyone. There's something horribly creepy about that man. I'd really like you to have left before he comes snooping round again.'

*   *   *

'No, no, it won't take a tic, I promise,' Nadia Fawns insisted. 'I've got a copy of *A Knight* here.' She all but pushed Mr Golightly before her up the stairs. Across the room she had observed Paula's midriff, bare but for a large glinting 'ruby' in the navel.

*   *   *

'Still not there,' said Johnny, who was watching Spring Cottage. 'What'll we do? We oughta get going before that screw sticks his face in here.'

'Give it five more minutes,' Ellen suggested.

*   *   *

'No,' said Nadia, 'it has to be ink for signings. My fountain pen's in here somewhere. You know how it is with handbags . . . ?'

'Really, I must—'

'Madam,' said Barty Clarke, looming beside them, 'when you have a moment, a word in your shell-like . . .'

*   *   *

'OK,' said Ellen. 'Look, you go on ahead. And will you give your mother this?'

273

'What is it?'

'It's from the man who wants to talk to her. Tell your mother he isn't angry, he just wants to talk to her.'

Johnny unwrapped a handkerchief and stared at the dirty disintegrating scrap of crimson material inside. 'What is it?'

'I think it was a rose.'

'Why's he want to give Mum this?' asked Johnny, suspiciously.

Ellen consulted her conscience. If Johnny was to convey the treasured keepsake it seemed right he should know why. 'Years ago, your mother and he were friends. She gave that to him then. He wants her to see he still thinks the same of her.'

'It's not my dad, is it?'

'I don't know,' Ellen said. 'Truly, Johnny, I don't know the answer to that.'

*   *   *

Wolford had woken that morning from a dream about crushing a rabbit under his boot. The rabbit had bled from the mouth and looked up at him with beseeching hazel eyes. When he spotted Johnny Spence leaving Ellen Thomas's house it was as if his mind had disgorged a dangerous secret.

Wolford's rational self told him it was improbable that Ellen Thomas was harbouring anyone, let alone an escaped con. Jackson was unreliable—very likely he'd caught sight of a stray visitor, maybe even a lover, who the woman might understandably be shy about. Either that or the whole story was a drunk's fantasy. Far more potently than any prisoner, it was the boy she had working there, Johnny Spence, he was curious about.

He'd promised his mother to look in to some drinks party that morning. Walking back up the high street, after parking his car, Wolford decided to call in at Spring Cottage. He didn't buy that story Golightly had spun him about the boy—he could tell it, there was something dodgy going on there.

*   *   *

Johnny's stomach was tight as he set off for Buckland Beacon. It was a long time since he had seen his mum and he felt almost afraid to see her again. The message he had for her, and the scrap of velvet in his pocket, bothered him. The mist had come down heavy by the time he reached the cattle grid so's you couldn't hardly see your hand in front of your face. He missed Mr Golightly and wished he'd waited that bit longer. He'd have felt safe with Mr Golightly.

As Johnny crossed the boundary of the moor, a car slowed down behind him, making a rattle on the metal bars. He waited for the car to pass but it drew up beside him and the window was brought down.

'Well, now, Mister Spence, and where might you be tripping off to so lightly in the mist and the snow.'

'It's not snowing,' said Johnny, blunt, but scared.

'Ooh, he's shrewd as well as bonny. Hop in,' Wolford said.

Johnny stood by the car and the mist danced

towards him and away again in soft seductive swirls. He had never felt more alone. His instinct was to bolt. The screw wanted something from him he could tell; but his mum was waiting. If he went straight to her now the screw would certainly follow and although he didn't exactly know why this mustn't happen he knew it mustn't and it was up to him to see it didn't.

'OK,' he said, suddenly, and opened the passenger door and got in beside Wolford.

Wolford had not continued up the road to the party after leaving Spring Cottage. He'd hung around, near the lambing pen, where you could see who was coming and going. When Johnny emerged from Foxgloves, Wolford's heart had contracted so violently he thought for a moment he was having an attack—his dad had died of his heart. He'd gone, almost mechanically, back to the car and had followed the boy up the road. But he'd no formed plan as to what he was doing. Johnny's sudden swift compliance rattled him.

'So, where are you off to then, Mister Spence?' he enquired, cautiously. Any slight resistance and he was ready to drop the boy and drive on.

Johnny fingered the scrap of red velvet in his pocket which had once been a rose. 'Southbrook,' he said, calculating fast—he reckoned he could cut back up to the beacon from there. 'You can drop me off if you like.'

CHAPTER FIVE

It was warm when Rosie had set out and she'd brought no coat or cardigan. Waiting in the mist on the top of the beacon, she shuddered beneath her thin dress. She was half desperate, half reluctant to see Johnny. If only, she thought, you could start over again, you might get it right next time . . .

She sat down on the boulder by the Ten Commandments and lit a cigarette. Someone had been cleaning the carving. Grandma would have been pleased. Incredible in this day and age that there were people whose job it was to clean the Commandments. The clearing operation seemed to have stopped at the commandment not to bear false witness. Well, she'd broken that one, for sure, along with all the rest . . .

*   *   *

'Listen,' said Ellen. She thought she'd seen a figure up the road by the lambing pen as she saw Johnny off, but it had disappeared now. 'I think we should get out of here. The mist is so heavy no one'll see us. I don't want you here in case that vile man comes back. He might have reported this to someone.'

She'd gone to Bainbridge's room where he was lying flat in his usual position, except he seemed to take up even less space than usual.

'Whatever you think . . .'

He left it, his tone said, to her—for himself he didn't care. But she now, after all this time, was filled with a sense of vital urgency. 'Where can I take you that will be safe? I'll leave Mr G. a note.'

It was funny, they had hardly spent any time together, she and Mr Golightly, yet when they met it was as if he were her oldest friend. She would miss him, too, when he left Spring Cottage—she almost regretted they weren't having, as that horrible man had insinuated, a love affair.

'I don't know.'

'Think—where's safe till they've spoken to Rosie?'

'I don't know—the mire maybe . . . ?'

*   *   *

At Southbrook, Wolford said, 'The weather's pretty rough. I'll take you on where you're going.'

Johnny had prepared what he was going to say next. He wasn't having the screw track him to where his mum was waiting. Mr Golightly could tell her about the man. His job was to lose Wolford and make sure Wolford didn't find her. 'Yeah, OK. I'll show you.'

Directing the screw, mostly by instinct, because the conditions made it hard to see, Johnny remembered the day he had taken Mr Golightly to the mire and told him about the sheep. He got Wolford to drop him by the track which led to the old sheep cot. It was so quiet in the baffling mist they might have been on Mars.

'Yeah, well, thanks,' Johnny said, getting out of the car, and his heart hit the soles of his feet when Wolford got out too.

'Lonely spot this. What you plan to do here, then, son?'

278

'I need a piss,' Johnny said, and walked off deliberately up the track to behind the sheep cot. He'd undone his flies when he felt a hand on his waist.

Johnny turned and kicked hard in the direction of Wolford's groin. Then he ran towards the mire. He knew it well enough during the hours of daylight but with the mist down it was trickier to see the lie of the land.

Johnny's kick knocked Wolford off balance but it missed its target. Thwarted desire, mingled with alarm at what he'd been about to do, flamed into bare panic and rage and he plunged after the boy. Unaware where he was following, he made some progress by sheer momentum, across the marsh, then staggered, swore, and began to founder. With his athletic strength he had almost managed to haul himself out, when Johnny, approaching along a solid spur of land, kicked him again, this time full in the face.

Wolford screamed, flailed around, and then grabbed at Johnny's ankle, pulling the boy towards him.

*   *   *

Inside the sheep cot they heard the cries. 'Wait there,' Ellen said. 'Don't move till I come back. Just wait here. Promise me you won't move . . .'

The last thing she saw of Jos Bainbridge was his assenting eyes, like great drops of dark rain.

CHAPTER SIX

It was felt by many as regrettable that the latest edition of the *Backbiter* should appear with the headline SHOCKING SCENES AT FILM DIRECTOR'S PARTY so hard upon the terrible catastrophes which hit Great Calne. It was Barty Clarke, himself, people said, who started the whole thing, telling Nadia Fawns that it was Paula's dad, Jenson, who had been up in court down in Plymouth, for living on immoral earnings. But then Nadia Fawns shouldn't have said what she said to Paula—though, as Kath Drover said, by rights the little madam shouldn't have been at the party at all.

'Mr Samuel Noble, the eminent local film director,' ran the story 'spoke of his dismay when two of his guests attacked each other at his home in Great Calne on Sunday. "I was having a few friends over for drinks," said Mr Noble, whose film about lady footballers was once tipped for a prize at the Cannes Film Festival, "when suddenly a fight broke out. Until then it was a most civilised occasion. I can only put it down to a misunderstanding between two of the ladies which unfortunately got out of hand."'

Sam rang Barty. '*Nice Girl* was a film about jockeys, not footballers,' he said, very irritated. Barty was apologetic but explained he could do nothing till the next edition. He advised Sam to write to the editor, correcting the error.

Nadia Fawns read the article while at Georgina's having a pedicure. The recent tragedies took up the greater part of the conversation, but Di also had happier news to impart. Her boyfriend, Steve, a tattooist, who'd gone off unexpectedly to Western Australia, had e-mailed, equally unexpected, to say he couldn't live without her and if she would join him out there he would make an honest woman of her—or at any rate they could try setting up a Body Beautiful Boutique together and see how they shook down. On balance, Di said, she thought he was sincere—so far as anyone who practised an artistic profession could be. She was selling up and moving on and guess who was buying the business?

According to Di, the vicar had written to the bishop, explaining that she had lost her faith, or, more accurately, that she had found she had never had one. She had spoken to the college down at Plymouth and had arranged to switch next term from her counselling course to 'Beauty and Hairdressing'. It was Paula who had suggested that the vicar should take over the running of Georgina's; the vicar was still in two minds about whether she should also take over the name.

The bishop had received the vicar's news with his usual calm; it was Keith, the husband—wasn't it always the way, Di suggested, giving Nadia's big toenail a going over with an emery board—who was making the fuss. But the vicar, now freed of hampering Christian sentiments, had apparently told her husband she had been looking through the bank statements and if he didn't push off—though in fact, Di confided, she understood much stronger language than *that* had been used!—the vicar would take legal steps to recover her missing share of their joint funds.

Nadia, with toenails freshly scarlet, drove straight from Oakburton to Sam's to recover her kitchenware. 'My kitchen's nearly finished so I'll get this out of your way.' Not that Sam Noble would be seeing much of her cooking in future. Dear Barty, who had told her that that common little slut's father was a pimp, had also given her to understand that Sam had spoken most disrespectfully about her novel. The moment she'd got her new kitchen organised Barty would be the one coming over for dinner. Blood will out, as she had remarked to that trollop! It certainly wasn't Nadia's fault that things had turned so nasty. She had had to defend herself, Barty had assured her; everyone knew that that was why she had pulled Paula's hair. She was sorry Mr Golightly had got caught up in the crossfire but, then, like her he was a writer and everything was grist to a writer's mill ...

Di had also divulged that Patsy and Joanne had called in on Hugh, during their recent visit to their old stamping ground. It seemed that Morning had been studying crithomancy and proposed reopening the tearooms so that she could run classes on the ancient art of divination by dough. It looked as if Patsy and Joanne would be coming back to manage the tearooms in conjunction with some of Morning's workshops, so that put paid to any ridiculous ideas Sam Noble might have had about that particular little tart!

*   *   *

'Why didn't you tell me? Is Jenson me proper name, then?' Paula had not gone straight round to her mum's from Sam Noble's party. After slapping Nadia Fawns's stupid face for her she had needed time to calm down.

282

'How was I to know he was the same Jenson as your father?' sobbed Paula's mum, weakly. 'It was all such a long time ago.'

'Oh, thanks, mum,' said Paula. 'I'm only twenty-four, for Christ's sake!'

'Who could know he'd gone to the bad, like that? I was in love with him, you wouldn't understand,' said her mum, blowing her nose into some kitchen roll.

'No,' said Paula, 'thank Christ I wouldn't!' If she had needed it, this would have convinced her that people did the most unbelievable things in the name of love.

CHAPTER SEVEN

Mr Golightly did not attend Ellen Thomas's funeral. He had another appointment that day but he met Rosie and Johnny Spence as they came out of the churchyard together, hand in hand. Most of the villagers, many of whom had never spoken to Ellen Thomas, were present. With the departure of the vicar, the bishop had conducted the ceremony himself, feeling that the tragic events which Calne had suffered merited recognition from the highest quarters.

Mr Golightly had not seen Johnny or his mother since the day of the catastrophe. Both looked pale and Rosie was plainly under pressure, but she told him she was managing and that till things got sorted she and Johnny were staying where she'd been before, in Plymouth, with her old friend, Jean. Mr Golightly invited Johnny for a drive. He

283

promised to run him back to Plymouth afterwards.

The old man and the young boy walked wordlessly down the high street to Spring Cottage where the Traveller was parked in its familiar place in the front garden. Mr Golightly waited till Johnny was settled in the passenger seat. 'Where shall we go?' he asked.

Johnny felt unaccountably shy. 'Don't mind,' he said, looking at the floor of the van.

'What would you say to going to the mire?'

'Yeah, all right,' said Johnny, obscurely relieved.

They drove, and this time Mr Golightly needed no directions. Johnny stared through the window. Small birds threaded through branches of gorse; bands of shaggy ponies stood stoutly among bracken, cropping the velvety grass; the sky was robin's-egg blue. 'A God day,' one of the old bell-ringers had said in church, 'Mrs Thomas has a God day for her send-off!'

It couldn't have been less like the scene of the previous Sunday as they drove up the lumpy track and parked by the path which led to the sheep cot.

Mr Golightly and Johnny walked together down to the edge of the mire and for a long while nothing was said.

It was Johnny who broke the silence. 'Mrs Thomas stopped that bastard from killing me.'

'Yes,' said Mr Golightly. 'I guessed that was the case.'

'I was trying to get away from him,' said Johnny. He looked ill. 'He was, you know, after me . . .'

All about them was deep quiet. Mr Golightly returned his gaze to the mire where a curlew had alighted and was delicately foraging with its long curved beak.

'I tried to kick him under,' Johnny said at last.

The curlew stopped its foraging and stood, head poised, as if to catch their conversation.

'Well,' said Mr Golightly, choosing his words, 'to hold fast to life is life's most powerful instinct and, as I suggested once, death improves some people.'

'But Mrs Thomas died too. If I'd waited for you it wouldn't have happened, would it?'

For the want of a nail the shoe was lost, for the want of the shoe the horse was lost . . . Mr Golightly's heart contracted. 'That's brave,' he said. 'Not many people are able to do that.'

'What?' asked Johnny. If Mr Golightly hadn't known better he might have imagined the boy was angry.

'Not many people can own their part in a chain of error.' For the want of the horse the battle was lost . . . 'If I'd not got distracted I would have been there for you in time, and if—'

'And if my mum had stayed with my dad we wouldn't have fetched up with my stepdad.' Johnny still had in his pocket the remnants of the rose, that the man he'd learned was his dad had given Mrs Thomas to give him to give his mum.

'Possibly that too. But all these "and ifs"—they are what life is: a series of decisions we can't know the consequences of in advance, and who's to say finally which are "good" and which "bad"?'

'But Mrs Thomas is dead.'

And all for the want of a horseshoe nail . . . ?

'I know. That's a hard one.'

'I thought I was dead, too.'

In his mind's eye, Mr Golightly saw a small boy in a carpenter's shop, his head bent, engrossed in shaping a piece of wood to fashion a catapult, with

285

no thought for the world to come.

'I didn't want to die,' Johnny said. For the rest of his life he would see Mrs Thomas hauling him away from Wolford's grip and herself being pulled into the mire. 'Run,' she had cried out, 'run, Johnny,' and when he had started instinctively towards the sheep cot, 'no, not there . . .'

It was where, later, they found his dad.

'She told me not to go to where, you know, he was.' Johnny, unwilling to give his new father a name, nodded towards the sheep cot. 'We might've have saved her, him and me.' He fingered in his pocket the rose, the last thing, almost, Mrs Thomas had touched—except for him, and Wolford.

Mr Golightly's eyes, which were usually half-lidded over, looked full into Johnny's—a steady, slow-piercing look. 'I understand. As death is most violent in taking away, so love is most violent in saving us. It isn't easy to be the recipient. But she didn't want your father found either—she wanted him safe too.'

'From that fucking bastard cunt! He fucking killed her. I saw . . .'

What had he seen? He hadn't quite dared to picture it. He'd run till his lungs were busting and then he'd stopped and looked back. The screw was struggling and screeching out and Mrs Thomas had seemed to put her arms round his neck, almost as if she loved him and . . .

'There was this horse,' Johnny said. The curlew cocked its head to one side. 'From over there.' Johnny pointed across the moor towards High Tor. It had galloped towards him, a large horse, not one of the ponies, its pale mane flowing, and passed so close he was afraid it might trample him with its big hooves; and he had smelled the breath from its nostrils and then . . .

And then when he'd looked she'd gone. Disappeared. And he hadn't known what he should do—go back, or run on. He'd run with his heart like a lump of coal in his chest, till he'd reached the nearest farm.

Suddenly, he saw Mrs Thomas's painting: You don't happen to know why a raven is like a writing desk? She'd smiled at that daft answer he'd given her. She looked nice when she smiled.

By the mire, from which, days earlier, the water-logged bodies of Ellen Thomas and Brian Wolford had been dragged, Johnny Spence sobbed, while Mr Golightly held him in his arms and the curlew took off over their heads, keening for no other reason but that it was alive.

CHAPTER EIGHT

Jackson was in the Stag and Badger the evening of Ellen Thomas's funeral. People said afterwards that he showed no sign of emotion but drank steadily till closing time. Paula stayed over at her mum's that night, so Jackson returned to an empty house, where he set about making a bookshelf for her. But it wasn't Paula who was on Jackson's mind.

It is no real loss when a feverish fantasy is replaced by a cool truth, but Jackson was not alone in feeling it to be an irreparable one. Although he had never entertained any serious belief that Ellen could be his, that there might be others to whom

287

she was closer was too great a blow to his sense of imagined singularity and to a future which had given the illusion of being his to control. He had already lost himself in the service of Ellen Thomas, and it was the sense of recovering some of his old power that had prompted him to give away her secret to Wolford.

That Jackson was aware of what he had done became apparent when, the morning after Ellen Thomas's funeral, he was found hanging from the pear tree in her garden. On the long grass beneath his dangling boots, where next spring the daffodils and narcissi she had planted would rise again, lay scattered the torn pieces of a ten- and twenty-pound note. Like confetti, Paula said, when she came to see him.

She insisted on going there, though her mum was all against it and said that if she stayed away no one could blame her. Jackson's puffy, swollen-throated body was laid out, where the living form of the woman he had loved had once lain, on the sofa, by her painting of the ravens—which gave Paula's mum a nasty turn, reminding her, as it did, of the big black bird which had settled on a tree outside her sister Edna's when Ron died.

It was the tragedy that must have unhinged him, people said. It was wonderful how attached the work-shy Jackson had grown to poor Mrs Thomas, who now had no need of his rickety construction, which, in his last hours, its architect and builder had torn down.

CHAPTER NINE

Jos Bainbridge was alone in his cell when he heard the bird at midnight—close as his own breath, simple as a sheepbell, pure as starlight on a frosty night it lanced his heart till in grief and gratitude he cried aloud—and way across the quiet moor a black Labrador dog howled in concert with the convicted man, to the graceful incomprehending moon.

CHAPTER TEN

On the night before Ellen Thomas's funeral, Mr Golightly did not retire to bed in the black-painted iron bedstead in the bedroom of Spring Cottage. Instead, he stayed up, drinking whisky and rereading the pages Johnny Spence had provided him with. Early the following morning, he sent off an e-mail and, without waiting for a reply, he set out to walk to his old haunt on High Tor.

'You got it then,' he said, as he breasted the top, breathing slightly hard from the effort. 'Thank you for coming. It's been a time.'

His rival, who had come from business which took him to and fro and up and down the earth, looked every bit as ordinary as Mr Golightly. He stood turned away, as if inspecting the river which was purling beneath them.

'Oh well,' he said, 'like you I'm always about.'

'Certainly you have managed to track me here.'

289

The other, still with his back to him, visibly shrugged. 'Do you imagine the likes of us can really take a break—in my case I can scarcely call it a "holiday"?'

'Mine seems to have become more of a wake,' said Mr Golightly. The line his old enemy had e-mailed him returned, mockingly: *Have the gates of death been opened unto thee?* 'I should have realised sooner. A clever trick to pose the questions back at the questioner.'

'A trick? It is a method you yourself taught me. It is my role, isn't it? The role you summoned me to perform on poor Job.'

'You pity our servant, then?' asked Mr Golightly.

'Yes, I pity him,' said the other. 'I know from my own experience the anguish he suffered.' A sluggish breeze round the tor top slightly ruffled his hair.

'Is that, then, why you have chosen to torment me?' Mr Golightly's voice was measured. 'Because I don't, or didn't, "know" anguish . . . ?'

'Oh, you . . .' said the one beside him, 'no one torments you but yourself. The questions I sent you were only the ones you yourself asked the righteous Job. I merely reflected them back to you. What's sauce for the goose, you know? You might say I was being playful—part of your holiday recreation. It is what today I believe is called "consciousness raising". One of the older of my functions.'

Mr Golightly said nothing but stood sunk in thought. It was true—hedged about, safe from turmoil, he had not been tested by life, and he had come to see that he had been the poorer thereby.

'I wonder,' he said, 'forgive me, there is no one else with whom I can have this discussion and it crosses my mind that perhaps you may be able to help me.' He was thinking of the e-mail he had dispatched that morning. 'I have been wondering very much about suffering and love. You see—'

'I understand,' the companion at his side interrupted, 'as the fountainhead yourself, you had no individual experience of it and yet—'

'And yet there is my son,' Mr Golightly broke in, not wanting the other to broach the name.

For the first time, his old rival turned to face him fully and his eyes looked like ruined stars. 'I was going to say,' he suggested mildly, 'that, from my rare observations of the phenomenon, to love another means in some sense to put oneself in their person; and for that to be possible there must first be the extinction of the self. I offer the idea in pure humility—' Mr Golightly gave a slight nod—'this, perhaps, is what your son—'

'Was that why you had him killed?' broke in Mr Golightly.

'I was no more responsible for your son's death than you were for saving the life of that boy you are so fond of!' replied the other, sharply.

Somewhere a rock tumbled noisily down to the river.

The other resumed. 'If nothing else, I know what is due to a kinsman. Don't lay that barbarity—or this latest local disaster—' he waved his hand in the direction of the mire—'at my door.'

'Whose then?' asked Mr Golightly, feeling a flash of anger that the death of his friend and neighbour should be so summarily dismissed.

'Do you really not know?' said the other. 'Surely you see that it was neither you nor I but your own creation, your pride and joy, that brought about the death of your friend and killed your own son: pinned his human flesh through with nails to hang in the hot sun till his unsupported neck fell on his own windpipe and slowly suffocated him. A particularly unsophisticated method of dispatch.'

'It wasn't you who put them up to it?'

'No more than you. You allowed them a choice—remember? And they chose to save the life of a common murderer instead. Do not presume; one of the thieves was damned. Do you mind if we sit down?'

'So long as you don't start a forest fire,' said Mr Golightly. 'We'd best sit on this—' indicating the desk-shaped rock—'the place'll go up like dry tinder if you don't watch yourself.'

They sat, side by side, on the rocky tor.

'Then what is the truth?' asked Mr Golightly, finally.

'As one who had a hand in that affair of your son's death once asked, and went on, in that bourgeois way I so despise, to wash his hands of the question. You speak as if "truth" were everything. Has it ever struck you that a lie might be as immortal, and therefore as much a cornerstone of creation as a truth?'

'But who laid the cornerstone thereof?' The ancient boast sounded pathetic now in his own ears.

'Well, the raven must also be provided with food, to paraphrase some more of your words. After all, some would say,' said his companion, 'that the fiction we both create is merely a sophisticated version of lying.'

'Only if it seeks to mislead,' said Mr Golightly, a shade huffily.

292

'Let's call it "fabrication", then,' said his rival, taking from his pocket a flat tin—'Will you have one?' and then as he extracted a small cigar and lit it—'Yes, yes, I'll be careful. You have to concede, though, it's a fine line: where does art end and falsehood begin?'

'I would say when the intention is crooked,' said Mr Golightly.

'But who's the judge? That is the question. A story is spun—you have done it, magnificently; I, in my lesser way, have merely sought, let us say, a diversion—'

'I'm tempted to say a distortion,' interrupted Mr Golightly.

'To be sure,' the other went on, in his more languid tone, 'but that's my very point, and, by the way, temptation itself, as you know, means to try the strength of. You had me test your servant to prove his mettle. Who hath put wisdom in the inward parts? You yourself asked your servant Job. You might say it was I who did, and that all he suffered made a man of him—or, equally, a woman of your friend. You may call it distortion if you like, I would call it development; you say tom*ay*to, I say tom*ar*to . . .'

'So "let's call the whole thing off!"' said Mr Golightly, impatiently. He was no metaphysician.

'You suppose I am playing with you,' said the other, 'but as someone said: "The play's the thing." The point is, everything created, and recreated, I should add, in deference to your latest enterprise, is capable of different readings—alternatives, if you like: mine is the tragic, yours the comic turn. Humankind, your own great fiction, must determine between the ends we each offer them.

293

All that time ago, when we fell out over that other woman, it was not that I misled her, certainly not that I seduced her in your precious garden, as you claimed—' here Mr Golightly looked a little sheepish—'I merely gave her another interpretation—an alternative version of the story you had told her. Both have a place in the whole drama, neither was right or wrong, positive or negative—' he always was long-winded, Mr Golightly reflected—'as I need hardly tell you, although you have been kind enough to flatter me by asking my views on this topic. I thought, by the way, that flattery was supposed to be my province?'

'Yes, well, love is deeper than flattery,' said Mr Golightly, shortly, 'and for all your sophistry the plain fact is that in your ending men and women, and children too, die. It seems to me that nothing lends itself to lies like death.'

'Oh, as to that, as one of them remarked, in the long run they are all of them dead. At your own request I spared Job's life, but I wonder if he mightn't have got the worst of it. Your friend could have told you there are blessings in mortality.'

'It is true,' said Mr Golightly, 'that death has its points. But not to the survivors.'

His companion continued to smoke, tapping the ash into the palm of his hand. It was pale and slightly fleshy, unlike Mr Golightly's more workmanlike hands.

'But it is to the survivors you have given this peculiar choice. There are those who have elected to make the death of the carpenter's son—I am giving him the pseudonym you also gave him—a comedy. It is a remarkable decision, one, if I may say so, that defeats my own modest dramatic

294

purposes. But one that, against all reason, you yourself made available.'

'He did give them a lead,' said Mr Golightly, contemplatively.

'One might say your son rather flung himself into the part,' said the other. 'But he, too, was a great dramatist. An original. Truly his father's son.' Mr Golightly made a gesture of deprecation. 'No, no, I meant it—the darkness and the light were also alike to him.'

Mr Golightly, for whom a thousand years were as a day, saw in his mind's eye the sun, in that distant land, standing still, withdrawing its light from the world. In the sky over High Tor that day, there was a bright blur. A different perspective, but the same sun. 'So his death is, was, what people choose to make of it, comic or tragic, is that what you are saying?'

'I thought it was I who was supposed to be the "diabolic" one,' said the figure with destroyed starlight for eyes. 'I am saying that the awful choice you gave your own creation was surmounted by your son, who took upon himself both ways.'

'It still killed him,' pointed out his father.

There was another pause and then his companion spoke again. 'It has been alleged that the "death" was not for ever . . . ?'

'Ah, as to that,' said Mr Golightly, 'that was not in the plot as I conceived it . . .'

'But as we both know,' said the other, 'no author has the last word on his own work. Once in the world it is the world's for the taking, or, if I may say—as one whose motives are so often misperceived—the mistaking. As you have been seeing for yourself, there is a great deal of hazard in human affairs.'

'Is there no help for it, then?' asked Mr Golightly, and his voice on the tor top sounded very small.

'Only you, if I may say so,' replied his companion, 'as the author of all goodness, can answer that. This boy is saved—your son, and others, lost. If things go on as they are doing many parents will soon weep and know why. But look at it this way—your creation is capable of more than its creator. You and I have no life—so we cannot give it, in that reckless fashion, to save a world, or a friend. However it came about that this extraordinary faculty of human affection was implanted, I have to admit that in its foolhardy way it is rather wonderful.'

'Yes,' agreed Mr Golightly, 'I have been thinking that there are many ways in which my characters are superior to their author.' And he sighed, thinking of Ellen Thomas and his beloved son.

'You know,' said his colleague, 'you remind me of the great clown Grimaldi. Do you remember?'

'As we have established, you have a better memory than me,' said Mr Golightly, humbly. 'As time goes on, I find I cannot always bring every last thing to mind. I'm afraid that I have uttered all kinds of things which nowadays I know not.'

'Grimaldi,' said the other, smoothly continuing, 'in despair, anonymously consulted a doctor. He described, at length, his condition, which was one of considerable and sustained melancholy. Clinical depression, as it would be diagnosed today. The doctor listened carefully and then offered his prescription. "You are careworn," he said, "and bowed down, and have forgotten that life has

296

another face. What you need are the benefits of laughter. The remedy is easy; go to see the greatest comedian of all time—go and see Grimaldi."

'Perhaps,' he concluded, gently, 'when your holiday comes to a close, and you finish your soap opera, you will find a happy end . . .'

'For a time, maybe,' said Mr Golightly.

'Well, but,' said his partner and rival, 'as we both know, everything here is only for a time . . .'

CHAPTER ELEVEN

Paula had been given compassionate leave from work and it was to Paula's mum's, and not the Stag and Badger, that Mr Golightly went one late June evening in search of Luke.

Luke was delighted when his old crossword companion appeared asking if he could spare a few words.

'Sure thing,' said Luke, ever agreeable. 'Come into the kitchen.'

Luke admitted he had been missing *The Times*. Paula's mum took the *Mail*, which, Luke observed, had a different mindset behind its crossword. He showed Mr Golightly one of the clues: 'His bite could be worse than His bark if you confuse him (3)', which reminded Mr Golightly that he had come to say that since his tenancy of Spring Cottage was almost at its end he wondered if Luke could look after Wilfred for a time. Johnny was going to have him eventually, but that would have to wait till Rosie Spence found a place to live and things got sorted over Johnny's new dad.

Apparently, Rosie was talking to solicitors and it looked as if it mightn't be long before Jos Bainbridge would be free again.

Luke said he'd be glad to look after the Labrador, though he'd have to clear it with Paula's mum—not that she ever put her foot down, especially now Paula was back. He offered his guest a Nescafé.

Mr Golightly reminded Luke he only drank real coffee. He had come, he said, mainly to say goodbye. Tomorrow he would be packing up and, having a dislike for farewells, he preferred to get them over with in advance.

'Oh, right,' said Luke. He was sorry his writing colleague was leaving. But he had an optimistic nature and expressed a hope they might meet up again.

'Undoubtedly,' Mr Golightly assured him. 'I never forget a friend.'

Luke apologised if he had seemed unsociable lately. He'd been hard at it, he explained, finishing his new work.

'My own idea I've decided to set aside,' Mr Golightly explained. It seemed to have found its own way of reproducing itself.

He was about to ask after Paula when the kitchen door opened and she appeared lugging a rubbish sack.

Paula had not been too thrilled by the discovery that her absconding father was in the same line of business as the man who had apparently beaten up Johnny Spence's mother all that time ago. For a while there was an excited rumour that Paula's father might also be Johnny's; but this turned out to be local wishful thinking.

'Shit, that's a relief!' Johnny said when he called by to borrow Paula's Dread-Fox Bitch CD and heard the latest gossip. 'You'd be on at me something horrible if you was me sister.'

'You bet your sweet arse I would if you use language like that!' Paula had said, whacking him on the backside. She told him he could come and play her keyboard any time. 'You're not like other kids. You're like I was, you are.'

Her father had been missing most of her life and Paula had given him up long ago. Jackson's death hit her harder. It revealed a side to him she hadn't detected and the discovery made her thoughtful.

However, a little after his death, a note was found to have been left by Jackson. In ill-formed capitals, apparently printed just before his suicide, it read:

I LEAVE EVERYTHING TO PAULA JENSON.

The note was dated, and signed, also in capitals, J. JACKSON.

Since Jackson had no relatives, or, other than Paula, close friends, the full extent of his illiteracy was not widely known. It was shrewd, and considerate, of the desperate man to use the surname which Paula herself had only lately discovered.

The day that Jackson's body was found in the pear tree Paula had returned to Rabbit Row to find Luke in a ferment over his writing. Luke had scarcely taken in the details of the true-life drama he was living among. Never much in touch with flesh-and-blood human beings, he was wholly preoccupied by the tragic tale he now believed—all memory of Bill having vanished—he had single-handedly constructed. Hungry for an opinion, and oblivious to her personal tragedy, he pressed it on Paula, who read it through in one sitting over her mum's kitchen table.

' 'S a good story,' said Paula, finally responding to Luke's repeated requests to know how she found it. She stacked the exercise books smartly into order on the table. 'You'll need to get it looking tidy and properly word-processed before you show it to anyone. It starts off well. 'S good the way the baby's a bastard, and all that bit about the dump he's born in, and not knowing who his real dad is and that he comes from a mysterious background, and that. That's all good romance—the readers'll like that. And the main character, the one who don't mind what he says and tells them what's what and gets himself killed for it—he's got balls, I like him. But the ending won't do.'

'Why not?' asked Luke, stung into protest. 'I mean, it's a fantastic ending—being put to death by the people you're trying to save and left to die in humiliating agony.'

He was deflated by this unexpected criticism of his tale of tragic suffering.

'Won't do,' said Paula, firmly. She knew from the best-seller lists at Tesco's that sad endings were not at all popular. 'It'll never sell, not the way you tell it, anyway.'

Luke was downcast. 'What'll I do, then? I can't change the ending. He has to die—that's the whole point.'

'You could add a bit on,' said Paula, pragmatically. 'He could die, right? Everyone could think he was dead—but he isn't. He comes back and only a few people see him. Then people start to talk—he becomes a cult hero, like Elvis, and that way you can keep the death, for the sob stuff, but still have a happy end.'

She had been in her room, tidying things away, when Mr Golightly called. It was her doll's house and the remaining toy animals, she told him, she had in the rubbish sack. 'Luke's going to put them up in the loft,' she explained. 'So there's room for us both when I move me other bits back. They was OK when I was a kid, but, you know, you can't stay a kid, you gotta move on . . .'

'I understand,' said Mr Golightly, wondering whether congratulations to the couple were in order. 'There's a time and place for all things.' It was a sentiment he had written of once himself, long ago, in one of the more poetic passages of his own work.

Paula said she would be selling Jackson's place once all the legal stuff was tied up but that she couldn't bring herself to spend another night there. For the time being she and Luke were going to squeeze in together at her mum's.

Mr Golightly absorbed this new turn of events unsurprised. He was glad that two of his friends should strike up an association and his visit to Calne had taught him that human affairs had their own momentum.

Luke's amiable indifference had conquered Paula far more effectively than any show of devotion could have done, but she was also impressed by the potential she saw in his writing. She took the opportunity to canvass their visitor's view on Luke's new project.

'I told him, it won't sell 'less he does something

about that ending. You got to look at the market. Change the ending and it could be a best-seller. I'm right, en't I?'

Mr Golightly looked at Paula in her jeans and sequinned T-shirt and her several gleaming nose studs. She had a far more discriminating worldly sense than ever he, or Luke, could hope to have.

'I expect you are right, child,' he said. And to Luke, 'I'd follow her lead on this, old chap—she sees these things more clearly . . .'

CHAPTER TWELVE

By the time he had finished packing up Spring Cottage it was early evening, but Mr Golightly did not stroll up to the Stag and Badger. He'd had his fill of endings. Luke, or, better still, Paula, could look after those.

He went outside to give Samson the sugar lumps he had pilfered for the horse from his last visit to the pub. Samson stood sturdily oblivious to the ceremony of departure as Mr Golightly ran a finger down the plush nose. 'Say "Ha, ha, among the trumpets" for me.'

He had promised Nicky Pope, who had her sister's husband's cousin staying and was up to her ears, to make sure that all was in apple-pie order to greet the new tenant, the tarot-card reader. The cottage hardly needed cleaning—Mr Golightly had discovered a fondness for housework. In any case, he gave the avocado bath and basin an extra going over, sprayed the kitchen hob with the last of the Mr Muscle that he and Johnny had bought together in Oakburton and got down on his knees to peer under the bed to see if there were any stray socks hiding. It was part of his rival's cunning to whisk away trivia into dark corners; but on this occasion his socks had been spared. He had already packed away the laptop with its e-mail dialogue and the final message—for the moment anyway—which had led to the meeting with his old associate:

shall he that contendeth with the Almighty instruct him?

Perhaps this had brought on a fit of leniency? But it couldn't last; they each had their own drama to play.

Walking back from Luke and Paula's, beneath a lambent midsummer sky, he'd reflected how quick life was to heal the breaches, to close over the ragged wounds of loss. He would miss Ellen Thomas, as he missed his son; but they would not miss him. They were part of the teeming tribute of the earth, ephemeral, evanescent but, in its way, boundless and enduring. Nature doesn't hold with tragedy, he thought, it has its own memorials: the green light of the dawn sky, the warmth of the spring soil, the spears of wheat, the blossom of a fruit tree, the clack of hooves, the clamour of starlings, the cool of rain, white stars and violets, the bark of an otter, the fall of dew, the abandoned dance of a girl, or the tears of a young boy as he wept for a world which had shown its best and its worst to him.

The tragedy was not his son's or Ellen Thomas's—it was poor demented Jackson's, and Brian Wolford's, and his mother's. Cherie Wolford

303

was beside herself for the son who had been the apple of her eye; it was thought she might never get over it, Nicky Pope had said.

Johnny Spence lived; and soon would have a father to quarrel with, and laugh about, and miss; and, no doubt, be ashamed of and bothered and anguished by. The beam of the balance of the universe, though slow, found its own level. For the while, it had righted itself; but neither he, nor his old rival, was the agent. If nothing else, he had learned that on his holiday.

Looking out through the window on to the garden, Mr Golightly saw one of Ellen Thomas's geese, its orange bill rootling in the grass through the barbed wire, and remembered that Mary Simms, who had promised to see to the livestock, was to call by. It would be a tonic to see Mary again before his departure.

There was tapping outside, so faint that, for a moment, Mr Golightly mistook it for the sound of the apple tree's branches scraping on the window, but its persistence made him look out. Across the way he saw Keith, with a face like thunder, reversing the Renault, packed to the windows, down the vicarage drive.

By the open window stood a man, open-faced and shambling. 'Evening, sir. I've come for the garden.'

'What?'

'The garden, sir. Mrs Pope said to come.'

'Well,' said Mr Golightly, 'I have heard of thee by the hearing of the ear: but now mine eye seeth thee it's all yours!' He gestured at the prodigal dandelions.

He had almost finished loading the Traveller

304

when Mike and Bill arrived, Mike riding pillion on the bike.

'Michael—Gabriel,' he embraced them fondly, his faithful assistants.

Before they left, Mr Golightly said goodbye to the gardener, who said his name was Joe, and that besides gardening he did a spot of woodwork. In fact, it was fixing up the fitted kitchen for Mrs Fawns, over Backen way, that had held him up so long from coming to do Spring Cottage.

Mike hopped in beside the driver's seat and Bill revved up the bike and rode off ahead of the Traveller. So he missed seeing Mary Simms, who was in time to wave the others off.

Mary was looking well. She had brought with her a memento of Oakburton, a milk jug in the shape of a cow, a present from the vicar, who was busy setting up 'Meredith's', her beauty salon, and couldn't get away, but sent her love and asked to be remembered.

And the sight that Mr Golightly took away with him, when he turned to look back at Spring Cottage, where he had spent his holiday, was Mary Simms, leaning on the gate, with the light of the vanishing sun on her copper-coloured hair, chatting, in her good-natured way, to Joseph the gardener.

*   *   *

Later that evening, Tessa Pope claimed to have seen two angels—each with six wings—conducting a fiery car across the sky over High Tor. But no one believed her.

Do you not see how necessary a World of
Pains and troubles is to school an Intelligence
and make it a soul? A Place where the heart
must feel and suffer in a thousand diverse
ways! Not merely is the Heart a Hornbook, it
is the Mind's Bible.

KEATS

THE RESEARCH NOTES
OF JOHNNY SPENCE

From the Old Testament Book of Job

CHAPTER 1

6   Now there was a day when the sons of God came to present themselves before the LORD, and Satan came also among them.

7   And the LORD said unto Satan, Whence comest thou? Then Satan answered the Lord and said, From going to and fro in the earth, and from walking up and down in it.

8   And the LORD said unto Satan, Hast thou considered my servant Job, that there is none like him in the earth, a perfect and an upright man, one that feareth God and escheweth evil?

9   Then Satan answered the LORD and said, Doth Job fear God for nought?

10 Hast not thou made an hedge about him, and about his house and about all that he hath on every side? thou hast blessed the work of his hands, and his sustance is increased in the land.

11 But put forth thine hand now, and touch all that he hath, and he will curse thee to thy face.

12 And the LORD said unto Satan, Behold all that he hath is in thy power . . .

CHAPTER 38

1   Then the LORD answered Job out of the whirlwind, and said,

2   **Who is this that darkeneth counsel by words without knowledge?**

3   Gird up now thy loins like a man; for I will demand of thee, and answer thou me.

4   Where wast thou when I laid the foundations of the earth? declare, if thou hast understanding.

5   Who hath laid the measures thereof, if thou knowest? or who hath stretched the line upon it?

6   Whereupon are the foundations thereof fastened? or **who laid the corner stone thereof**;

7   When the morning stars sang together, and all the sons of God shouted for joy?

8   Or who shut up the sea with doors, when it brake forth, as if it had issued out of the womb?

9   When I made the cloud the garment thereof, and thick darkness a swaddlingband for it,

10 And brake up for it my decreed place, and set bars and doors,

11 And said, Hitherto shalt thou come, but no further: and here shall thy proud waves be stayed?

12 Hast thou commanded the morning since thy days; and caused the dayspring to know his place;

13 That it might take hold of the ends of the earth, that the wicked might be shaken out of it?

14 It is turned as clay to the seal; and they stand as a garment.

15 And from the wicked their light is withholden, and the high arm shall be broken.

16 Hast thou entered into the springs of the sea?

or hast thou walked in the search of the depth?

17 **Have the gates of death been opened unto thee?** or hast thou seen the doors of the shadow of death?

18 Hast thou perceived the breadth of the earth? declare if thou knowest it all.

19 Where is the way where light dwelleth? and **as for darkness, where is the place thereof,**

20 That thou shouldest take it to the bound thereof, and that thou shouldest know the paths to the house thereof?

21 Knowest thou it, because thou wast then born? or because the number of thy days is great?

22 Hast thou entered into the treasures of the snow? or hast thou seen the treasures of the hail,

23 Which I have reserved against the time of trouble, against the day of battle and war?

24 **By what way is the light parted**, which scattereth the east wind upon the earth?

25 Who hath divided a watercourse for the overflowing of waters, or a way for the lightning of thunder;

26 To cause it to rain on the earth, where no man is; on the wilderness, wherein there is no man;

27 To satisfy the desolate and waste ground; and to cause the bud of the tender herb to spring forth?

28 **Hath the rain a father?** or **who hath begotten the drops of dew?**

29 Out of whose womb came the ice? and the hoary frost of heaven, who hath gendered it?

30 The waters are hid as with a stone, and the face of the deep is frozen.

31 Canst thou bind the sweet influences of

Pleiades, or loose the bands of Orion?

32 Canst thou bring forth Mazzaroth in his season? or canst thou guide Arcturus with his sons?

33 Knowest thou the ordinances of heaven? canst thou set the dominion thereof in the earth?

34 Canst thou lift up thy voice to the clouds, that abundance of waters may cover thee?

35 Canst thou send lightnings, that they may go, and say unto thee, Here we are?

36 Who hath put wisdom in the inward parts? or **who hath given understanding to the heart?**

37 Who can number the clouds in wisdom? or who can stay the bottles of heaven,

38 When the dust groweth into hardness, and the clods cleave fast together?

39 Wilt thou hunt the prey for the lion? or fill the appetite of the young lions,

40 When they couch in their dens, and abide in the covert to lie in wait?

41 **Who provideth for the raven his food?** when his young ones cry unto God, they wander for lack of meat.

CHAPTER 39

1 Knowest thou the time when the wild goats of the rock bring forth? or canst thou mark when the hinds do calve?

2 Canst thou number the months that they fulfil? or knowest thou the time when they bring forth?

3 They bow themselves, they bring

4 Their young ones are in good liking, they grow up with corn; they go forth, and return not

unto them.

5 Who hath sent out the wild ass free? or who hath loosed the bands of the wild ass?

6 Whose house I have made the wilderness, and the barren land his dwellings.

7 He scorneth the multitude of the city, neither regardeth he the crying of the driver.

8 The range of the mountains is his pasture, and he searcheth after every green thing.

9 Will the unicorn be willing to serve thee, or abide by thy crib?

10 **Canst thou bind the unicorn** with his band in the furrow? or will he harrow the valleys after thee?

11 Wilt thou trust him, because his strength is great? or wilt thou leave thy labour to him?

12 Wilt thou believe him, that he will bring home thy seed, and gather it into thy barn?

13 Gavest thou the goodly wings unto the peacocks? or wings and feathers unto the ostrich?

14 Which leaveth her eggs in the earth, and warmeth them in dust,

15 And forgetteth that the foot may crush them, or that the wild beast may break them.

16 She is hardened against her young ones, as though they were not hers: her labour is in vain without fear;

17 Because God hath deprived her of wisdom, neither hath he imparted to her understanding.

18 What time she lifteth up herself on high, she scorneth the horse and his rider.

19 Hast thou given the horse strength? hast thou clothed his neck with thunder?

20 Canst thou make him afraid as a grasshopper?

the glory of his nostrils is terrible.

21 He paweth in the valley, and rejoiceth in his strength: he goeth on to meet the armed men.

22 He mocketh at fear, and is not affrighted; neither turneth he back from the sword.

23 The quiver rattleth against him, the glittering spear and the shield.

24 He swalloweth the ground with fierceness and rage: neither believeth he that it is the sound of the trumpet.

25 **He saith among the trumpets, Ha, ha**; and he smelleth the battle afar off, the thunder of the captains, and the shouting.

26 Doth the hawk fly by thy wisdom, and stretch her wings toward the south?

27 Doth the eagle mount up at thy command, and make her nest on high?

28 She dwelleth and abideth on the rock, upon the crag of the rock, and the strong place.

29 From thence she seeketh the prey, and her eyes behold afar off.

30 Her young ones also suck up blood: and where the slain are, there is she.

CHAPTER 40

1 **Moreover the LORD answered Job, and said,**

2 **Shall he that contendeth with the Almighty instruct him?** he that reproveth God, let him answer it.

3 Then Job answered the LORD, and said,

4 Behold, I am vile; what shall I answer thee? I will lay mine hand upon my mouth.

5 Once have I spoken; but I will not answer: yea, twice; but I will proceed no further.

6   Then answered the LORD unto Job out of the whirlwind, and said,

7   Gird up thy loins now like a man: I will demand of thee, and declare thou unto me.

8   Wilt thou also disannul my judgment? wilt thou condemn me, that thou mayest be righteous?

9   Hast thou an arm like God? or canst thou thunder with a voice like him?

10   Deck thyself now with majesty and excellency; and array thyself with glory and beauty.

11   Cast abroad the rage of thy wrath: and behold every one that is proud, and abase him.

12   Look on every one that is proud, and bring him low; and tread down the wicked in their place.

13   Hide them in the dust together; and bind their faces in secret.

14   Then will I also confess unto thee that thine own right hand can save thee.

15   Behold now behemoth, which I made with thee; he eateth grass as an ox.

16   Lo now, his strength is in his loins, and his force is in the navel of his belly.

17   He moveth his tail like a cedar: the sinews of his stones are wrapped together.

18   His bones are as strong pieces of brass; his bones are like bars of iron.

19   He is the chief of the ways of God: he that made him can make his sword to approach unto him.

20   Surely the mountains bring him forth food, where all the beasts of the field play.

21   He lieth under the shady trees, in the covert of the reed, and fens.

22   The shady trees cover him with their shadow; the willows of the brook compass him about.

23 Behold, he drinketh up a river, and hasteth not: he trusteth that he can draw up Jordan into his mouth.
24 He taketh it with his eyes: his nose pierceth through snares.

CHAPTER 42

1 Then Job answered the LORD, and said,
2 I know that thou canst do every thing, and that no thought can be withholden from thee.
3 Who is he that hideth counsel without knowledge? **therefore have I uttered that I understood not; things too wonderful for me, which I knew not**.
4 Hear, I beseech thee, and I will speak: I will demand of thee, and declare thou unto me.
5 **I have heard of thee by the hearing of the ear: but now mine eye seeth thee.**

AUTHOR'S NOTE AND ACKNOWLEDGEMENTS

Mr Golightly's Holiday is set on Dartmoor, in Devon, in the south-west of England, and most of the locations described are factual. For the purposes of the story, I have slightly altered the position of the mire, and Great Calne, Oakburton, Backenbridge and High Tor are fictional creations, as, of course, are all the characters. There are, however, words of other authors, which, from time to time, issue from the mouth or occur in the thoughts of my principal character, Mr Golightly. To put these allusions in quotes would not only have been clunking but would have spoiled a point. My hope was that these authors—none of them living—would not have considered it an insult if I implied that their words had originated from my, so to speak, supreme author. A perceptive reader will come across, variously, as well as quotations from Mr Golightly's own 'Great Work', echoes of John Chrysostom, St Augustine, William of Ockham, Jakob Boehme, Shakespeare, Marlowe, George Herbert, John Donne, William Blake, John Keats, Gerard Manley Hopkins, Matthew Arnold, Robert Frost, ee cummings, Saki, C. S. Lewis—if there are others I have overlooked it is because they have become part of my unconscious furniture. I hope the authors, whoever they are, wherever they are, will forgive me, and take it as a compliment rather than an act of theft. It has been pointed out to me that a God in the shape of a middle-aged man also visits an English village in

315

T. F. Powys's *Mr Weston's Good Wine*. As Mr Golightly and Mr Weston would probably agree, there is nothing new under the sun and I can only say that the idea came to me independently. I believe anyone who reads the two books will see that the themes are very different.

There was, however, one particular influence on this novel: I owe to the critic Northrop Frye the brilliant observation that, temperamentally, we tend to favour either the tragic or the comic outlook. It was his contention that Dante, Shakespeare and the authors behind the New Testament were, in essence, finally comedians— hence *The Divine Comedy*—by which he meant not that they were a fund of belly laughs but that ultimately they saw life as more powerful than the forces which conspire against it: that the canon of their works—for all their equivocation and deep ambiguity—evolves towards 'happy' ends. Happy ends are not fashionable nowadays, but a 'happy' end does not necessarily imply Pollyanna or Panglossism—that an author believes that all of life is agreeable, or that everything is moving inevitably towards the best possible conclusion. It merely implies a particular slant of vision, one which sees the potential, deep in the core of human affairs, for misfortune's alternative—a view which may in fact encourage just that possibility. For while art can never replicate life itself, it does affect and influence it. It is arguable, therefore, that there is a responsibility at least not to overlook the comic as a component of the real.

In its small way, *Mr Golightly's Holiday* is an example of this outlook, not just in its subject matter and conclusion but in its inception. It arose out of a period of turmoil in my life. I was, in fact, writing a different novel when events cut the threads of my concentration, so that book was set aside in the distractions of the personal drama I found myself acting in. At the lowest point, when things stood around my bed in the small hours looking worse and worse, and I thought I may never write again, the idea of *Mr Golightly's Holiday* stole upon me and I am convinced that it was the wreck of my former plans which allowed its admission.

But the book has several godparents, too, without whose particular contribution it could not have been conceived and born. Gerald Beckwith told me the joke about the need for even the Highest Powers to take a rest from their eternal activity; I owe to Nicholas de Jongh the idea that my own life was best understood as a TV soap opera, one scripted by an inaccessible authority; my two publishers, Christopher Potter of Fourth Estate and Jonathan Galassi of Farrar, Straus & Giroux—even when I owned up to abandoning the book they had bought and believed in—supported me in ways I know to be wholly unusual in current publishing circles. Publishers are the midwives of books and, as with children, early experiences affect a book's future. Any author who is lucky enough to have two such publishers as Christopher and Jonathan is already blessed. They have been the most patient and benevolent as well as astute of midwives. Captain David Swales, the chaplain to Dartmoor prison, helped my researches but is not responsible for any misimpression of prison life my fictional representation may give. Dr Michael Gormley and Dr Peter Barwell advised on epilepsy.

317

Lily Smith kept unwarranted distractions at bay. My sons, Ben and Rupert, were, as always, my best teachers: they are living proof that the 'creator' needs, and learns from dialogue with, the 'created'.

There are three people to whom I owe a special debt. Ru Roberts, with exceptional generosity, provided the two things I needed most: she gave me a place to write and let me alone. Paul Rhys offered further sanctuary and fine insights which nourished many of my own. Finally, Gillon Aitken, my agent, went far beyond the call of duty. Without his strong and unobtrusive encouragement over the past two years, I would have gone over to the side of Mr Golightly's rival, which would have resulted in a tragedy.

CHIVERS LARGE PRINT
-direct-

If you have enjoyed this Large Print book and would like to build up your own collection of Large Print books, please contact

Chivers Large Print Direct

Chivers Large Print Direct offers you a full service:

• Prompt mail order service

• Easy-to-read type

• The very best authors

• Special low prices

For further details either call
Customer Services on (01225) 336552
or write to us at Chivers Large Print Direct,
FREEPOST, Bath BA1 3ZZ

Telephone Orders:
FREEPHONE 08081 72 74 75